**Dalton dropped the handcuffs and kicked them across the floor to her. "Put those on."**

"A frequent fantasy of yours?" Kira had been aiming for a sarcastic tone and instead, the words came out breathy. Like an invitation.

"Definitely." His raised eyebrow spoke volumes and she balanced on the thin line between anger and appreciation. He was good. Scratch that. He was very bad, and he knew it.

"I meant, use them on your friend. We need to get out of here before the fire closes in."

"And if I refuse?" She swiped her cheek across her forearm and stifled a groan when her skin burned from the action.

"Then you deserve each other," he drawled. His warped sense of humor added to his raw appeal. Laughter and looks were a dangerous combination.

His silky brown eyes slid down her body and then to the gun in her hand.

"You're making me nervous. How about a truce?"

\* \* \*

If you're on Twitter, tell us what you think of Harlequin Romantic Suspense! #harlequinromsuspense

Dear Reader,

Thank you for picking up my book and taking a chance on a brand-new author! You're holding this book because, like me, you're drawn to action, suspense and strong characters with seemingly nothing in common.

Kira Kincaid is a woman who has been vulnerable for far too long. A product of the foster care system, she walks the straight and narrow road to guarantee a safe journey through life. Until fate intervenes and she meets a man who treats her like a queen. Life becomes everything she'd been afraid to hope for and then, just as quickly, it's taken away.

Dalton Matthews is a coffee mogul turned recluse. He has no desire to rehash his wife's suicide or play the blame game with the tabloids. But when he catches Kira snooping around his property, he's forced to leave the safety of his wilderness retreat to protect a woman who is keeping far too many secrets.

My favorite stories are those that make me forget I'm reading a book. My fondest hope is for you to get lost in Kira and Dalton's story and believe that no matter what obstacles may stand in your way, love happens when you least expect it.

*Jan*

# PROTECTING HIS BROTHER'S BRIDE

---

## Jan Schliesman

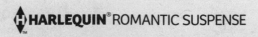

HARLEQUIN® ROMANTIC SUSPENSE

Recycling programs
for this product may
not exist in your area.

ISBN-13: 978-0-373-27920-3

Protecting His Brother's Bride

**Printed in U.S.A.**

**Jan Schliesman** became addicted to Harlequin Superromance novels in high school, often swapping bags of books with her girlfriends. Shortly afterward, Mr. Wonderful walked into her life, and it was love at first sight. At least for her. It took a few months for him to realize that she was mowing the grass in tight spandex to get him to notice her. They married and started a family and she became a stay-at-home mom. Not as much time to read meant Harlequin Desire books were her new best friend, especially when they started including wineglasses in the monthly shipment. After their son was diagnosed with autism, it was also vitally important that somebody, somewhere, was getting a happy ending. She returned to college in pursuit of an English degree, but working as a police dispatcher provided too many story ideas. The Romantic Suspense line became her new love, and a degree in criminal justice followed many years later.

Most days you'll find Jan listening to love stories and helping couples choose the perfect engagement ring. Most late nights she's in her office, getting new words on the page. Born and raised in Iowa, she's the mother of three semi-grown children. Jan lives in Kansas with the man she still calls Mr. Wonderful. Find her on Facebook, follow her on Twitter or check out her website at janschliesman.com.

### Books by Jan Schliesman

### HARLEQUIN ROMANTIC SUSPENSE

*Protecting His Brother's Bride*

Visit Jan's Author Profile page at Harlequin.com or janschliesman.com for more titles.

Sixteen years ago I drove sixty miles on a Thursday night to attend a Heart of Iowa Fiction Authors meeting. I brought along ten single-spaced pages of my manuscript, which I'd printed on lavender paper. No one laughed at me. I received nothing but encouragement and amazing advice. Thank you, Roxanne Rustand, Kylie Brant and Cindy Gerard for being such great roomies at the conference and for including me in all your fun.

When we moved to Kansas nearly six years ago, I connected with a critique partner, Sarah Cannon. We kept each other going when it might have been easier to give up. And thank goodness we didn't give up, because 2014 was the year we both sold manuscripts to Harlequin. It's been an exciting ride and one that wouldn't have been possible for either one of us without the unwavering support of Harlequin Intrigue author Angi Morgan. Besides being my toughest critic, she's also my best friend. I am lucky beyond measure to have her in my life.

# Prologue

"I am not a criminal," Kira Kincaid announced to the female FBI agent who watched her every move. On the contrary, Kira was an upstanding example of citizenship. "I never even drive over the speed limit." The fact that she didn't own a car was inconsequential.

"Save it for the judge," her keeper barked.

Kira pressed the cup to her lips and finished the last drop of water. She wished she had more. The third-floor interrogation room faced west and the late-August sun was outpacing the air-conditioning.

Rocking back and forth in the seat, she focused on trying to calm her nerves while preparing for what would happen next. Every police drama she'd ever seen replayed in her head. *If you cannot afford an attorney, one will be appointed for you.* The only attorney she knew was Marissa Reynolds, a neighbor in her apartment complex.

Sitting there in shock, Kira didn't know how much time

passed. She also didn't know how she remained so calm. Shock could do that to a person, she guessed. Even so, she had enough sense to refuse answering any questions until her attorney arrived. She sat quietly in the interrogation room, handcuffs removed, but with one agent left to supervise her actions. Where would she go?

She'd gone out of her way to avoid direct contact with Marissa, but Kira could deal with the interaction if it meant the difference between going home and spending the night in jail. After having messy fingerprints and a horrible mug shot taken, she had used her one allotted phone call.

The door swung open and Marissa Reynolds hurried in, giving Kira a quick once-over before a glance to the agent sent the woman from the room.

"I'm sorry you had to wait. I was right in the middle of an adoption."

Kira pressed a fingernail into her palm to keep the tears at bay. Adoptions meant babies were getting new families. Marissa dealt with children every day, which was part of the reason they could never move beyond the boundaries of exchanging pleasantries in the hallway of their apartment complex.

Kira had stopped at Marissa's once to borrow Scotch tape and nearly had a meltdown in her kitchen. Marissa's refrigerator was covered in pictures. Snapshots of babies and toddlers offered an unwelcome reminder of what Kira had lost.

"I didn't know who else to call."

Marissa pulled out a chair, sat and dropped the notepad she'd been holding on the table. "I'm not a criminal attorney, but I can refer you to someone who is."

"I've been set up," Kira insisted. "I know who's responsible."

"Then you need to cooperate with the FBI." Marissa

was all business as she paused to straighten her lapel and brush away invisible lint.

Cooperate with the FBI? Kira had come too far for that option to sound feasible. And if they had any proof against her, dollars to doughnuts it was Griffin who'd once again left her a hair's breadth away from learning his true identity. He'd also promised a fate worse than being arrested.

Two men entered the room after a quick tap on the door. Their FBI badges were flipped open on their jacket pockets. Marissa stood to greet them. Introductions and handshakes were exchanged, and Marissa asked to see the warrant for Kira's arrest. Kira already knew what it said—the United States Government, Judicial District 47, was charging her with twenty-two counts of insurance fraud and fifteen counts of identity theft. And to add insult to injury, there were three counts of embezzlement. All Kira could do was sit and stare in dumbfounded silence.

"Mrs. Kincaid, you seem to have gotten in quite a pickle," Agent Nissen said, sitting at the table with them. "Fortunately, it's not you we're after."

He dropped a file in front of Marissa. She opened it and scanned the page.

"Eleven million dollars?" Marissa snapped the file shut and looked at Kira, not questioning the agent.

The second agent leaned against the wall. "We're after the bigger fish and the money."

"Meaning Justice is ready to make a deal to recover the cash," Agent Nissen said.

Three pairs of eyes turned to Kira.

"You seriously think I embezzled eleven million dollars? I'm an insurance investigator. I only have three hundred dollars in my checking account. I didn't steal anything."

"Tell us what you know," Agent Nissen insisted. "Start

with the account under your maiden name holding eight hundred thousand dollars."

"You're married?" Marissa tipped her head to the side, her eyes reflecting betrayal. No one in their apartment building knew Kira was married. It was a lot easier not to discuss how she'd been abandoned.

"It's been a while. Things didn't work out." *Understatement of the year.* "If an account still exists, then it's news to me."

"Here's a listing of wire transfers into that account spanning the last four years, including one just two weeks ago." Agent Nissen slid a sheet of paper across the table.

Kira would never in a million years waste fifty dollars on a single wire transfer, let alone continue doing it for several years. Her thrifty nature was common knowledge. She always packed a lunch and rode the bus rather than wasting money on a car, insurance and gas.

The numbers staring back at her contained too many commas and zeroes. But the paper also listed her full name, with the last four digits of her social security number. "Anyone can rent a PO box under my name and pay cash to hide their identity."

"Is that how you did it?" Agent Nissen asked.

Kira ignored the jab. "What about this account in the Cayman Islands? Whose name is listed on it?"

Another sheet of paper sailed across the table. "Recognize that signature?"

"I recognize the name," she conceded. "But that isn't my signature." She grabbed Marissa's pen and signed her name on the first sheet of paper, shoving both across the table to Agent Nissen.

After studying the page for a moment, he shrugged. "We have plenty of other evidence linking you to these crimes." He pulled a few more sheets from the folder.

"Video of you from the bank in Denver, airline manifests showing frequent trips to Colorado, the Cayman Islands and your condo in Florida."

"Stop." She squeezed the bridge of her nose and took a cleansing breath. "This is absurd. Beyond absurd, it's ludicrous. I've never been to Florida, let alone the Caymans."

"The evidence tells a different story." The second agent had a note of superiority in his voice, almost as if he was taking too much pleasure in tightening the invisible noose around her neck.

Whatever fear existed in her before was gone, along with her initial shock. This was wrong, plain and simple. "What is it you want from me?"

"We want evidence against your partners. This scheme is too well orchestrated for one person." Nissen ticked off his list by unfolding his fingers. "We want to know how it was done. Obviously, the safeguards in place at the federal level are not enough to deter every criminal."

"Terms for immunity?" Marissa's voice was clipped.

"The money, or nothing else is negotiable."

"What if she agrees to sign over the funds in those accounts?" Marissa held up her hand before Kira could protest.

"This isn't a fine on an overdue library book, Ms. Reynolds. Your client is looking at some serious time behind bars, whether or not the money is returned." Agent Nissen tugged at his shirt cuff and checked his watch. "We'll give you a few minutes to confer with her."

Marissa followed them to the door and verified that it was closed before turning to Kira. "I'm really disappointed in you."

"Why?" It hurt knowing Marissa believed anything Agent Nissen said.

"You've got a condo in Florida and haven't invited me

along even once?" She shook her head. "I thought we were friends."

"I didn't do this," Kira insisted. "Marissa, you have to believe me." Kira needed to know that at least one person was on her side. No one from Midwest Mutual had rushed to her defense when she'd been handcuffed and marched out of the office earlier today.

"I obviously don't know everything about you." A smile worked its way across the attorney's face. "But I do know that you're afraid to fly."

Kira's relief was evident in the hug she offered Marissa. "Thank you."

"Don't thank me yet," she insisted. "First we need to get you arraigned and released."

Kira had to pull herself together. Equal parts anger and angst rolled through her veins. Anger at Geoff Griffin, the man who'd managed to elude all her attempts to link him to the stack of claims the audit department funneled her direction every month. Griffin was the only one who'd figured out that she'd spent quite a bit of her free time away from Midwest Mutual, working every angle she could come up with. How in the world had he known about her off-the-books investigation?

The only positive in this fiasco was that she now had confirmation that her activities were making him nervous. Was it his goal to see her in prison? From every document she'd obtained, she knew the man covered his tracks too well. Someone inside Midwest Mutual must be helping him. It was the only explanation for his ability to know her every move.

The bank account was a bonus. Just further proof that her husband was a control freak and had failed to follow through on one more of his promises. Kira thought of the divorce papers that were gathering dust in her bill organizer. Even when she'd made the effort to erase his memory, he'd avoided the sheriff's attempt to serve him with the papers.

Why hadn't she tried harder to track him down? She wanted to forget their *relationship*, right? So what did it say about her that she remained linked to him?

And now, angst over the latest revelation that she was somehow involved. The bank account the FBI had found was much too convenient. It also meant she'd have to make a concerted effort to find her almost ex-husband. Josh could sweet-talk his way out of walking naked through a ladies' Bible study. Yes, he was that charming. Totally untrustworthy, but charming…like a snake.

She had only herself to blame. This is what happened when you trusted the wrong person. This is what happened when impulse overruled common sense. And this is exactly what happened when you lived a lie without giving any consideration to the consequences.

She'd survived far worse than this, hadn't she?

It was time for her to demand answers from the man who'd left her broken and alone. If it meant the difference between prison and freedom, she would use every morsel of information she'd gathered to track him down.

# Chapter 1

Dalton Matthews slapped the sawdust from his well-worn jeans and scowled at the gray Ranger pickup parked a half mile or so down the gravel lane to his house. It was a little late for the welcome wagon to come knocking, since he'd no longer be considered a newcomer. If his streak of bad luck continued, another snooty reporter from News Channel 9 was probably close enough for him to strangle.

He scanned the area and then jogged down the road to check for the intruder. Anger swelled and added to his frustration when he found the truck unoccupied. He stared inside the unlocked cab. The keys hung from the ignition and a black leather purse was sideways on the seat amid some fast-food wrappers and a few empty water bottles. But the most interesting item of all was a digital camera partially hidden under a road atlas.

Damn the paparazzi for their never-ending attempts to breach his privacy and twist the knife deeper in his gut. He should have known they wouldn't allow him a moment's peace. Not with *Gossip Girl* magazine offering three hundred grand for any picture of him in exile.

He swiped the keys from the ignition and pocketed them. Let the owner hike to the main road and hitch a ride. Or maybe he'd call the sheriff and have them arrested for trespassing. As an afterthought, he removed the memory card from the camera and pocketed it, as well.

As he retraced his steps to the house, he noticed the door to the storage shed swaying in the breeze. He was certain he'd closed it earlier after placing extra lumber inside. He scanned the yard once more before checking his pockets for his phone. Maybe he ought to call the sheriff first and delay a confrontation.

Instead, he rushed to the building's entrance and shouldered his way inside. His annoyance ratcheted up another notch when, even in the dimly lit space, he spotted the trespasser picking her way through various pieces of scrap wood littering the floor.

A woman with blond hair falling below her shoulders and a shapely rear end clad in faded blue jeans.

"What are you doing out here?"

The startled woman pivoted and stumbled, tripping on the uneven surface and pitching sideways. He instinctively extended his arms, but he wasn't nearly close enough to break her fall. She whacked her head on one of the wide wooden support beams and crumpled to the floor.

He was paralyzed by memories of another time and another woman. His attempts at revival had been futile back then. The sickness of that moment clogged his throat, as it had so frequently in the early days. He'd clutched a lifeless form in his arms while he'd bargained with God for another chance.

Hurrying forward now, he knelt beside the stranger and

moved a length of hair from her brow while avoiding the cut over her right eye. Blood flowed down her temple, forming a small puddle near her ear. He lifted her in his arms and strode outside, hoping the late-afternoon sun would provide a better view of her injury.

She was softer than he remembered a woman being, probably because his memories of the opposite sex were in the distant past. A pink lacy bra was visible beneath her green short-sleeved shirt. Only a pervert would recognize a front-hook bra on an unconscious woman. One more reason for annoyance to fuel his actions.

He shifted her in his arms and forced his eyes away from her undergarments as he crossed the last thirty feet to the house. Spying another large scrape on her forearm brought him to a halt. What if she needed an ambulance?

He didn't relish the thought of alerting anyone to his location or having her arrested so she could blab to the highest bidder. Right now he needed to make sure she was all right and stem off any possible lawsuit she might have in mind. People got a bit crazy when they had their sights set on some easy money, a lesson he wished he'd never learned.

After taking the front porch steps two at a time, he caught the bottom corner of the screen door with his booted foot and kicked it open. His living room rivaled an obstacle course. All the kitchen appliances and furniture had been relocated to the small room because the new granite countertops hadn't arrived yet. The path to the stairwell was tight, forcing him to turn sideways and adjust his hold on the woman when her feet caught on his oversize recliner.

He maneuvered the narrow stairway to the second floor, slipped into the first doorway and laid her on the unmade bed. She looked so out of place, and so pale, with the dark circles rimming her eyes matching the shade of gray from the sheets covering the mattress. He caught himself reaching for her wrist and counting the beats before he comprehended he'd been holding his breath. This woman had a pulse, unlike Lauren.

He dropped her hand and stepped away from the bed, working to calm his racing heart. He never relived the day he'd found Lauren without the benefit of a strong drink. But all the same, the image was there, sinking into the gap in his brain he hadn't managed to fill despite the physical labor blending the days together.

The woman moaned, one ashen forearm covering her eyes as she rolled closer to the side of the bed. He jerked forward, catching her shoulders before she could topple to the floor. She shuddered in his grasp as he settled her against the pillow and pressed a handful of tissues against her injury.

Her eyes opened a fraction of an inch and long lashes fluttered against the brow already shadowed with purple, predicting an impending bruise. Lifting her hand to her forehead, she winced, before glaring at him with utter contempt. "You hit me?"

"Of course not." Perhaps she'd used this ploy before.

"You must have," she said, as her gaze bounced around the sparsely furnished room. "Where am I?"

"You're lost," he offered, seriously tipping the scales in the generosity department. This little fiasco had *scam* written all over it, and he was through playing the game.

Removing his cell phone from his pocket, he scrolled to find the number of the local police department. Pausing before hitting the send button, he shifted his gaze to the trespasser, resigned to giving up his anonymity in order to get her out of his hair. "Maybe the sheriff can help you find your way."

A thunderous boom rocked the house, shattering the bedroom window and sending shards of glass and chunks of metal hurling through the air.

Dalton lurched forward, eliciting an ungrateful cry from the woman. She bucked like a bull out of the chute, rolling them both to the floor. He used his elbows to keep from crushing her with his full weight.

Evidently gratitude wasn't in her vocabulary, because Ms. Con-Artist-Extraordinaire kicked his shin and tried twisting out of his hold. He allowed his full weight to drop on top of her, pinning her to the floor. But if he thought the explosion in front of the house was his utmost worry, he'd been mistaken. The angry glint in her bright green eyes warned him the game wasn't over. She kicked once more, drawing his attention to a lump pressing against his kneecap.

"Get off me." Her painted fingernails were little spikes through his shirt as she shoved at his chest.

"Lie still." He held her in place as she squirmed beneath him. She was a lot stronger than he'd expected. Her labored breathing warmed his chin and her continued movements succeeded in firing more than his temper. Those sizzling emerald eyes promised retribution for her confinement. He reached between them, shoving the denim up her leg, revealing a leather ankle holster.

"What's this?"

Bad enough the scam artist had accused him of assaulting her and then managed to blow up a good portion of his house; she also had a concealed weapon.

"It's not what you think." She bucked her hips beneath his in a feeble attempt to break free.

"Don't even start." He double-checked the safety before releasing her and hauling himself to his feet. Inspecting the magazine, he half hoped it would be empty. No such luck. One bullet was chambered and another eight remained in the clip.

After shoving the clip into place, he kept the weapon aimed at her while sliding closer to the window. The woman's truck was fully engulfed in bright orange flames.

"Your truck exploded."

"What?" She sat up, appearing genuinely shocked by the news.

"Not part of your plan?"

"No. Why would I blow up a rental?" Inhaling a shaky breath, she swiped at pieces of glass stuck to her palms.

"Maybe you should have put more thought into your plan, whatever that may be." Sparks ignited the dry grass around the truck. His anger with the woman slid to a non-priority. Alerting the fire department was his first.

Dalton crossed the room, collected the remainder of his cell and disgustedly tossed it aside. "Where's your phone?"

"I don't have one." She remained seated on the floor.

"Empty your pockets." He didn't believe a word she spoke.

After wiping a spattering of blood on her jeans, she shifted to her knees and dug her hand into her pockets. A handful of change clattered to the floor along with a lip balm, a few dollars and a piece of gum.

"I told you the truth."

"I doubt it." Now what was he supposed to do with her? From the corner of his eye he noticed movement beyond the tree line. Another armed trespasser?

"Who else is out there?" He held the gun on the woman and watched her accomplice making his way to the back of the barn.

"How would I know?" Her eyes darted to the doorway and then returned to the weapon in his hand. "I want my gun."

He flat out laughed at the request. Smoke from the explosion reached his nostrils, reminding him of the urgent need to control the fire.

"Get up," he ordered, wordlessly promising to drag her off the floor if she didn't comply. He reached for the simple wooden chair that had survived more than a century of abuse at the hands of his family.

"You can't keep me here. What if the fire spreads?" Was that genuine fear or insolence lacing every word?

"Wanna bet?" He dropped the chair at her feet and shoved the weapon into the back of his jeans. He pulled out his pocketknife and cut through a section of sheet, quickly ripping it in half. A second later her shoe sailed through the air and bounced off his cheek, before she bolted for the door. He chased her into the hallway, catching her around the waist and pulling her back into his bedroom.

"Let me go," she hollered. Her elbows and feet connected with various parts of his body as she tried ineffectually to get free. "Ouch, you're hurting me."

"And you're really pissing me off, cupcake." He dropped her onto the chair. Pulling her arms together in back, he slipped a wide section of sheet around her wrists and tied a double knot. Then he moved in front of her to secure her legs to the chair.

"You're going to be sorry you messed with me," she threatened, already trying to work her way free.

"What's your friend's name?" Dalton demanded. Her immediate silence surprised him. He should've been grateful for the reprieve.

He glanced out the window once more. The blonde bomber's cohort was skirting the shed with a gun clutched in his hand. Armed paparazzi or kidnappers hoping to extract a big ransom? It didn't make sense for them to blow up their own getaway vehicle.

Dalton may have briefly forgotten the Coast Guard's motto, *Semper Paratus*, Latin for Always Ready, but having a gun in his hand again brought his training to the forefront. His muscles twitched in anticipation, not unlike the first time he'd boarded a vessel in the Gulf of Mexico and helped his team seize a shipment of cocaine bound for the United States.

He slipped off the safety and approached the open doorway. Glancing once more at the troublesome woman, he stifled a brief flicker of guilt over leaving her without a way to protect herself. But she'd already burned through his goodwill. Judging her an enemy instead of an ally was self-preservation in its simplest form. As jaded as it sounded, it was easy to slip back into the role that had shaped his early life.

Chair legs scraped across the floor, but he didn't have any more time to waste on her. He needed the landline downstairs and it would take a minute to push his way to it. Phone, firemen and, unfortunately, another round with the police. Maybe it was time to hire some private security and stop depleting the sheriff department's resources. Then again, his *donations* had already funded two new patrol vehicles and trained a K-9 dog. What next?

Smoke billowed in an upward spiral close to the house, tainting the breeze, which had earlier carried the scent of autumn. Kira's head pounded an irregular rhythm, and she squeezed her eyes shut in an effort to overcome the nausea bubbling in her stomach. Convincing herself that being sick wasn't an option, she tried piecing together a plan. This was the place, she was almost certain. That shed outside hadn't been here before, but there was something familiar about this room.

Why hadn't she blurted out the question she wanted answered? *Do you know Joshua Kincaid?* That's what normal people did—they asked questions. She was terrified the man would say no, because she'd run out of options, chances and luck.

Nothing to lose. She wiggled in the chair. The tiny thumb drive wedged in her bra beneath her left breast pinched, confirming it was still in place. Considering her jarring fall to the floor and being manhandled by the impatient ogre in a lumberjack shirt, it was a miracle. Maybe ogre was an exaggeration, but he looked and felt solid enough to play the man in the Brawny commercials.

Most people backed up their computer files. But some people, like Kira, went a little crazy. She had an external hard drive for her home computer and several flash drives she rotated through. The FBI thought they'd confiscated everything, but they didn't know about the online backup site she used. Some secrets would always be safe as long as they didn't fall out of her bra.

Straining her neck to the right, she shifted enough to see past the valance hanging lopsided from one of the two front windows. A six-inch pane of glass remained intact, but the rest was reduced to various sized pellets littering the hardwood floor.

Nearly four years had passed since she and Josh had spent the weekend here and he'd proposed. If Kira thought too much about how she'd arrived back here, she'd never dig herself out of the darkness.

Josh had effectively fallen into a black hole. She had no idea where he'd gone after their separation, and she had to find him. Her desperation had led her to the obituaries, numerous social networking sites and every phone number for every Kincaid in the Midwest. No one knew him or was related to him. Josh couldn't have disappeared without a trace. Okay, she'd found a trace in the form of a joint tax return he'd filed, managing to collect a refund.

He had also worked for one of Griffin's shell companies. The entire time Josh and Kira had been together he hadn't been the struggling artist he'd portrayed. He had earned nearly twenty thousand dollars and hadn't shared a dime with her. Not only were the Feds breathing down her neck, but since her arrest five weeks ago she'd acquired a shadow. If there were two feelings she'd never quite grown used to, they were being watched and being alone.

What had Josh gotten mixed up in? And why had she worked twelve-hour days to put food on the table while he'd spent their extra money on *studio time*? She'd seen only one of his paintings, and it hadn't inspired confidence that he'd ever support their expanding family.

Learning he had money and yet hadn't offered to do more shouldn't have surprised Kira. He'd never been a college student, either, at least not in Kansas City. The number of lies he'd told her expanded into double digits. When she finally tracked him down, she'd be armed with plenty of persuasive evidence to encourage some honesty. And a quick divorce.

Kira rocked the chair from side to side, determined to free herself. Tight bindings cut into her wrists. Swallowing a groan, she fought against the material holding her hands and legs in place.

Her truck was gone. Technically, it wasn't hers, but she assumed the obnoxious rental car manager wouldn't mind garnishing her wages for the next decade.

What did it matter? She'd be in prison, anyway… Which was negative thinking. She was supposed to send good vibes out into the universe and be rewarded for her efforts. Obviously the ogre wasn't a fan of Dr. Phil.

"I can absolutely, positively free myself," she chanted.

Her fingers found an opening in the bindings, and on the third try, the knot was gone and she was free. She heard noises downstairs and hurried to detach the bindings from her legs.

She stood and grabbed the chair, steadying herself while her head spun with troubling theories of escape. She couldn't stay here. The Brawny guy was determined to call the fire department, and probably the sheriff's office to charge her with trespassing. If she was arrested, they'd ship her back to Kansas City to face all the original charges, plus bail jumping.

A rush of adrenaline forced her awareness to strict survival skills. She needed a weapon.

Feathers from a down-filled pillow covered most of the floor and the box springs clung precariously to one side of the metal bed frame. Kira stepped closer and yanked at the center support bar underneath. It popped loose and one end dropped to the floor with a resounding clunk. She froze.

What if Brawny heard?

Seconds passed. No footsteps.

The four-foot piece of metal she held was heavy, awkward and difficult to grip. But she managed to swing it a couple times and pictured herself landing a blow to Brawny's kneecaps. Then she could retrieve her gun. She hated guns, but after the explosion, she needed all the help she could get.

A board squeaked and she scampered to a side wall. Her heart hammered as she tried breathing without making any sound. She needed the element of surprise on her side. A partial shadow crept across the floor. She swung, aiming low, pouring every ounce of her strength into connecting with his kneecaps.

But the man who came through the door wasn't Brawny. And she hadn't hit his kneecaps.

The new man howled as he doubled over, firing off three quick shots before collapsing to his knees. Kira swung at his shoulders, hoping to knock him out of the game. His gun skidded across the floor.

She dropped the metal bar and dived for it. Shards of glass and wood splinters bit into her arms and legs. Feathers scattered in her wake. As her fingers gripped the weapon, she rolled onto her back, pointing the barrel toward the newcomer's balding head.

Could she shoot him? Would it guarantee no more attempts to kill her? The man on the floor didn't move and relief engulfed her.

She'd never thought herself capable of killing anyone, so this was testament to how far she'd fallen on the sanity scale. Kira struggled to a sitting position, exhausted and swiping at the blood mixed with sweat dripping down her cheeks—battle scars from her earlier tumble.

"Guess your friend found you." Brawny stopped short in the doorway, holding her gun as if he planned to use it.

"You mean *your* friend. Put my gun down or I'll shoot." Okay, maybe she'd shoot. She'd never fired at a real person before.

Brawny was tall, probably over six feet, with a stance that said he expected compliance. A faint hint of stubble ran across his jaw. His dark brown hair held a few blond highlights, showing a bit of length in the back, leading her to believe he'd missed a haircut or two.

"Shoot your friend first, since he's the one trying to kill you."

A very rational request. "Maybe I should shoot you both." The gun wobbled in her hands. It was heavier than hers and she really shouldn't point it at anyone. What if it went off?

"Good luck with that. You know live ammunition does more than go boom, right?"

Was he mocking her? "Of course I know."

Brawny fired at the wall above her head and she ducked. When she glanced up again, he was dumping the shells into his palm before tossing the gun at her feet. "Your gun is loaded with blanks and I'm dying to hear why."

"I tried telling you, but you wouldn't listen." How would she explain that she didn't want to shoot anyone? To her they were practice bullets, meant to help her get used to the sound of gunfire without flinching.

"Why use a gun without real bullets?" Brawny rubbed his chin, drawing her attention to the five o'clock shadow that was much too sexy for his own good.

"I'm holding a real gun with real bullets now."

"If you shoot me, who's going to help you with these?" He held out a set of handcuffs, nodded toward the man on the floor. Then he unwisely took a step closer.

"Stay back," she ordered, visualizing herself handcuffed to another chair. "I don't want any more of your help."

He flashed a perfect smile, which under any other circumstances would have made her weak in the knees. He shrugged. "You destroyed half my house."

"*I* didn't destroy anything." She needed to hold on to the anger, make him think twice about laying another hand on her.

"And I know this isn't your house." She hated that her voice shook.

"Really? Then whose house is it?"

"I'll ask the questions." Her eyes darted to the man on the floor and then to Brawny. "How do I know you didn't send him up here to kill me?"

"You don't."

Not at all what she'd expected. "No song and dance about why I should trust you?"

"You shouldn't."

Well, good. At least they were on the same page. He took a lazy step forward and she adjusted her sights. She slid a few inches to the left and connected with a wall. "Don't move any closer."

"Shooting me is a waste of bullets." He dropped the handcuffs and kicked them across the floor to her. "Put those on."

"A frequent fantasy of yours?" She'd been aiming for a sarcastic tone, and instead the words came out breathy. Like an invitation.

"Definitely." His raised eyebrow spoke volumes and she balanced on the thin line between anger and appreciation. He was good. Scratch that. He was very bad, and he knew it.

"I meant, use them on your friend. We need to get out of here before the fire closes in."

"And if I refuse?" She swiped her forearm across her cheek and stifled a groan when her skin burned from the action.

"Then you deserve each other," he drawled. Brawny's warped sense of humor added to his raw appeal. Laughter and looks were a dangerous combination.

She lowered her gun a smidgen. Was she really going to shoot either of the men? And if she had to trust one, it would be Brawny. His silky brown eyes slid down her body and then to the gun in her hand.

"You're making me nervous. How about a truce?"

"How long until the police arrive?" she countered. The burst of adrenaline was quickly fading from her bloodstream, causing her hands to shake.

"Twenty minutes." His critical eyes swept her again. "Do you need an ambulance?"

Did she? The thoughts were getting jumbled in her head. She couldn't stay here, but didn't know how to leave. The man on the floor shifted, distracting her long enough for Brawny to pry the gun from her fingers.

He pointed the weapon at the man she'd temporarily sidelined. "I *will* shoot." He kicked the balding man's outstretched arm for emphasis, earning a grunt in return.

"Hand me the cuffs," Brawny said.

Kira reached for the handcuffs, stifling the urge to ask where he'd gotten them. Pressing her back against the wall, she struggled to stand, one bare foot crunching on broken glass. She winced, throwing all her weight onto her other leg while trying to extend the cuffs to Brawny.

"You ain't cuffing me," the other man bellowed.

"Shut up," Brawny said.

An obnoxious noise filled the room. Belching, maybe? But the man's lips weren't moving.

"Oh, that's classy," Brawny said. "Where's the phone?" He pressed the barrel of the gun against the balding man's head when he didn't reply. "Last chance."

"All right, all right, it's in my pocket."

As Brawny squatted to search the denim pockets, Kira stood holding the cuffs. She should do something to help, right? Maybe slip one of the silver bracelets onto the man's wrist while Brawny subdued him.

She took a step closer as Brawny located the phone and silenced the annoying ringtone. In a flash, the balding man wrapped his fingers around her ankle and yanked her off balance as he threw his elbow toward Brawny's face. Her bare foot was already unsteady as she tried kicking free.

Kira tumbled, her arms windmilling as she tried to catch herself. Hot pain hammered the back of her head as she fought to remain conscious. Her eyes slid closed against a backdrop of grunts and punches. She rolled to her side, unable to do more than lie there and listen.

Another punch, another curse, another gunshot, then silence. She felt more than heard the vibration against the floor. Sensed someone moving nearby. Her heart hammered in her chest, but she couldn't breathe.

"Tell me she's dead." An unfamiliar voice crackled through the phone.

Another gunshot exploded and Kira grabbed her head. The sound echoed in her ears, reverberated through her skull. Then silence.

# Chapter 2

"She's dead." Dalton mimicked the thug's voice to perfection, a skill he and his brother, Josh, had honed as kids. At the same time he was grinding his heel into the intruder's face for emphasis.

"Clean it up and get here by morning." Whoever Rico was, he disconnected before Dalton uttered another word.

He shoved the phone into his pocket. The surreal activities of the past twenty-odd minutes came into clear focus. The blonde bomber had told at least one truth: she didn't have a partner. She also didn't have a prayer of walking away without sharing the full, unabridged version of why she'd ended up at his door, and how she planned to stay alive.

For a moment, he allowed his gaze to roam her body, lingering on the cleavage exposed when her shirt had slipped off one shoulder. The thickening smoke reminded him they had to get out of here.

Dalton could consider himself every kind of fool for not letting the woman suffer alone, but she needed a doctor. A man with any functioning brain cells would've found out her name when she'd first opened her eyes. There *had* been an explosion, so maybe he should cut himself some slack.

The sound of rain splattering against the house, along with the crack of thunder that followed, had him breathing easier. The small fire would be out in no time. "At least something is going right."

He should have expected that the man would put up quite a fight. The bastard had gone after Blondie again, leaving no doubt he wanted her dead. Dalton had stopped short of killing him, but the thought still flickered in the back of his mind.

It would be self-defense, plain and simple. But he didn't want an ounce of scandal to touch his family's name ever again. His mom couldn't take another and would never forgive him. First Lauren, and the personal attacks that had seeped into his mom's life, then Dalton lying his way through his brother's death. The tabloids insinuated Josh had gotten what he deserved, and although Dalton felt the same way, he had to deflect their claims.

Josh had always been their mother's favorite. Maybe because he was the baby of the family, or maybe because his mother coveted his free and easy nature. He could do no wrong in her eyes. And since they'd fought the day before his death, his mother was convinced she'd played a role in sending him over that cliff.

Dalton grabbed the man's shirt collar and dragged him into the bathroom, anchoring him with duct tape to the cast-iron bathtub while he writhed in agony.

"Who are you and why do you want her dead?"

The portly man pressed his lips together, trying to look cocky. "You're a wrinkle in the plan," he said. "They want this place gone, burned to the ground. I'll be out of jail and back in a couple hours to finish the job."

"I'm shaking with fright." The man might have been intimidating to anyone else, but to Dalton, he was simply a bully. "Behave yourself and I'll call the cops tomorrow."

He returned to the bedroom and dialed the emergency services number again. He couldn't second-guess his decision to help the unconscious woman. Commitment was his middle name. "This is Dalton Matthews. I need to cancel the call for a grass fire. Looks like the rain put it out."

"I'll remove it from our list," the dispatcher replied.

"I'm heading out of town for a few days. Could I get an extra patrol to swing past tomorrow and make sure everything's in order?"

"We can do that."

The man in the next room gathered enough energy to bellow a string of curse words.

"Sorry. Forgot to mute the television before I called."

"No problem, sir. I've heard worse."

"Now that I think about it, switch the patrol to the day after tomorrow." Dalton grinned to himself. "Nothing exciting ever happens around here."

"Right. I've got you down. Have a safe trip."

He disconnected the call and stared at Blondie. She was out for the count and his ruse might have bought her a short reprieve. Getting her to a doctor or hospital would cover his culpability regarding her injuries. He dropped his bloodstained flannel shirt and pulled on the first available T-shirt.

"Now for sleeping Blondie."

All his efforts while he'd been in hiding the past several months would be wasted by tomorrow. There was no time to cover all the windows and prevent any further damage to the house. He released another, longer sigh and with it some of the anger kindling his blood.

He tossed an old afghan onto Blondie and secured her close to his body. He settled her in the front passenger seat of his vehicle, clicked the seat belt in place and climbed into the driver's side. He backed out of the garage and refused to look at the damage.

The rain had arrived in time to stop the fire. He adjusted the wipers and pulled onto the darkening county road with one final glance in his rearview mirror. No second thoughts.

Right or wrong, he was committed to securing Blondie's health and safety. She needed a hospital. She'd get a hospital. If she woke up before that, he'd get answers.

Dalton rubbed his knuckles, thinking of the bastard who'd taken a hit to the groin. The man's curse-filled tirade had confirmed that someone wanted more than death for Blondie. What did she want from Dalton? More than a few things didn't add up.

Dalton spotted the bright pink nails grasping the edge of the damp afghan he'd thrown over her. He caught himself reaching for her fingers, the familiar color causing his gut to clench. Instead, he anchored his hands on the steering wheel.

How many times had he seen such a color? Visiting the nail salon had been a ritual for Lauren. Until the day she'd taken her life. It was almost impossible not to think of his wife, and every time he did, he couldn't get past the circumstances framing her death or the blame levied at him.

"How many media *exclusives* can you people want?" An unlimited supply, when every person Lauren had known, past and present, collected a fee for their sorrow. Too bad they hadn't been half as involved in her life when her fame had started tearing her apart.

But paparazzi don't normally carry guns or have thugs blowing up their cars.

The woman beside him was too pale. Too fragile looking, as though she'd endured more than her fair share of pain. She moistened her lips and wiped her hand across her eyes before wincing and bolting upright in the seat.

"Let me out!" She tugged at her seat belt.

He glanced at the highway. "Out where?"

She pushed a strand of hair off her face and glared at him. "Just pull over and let me out."

Dalton hit the brakes and steered the sedan onto the shoulder, sending gravel flying against the undercarriage of the car and abruptly stopping them with enough force the airbags could have deployed.

She braced a hand against the dashboard before throwing off the afghan and releasing the seat belt. She yanked on the door handle and then beat her fist against the cherrywood trim in frustration. "Why won't this door open?"

Dalton placed the car in Park and turned off the ignition. "Because we have some unfinished business, because it's dark and rainy outside or because you aren't wearing shoes. Take your pick."

She shut up for six seconds and then immediately returned to attack mode. "I already said I was sorry. Now let me go."

"First tell me your name."

"Tell me *your* name." She might talk big, but her body language told a different story. She was shrinking to the corner of the seat.

"I have a feeling you already know it."

Pinching the bridge of her nose, she softly counted to ten. Then she reached forward, opened the glove box and started riffling through the papers inside. He'd give her points for resourcefulness, but she'd find nothing in there to help her.

Next, she flipped on the console light and held up three or four papers for inspection. "BCA. BCA. And BCA, Inc." She glared over at him. "What's a BCA?"

"Business name." He winked, hoping she could see it in the dim light. "Your turn."

"I pass." She crossed her arms, stubborn yet again.

"Are you sure?" he asked, typing in a request on the car's GPS screen and doing it with enough fanfare she had to be watching him. He flipped on the audio switch and waited for the announcement.

"Law enforcement located, ten point three miles northeast, downloading directions now."

She stared at the screen, chewed her lip nervously and then straightened her spine. "If you were going to turn me in, why didn't you do it already?"

He didn't need her calling his bluff. He needed her to crumble and spill her guts so he could determine her true motivation. It was like a really bad game of hot potato and he wanted to get rid of her as soon as feasibly possible.

"Simple answer, I was headed to the hospital, quicker than waiting for an ambulance." He invoked his most take-charge tone before continuing. "You could move things along by telling me your name and how you found me."

She shoved the mass of paperwork and fast-food napkins back into the glove box and slammed the cover shut. "I wasn't looking for you."

"Really? Then what were you doing, snooping around my property?"

She chewed her bottom lip again. "Exactly how long have you lived there?"

The air in Dalton's lungs turned to fresh cement and for several seconds he couldn't breathe as he remembered the day he'd escaped to the woods. Had he really been hiding out for over a year? He cleared his throat. "Answering a question with a question is a classic avoidance technique, one you probably already knew."

She blew the bangs from her forehead and turned toward him. "And yet it's a question I will ask again. How long have you lived there?"

"And I'll repeat, what were you doing snooping around my property?" Two could play her game.

She glared at him again. "I wasn't trying to snoop, but I'd actually been there several years ago. I was searching for…an old friend."

Dalton took a moment to absorb the information. This woman was asking him to believe she'd been there, legally, without his knowledge. There were only four people with a key.

"Maybe the exterior has changed a bit, but I'm 99 percent certain my friend still owns that property. We came here New Year's Eve almost four years ago." Her voice shook again and she blinked away tears.

"Blondie, my family has owned that house for sixty years." Dalton watched as her expression changed from anger to uncertainty. "You've either confused the location with another property or you were trespassing the first time."

He'd expected another string of denials to fall from her lips.

"Damn you, Josh," she softly cursed.

Dalton's blood ran cold at the mention of his brother's name. He gripped the steering wheel when he'd rather have hold of her neck. "Did you say Josh?"

"Yes, Joshua Kincaid." She swiped her tongue across her lips again, momentarily distracting him.

"And…" He tossed off his seat belt and leaned across

the console, anxious to hear what scheme his half brother had gotten her involved in.

"And what? He proposed to me in that cabin." She released a huge sigh. "Josh is my husband."

Dalton couldn't stop staring at her as if she'd admitted to being a topless dancer at an old folks' home. Then a laugh burst from his chest. "You're definitely not his type."

"Tell me something I don't know."

"Josh was never married." So this was her plan the whole time? She was sniffing around for a windfall, but not from him, from Josh. No wonder she'd turned up at his family's cabin, but claiming to be Josh's wife didn't help her credibility. At least not with Dalton. And there was no way in hell he'd let his mother hear. Lie or not, she'd take Blondie's word without a shred of evidence, just so she'd have some part of Josh again.

"We *are* married," Blondie said. "And I need to talk to him."

"Lady—and I use the term very loosely—there are many things you obviously need. But you'll never talk to Josh."

"Oh, you can bet I'll find him," she yelled, shoving forward and staring Dalton in the eye. "You don't know anything about me."

"Lucky me." He'd give her points for appearing wounded by his comment, but she was still a fraud. "Cooking up this whole story isn't getting you a dime. I guarantee it."

"It isn't a story and I don't want your money. Josh will help set everything straight. Do you know where he is?"

"Yeah, I know a lot of things." The words spit from his lips. "I know you're definitely not Josh's wife." Of all the ridiculous lies she could have created, this one knocked the breath from Dalton's lungs. He had to stop her before the situation snowballed out of control.

"I couldn't care less what you believe," she snapped, giving as good as she got. "Can you help me find Josh or not?"

"Find him? Oh, yeah, I can lead you right to him." Dalton slammed his fist against the console and drew a deep breath before he threw the car into gear, made a U-turn and tore down the roadway. He veered right on the second gravel road, so upset that he forgot about slowing down for the ruts.

"Where are you taking me?"

He couldn't answer her.

"When was the last time you saw Josh?"

"Seven weeks ago." He pushed the words out.

"Did he seem all right?"

"No." Dalton felt nothing now that the gate was in sight. "He seemed dead."

Blondie was silent for several minutes. "Tell me how." She kept her face turned toward the window, although he couldn't have judged her true reaction in the darkness, anyway.

"Does it matter?" Dalton refused to go into the whole story when it was the least of his worries. He followed the ruts in the road as the pellets of rain lessened to a fine mist. After kicking on the high beams, he adjusted the wipers to a slower interval and watched for washed-out spots in their path. He hadn't been here often, but the archway entrance to the cemetery couldn't be missed.

"It matters to me." She rubbed her palms against her eyelids. "Why is this happening?"

"You must have some idea."

"So far, every one of my ideas has turned to crap." She coughed. "Leave it to Josh to get the last word, even in death."

"So the honeymoon was over? I can't imagine why Josh would've kept your charming personality a secret from the rest of the family."

"Family? What are you talking about? Josh didn't have family. Who are you?" She fired the questions while bracing a hand on the ceiling to keep herself from jostling around each time they hit a bump.

Dalton ignored her question. He sped through the gate, gripping the leather steering wheel as he turned to the family's corner. He eyed Josh's *wife* with renewed annoyance and questioned her lack of emotion since he'd announced his brother was dead. If they really were married, shouldn't she have some remorse over his passing? What kind of wife referred to her deceased husband as getting in the last word?

The cemetery had been a private plot until his father sold most of the land thirty years ago. Dalton had hated the place as a kid. Hated it more now, since Lauren and Josh were buried here. Throwing the car into Park, he jumped out and opened the heavy iron gates separating their family from the rest of the cemetery.

When he climbed back inside the car, he realized Blondie could have locked him out and driven away. Instead, she was staring out her window. What was going through her mind?

He followed the pathway curving to the right. Towering green ash trees and a few rare bushes whose name he'd forgotten edged the lane. He parked near the large headstone serving as the grand centerpiece.

"Let's go."

"No." She shook her head. "I'm not doing this."

"I don't remember giving you a choice." He released the door locks, remembering to pull the keys.

The interior lights flickered when he tugged on his door

handle, then exited the car. Stepping away from the closest muddy rut, he waded through the grass and flipped open the trunk. He found the emergency kit and the flashlight before circling to the front of the vehicle, where he waited for Blondie.

She took her time, staring through the windshield at him for several moments before joining him in the halogen glare of the headlights. She dragged the afghan with her as she stalked silently beside him. The flashlight glimmered off the headstone at the center of the plot.

"I guess size matters a lot in your family," Blondie snickered.

"It's rumored to be sprinkled with real diamond dust. Probably not true, since no one has ever tried stealing it."

"Pretty flashy for the middle of nowhere," she said, continuing around the far end. "Why did you bring me here?"

Was she deliberately trying to goad him?

"The Matthews men were a prideful bunch, with a history of grand exits from the world. This massive headstone took two years and a lot of money during the Depression to complete. Nowadays, only the caretaker sees it on a regular basis."

"Nice history lesson, but my husband's last name is Kincaid. This has nothing to do with me and I don't care."

Dalton hadn't been the most respectful Matthews family member to set foot in this place, but Blondie's disrespect was ticking him off. Or was it being close to Lauren's grave?

Or even the fact that Josh had been buried next to Lauren, at his mother's suggestion. And Dalton couldn't object without voicing his suspicions about their affair and starting everything again. No, this had to end—right here, right now.

Then a stretch of bare earth appeared, and the pile of

flowers the wind and rain hadn't managed to carry away. No one visited, but his mother insisted a fresh arrangement be placed there every Sunday.

"Josh is over here." Dalton took her arm and tried pulling her a few feet closer to the site.

"Why should I believe a complete stranger who won't tell me who he is?"

"I'm Dalton Matthews. Josh was my half brother." It wasn't a term they'd ever used as kids. Their mother used to say that half of anything didn't matter. They were brothers. Period.

"No, you're not. Josh didn't have any siblings and you have no proof he's dead. My Josh can't be dead." She pivoted and took off running for the car.

Dalton was more than mad, but he couldn't lose it, not here. For some reason this woman got under his skin faster than any paparazzi. But she wouldn't fake that she was his brother's widow. What if she went to his mom?

Dalton easily caught up with her in a few steps and gripped her shoulder.

"Get your hands off me." She tried dodging his grasp.

He spun her around to look at him, shining the flashlight in her eyes. "How long were you married?"

"Four years in January."

If Josh had been married, that would explain his frequent absences. Or was Dalton clutching at any straw to keep his mind from straying to the thought of Lauren and Josh together? The flashlight beam swept their graves. He tried for calmness.

He failed.

"You haven't seen Josh's headstone yet."

"You're an ass."

"So I've been told."

# Chapter 3

"More diamond dust?" Kira yanked her arm from his grasp and fell sideways into the mud. She didn't realize what the mud was until the beam of light fell across the stone. Joshua Kincaid Matthews, loving son and brother.

Kira immediately wanted to scream what a bastard Josh was. She recognized yet another lie to add to the long list her husband had told her. But if he hadn't used his real name with her, had they really been married?

"Do you still think I didn't know Josh?" She stood, wiping her mud-covered hands down her pants. There wasn't anything physically similar about the two men.

"You aren't acting like the mourning bride."

"How I mourn is none of your business. What motive could I possibly have to stand here if I'm not married to that man?"

He couldn't be dead. He just couldn't. She refused to show any sadness for the man who'd abandoned her. But what made her want to sink to her knees in despair was knowing that her last hope to identify Griffin and clear her name was gone.

It was a long shot to begin with, and now she'd truly run out of options. There wasn't anyone left to turn to for help. No family to lend support or friends to phone for advice. Now her freedom hung in the balance.

Strong fingers latched on to the soft flesh of her shoulders.

"You're an imposter." He gave her a slight shake.

The eternity candle from the mausoleum was doing weird things with Josh's brother's features. It cast a glow that made everything appear more sinister.

Cemeteries in general were creepy. And visiting one in the middle of nowhere, with an armed stranger, was more creepy than usual. The likelihood anyone would stumble upon them was minimal, but being so far out in the boondocks only magnified the otherworldly feel.

Dalton Matthews looked angry enough to kill, and Kira's mind jumped into overdrive. A moment of sudden clarity struck. What better place to dump a body than in a private cemetery with a fresh grave? The longer she stood next to him, the more certain she was that leaving was less likely. He'd been furious when she'd mentioned Josh's name and then he'd immediately driven her to this isolated cemetery. Brother or stranger? BCA, Inc. could stand for Brawny Commits Assault for all she knew.

Stay or run? If she could get the jump on him and sprint to the car, she could lock herself inside and drive away. Then Kira remembered he'd pocketed the keys.

She wanted to punch something, and violence had never been an option in her life. Until today. She knew it was wrong, even before her fist connected with a set of rock-hard abs. Hitting him hurt her much more than she'd expected, forcing her nails into her palm with razor sharpness.

"What was that for?" Dalton grabbed ahold of both her fists and shook her till her teeth rattled.

Hysterical laughter escaped her lips. Was he serious? As if being chased, blown up and tied to a chair wouldn't cause the average person to become a little cranky? Kira tugged against his grip, but he held tight, startling her into throwing up a well-placed knee, barely missing its mark. Then training from her Saturday-morning self-defense class kicked in and she released a bloodcurdling scream, hoping to attract someone's attention.

Dalton spun her away from him and quickly pinned her arms at her sides, drawing her back to his chest.

"Knock it off or I'm finding a place for you in the trunk," he threatened, tightening his grip for emphasis.

"This is against the law," she said, trying to fight her way out of his grasp.

"Guess it depends which side you're on, right, Blondie?"

"Blondie?"

"I've got to call you something, unless you'd rather tell me your real name?"

"I'm so not amused by you, Brawny Boy."

The afghan fell to the ground, leaving her arms bare against the coolness of the night. His forearms crossed beneath her breasts, shoving her assets even closer to overflowing from her worn and torn shirt. His breath fanned against her neck, causing a chill to run down her spine.

"Let me go." Kira resisted the overwhelming desire to struggle, for what seemed like an eternity plus a day. In the span of fifteen or so seconds she knew exactly when her traitorous body shifted to the dark side, recognized that she would have been better off avoiding the heat he radiated and finally identified what a tactical mistake she'd made.

"You sure do love a good fight, don't you?"

"I wasn't fighting," she mumbled, "just expressing a difference of opinion."

Kira relaxed a tad, hating the fact she enjoyed the security of feeling his arms wrapped tightly around her ribs. Very bad. Or maybe she should consider the possibility that she'd suffered a concussion when she'd whacked her head. Whatever the reason, being pressed against Dalton forced her to catalog his attributes, which were many.

First there was the heat he radiated, and not gosh-he-feels-warm heat, but the honest-to-goodness hey-it's-hot-in-here-so-turn-the-furnace-down kind. Big difference.

And muscles. The man had muscles upon muscles. Kira flattened her palms against his thighs for balance. She should admit that she was cold and shoeless, and he might allow her to return to the car.

"Are you finished?" His rich baritone shot warm air across her ear.

Had she really allowed herself to relax against this superbly built man? He could be lying. *Remember the fresh grave?* What if he was another of Griffin's assassins? She jerked against his grasp once more.

"You can't haul someone out to a cemetery after dark and think they'll willingly go along with their own murder. Unless you've done this before?"

"Murder?" Great. He'd scared her more than the assassin at his house had.

Evidently Dalton's lack of human contact over the past few months had turned him into one of the bottom-feeders he claimed to detest. Was he really standing in a cemetery, attempting to exert some kind of control over a woman he hardly knew? He should say something reassuring, right? But her disposition made him edgy and off balance.

Before he could form a suitable explanation, he released her and she stumbled forward. One hand covered her mouth as she coughed, while the other signaled for him to give her space.

The flashlight beam silhouetted her figure and he caught himself staring at the damp T-shirt clinging to her heaving chest, leaving absolutely nothing to the imagination. All her struggling against him had caused the fabric to bunch below her breasts, exposing her midriff. Her pants had also shifted, revealing name-brand underwear.

Then his disbelieving gaze slid down her slim legs to her bare feet, planted in ankle-deep mud. He should have taken her to the hospital, not a cemetery.

"Don't. Touch. Me." Each word she spoke was emphasized by a cough.

"You shouldn't have gotten out of the car without shoes." He glared down at her, feeling like a Sunday school teacher trying to persuade an unruly child to see the light.

After one final cough, she jabbed a finger in the center of his chest. "You didn't get my shoes, remember?"

Yeah, he remembered. The first one she'd thrown at his head, and the other fell off as he'd carried her from his house. "Get in the car."

He shoved his hand into his pocket for the keys, clicked the remote and popped open the trunk. It was loaded with T-shirts, sweatshirts, coffee samples and water bottles. He carried several items to the passenger door.

"You sell T-shirts?" she rasped.

"No, they're freebies." He dropped most of the clothing into her lap, holding on to a camouflage shirt. He mopped some moisture from the roof of the car with it, then knelt down and used the shirt to clean the mud from her feet.

"I can do that," she said.

"I'm sure you can."

"Buckshot's?" She eyed the purple shirt in her lap. "Like hunting supplies or something?"

"Or something." It might have been a reasonable conclusion for somebody living on the moon, but how could anyone with a television, a smartphone or even one dollar to her name not know about Buckshot's? They were "world famous." Dalton had personally opened a dozen new stores in Europe before Lauren had died.

If Blondie had never heard of Buckshot's, she probably didn't know who he was or what he was worth. The idea that she'd shown up looking for some fast cash, from either him or Josh, was quickly losing merit. What if Dalton was wrong? After all, he'd bailed Josh out of more than one unpleasant situation. In school. In his choice of careers. His brother could weave a story and paint himself as the victim in less time than it took to microwave a bag of popcorn.

Dalton swallowed a sigh before it crossed his lips. Blood would always be thicker than water. Was he really going to let this woman disparage his brother's memory? God forbid his mother got wind of the latest attempt to tarnish the family name. She'd been through more than enough.

"Put on a dry shirt while I get a couple more things from the trunk." He slammed the door before he could blurt any of his thoughts aloud. It was probably safer to let her assume he dealt in hunting supplies.

How warped was it that Dalton knew his brother was capable of deception, but couldn't bring himself to admit it to anyone else? Fat raindrops fell on the back of his neck as he returned to the trunk. The light mist segued into rain, and he was about to be soaked.

He shoved the dirty shirt into an empty box and snagged a soft-sided cooler containing drinks. After giving the trunk lid a slam, he sloshed to his door.

"So you handle marketing for this company?" Blondie

had removed her wet shirt, which was now lying on the floorboard.

A true gentleman would feign interest in the moonroof or a dashboard gadget. A true gentleman wouldn't have hauled her out here at all. But Dalton had learned enough to make the trip worthwhile. He settled himself in the seat and watched. She didn't seem to care, confident with her long hair dripping onto her pink bra.

"Among other things."

"Travel a lot?" She struggled to get the clean T-shirt over her head.

"Not as much as I used to." He allowed his gaze to follow her curves. Their conversation was quickly fogging up the windows, something he hadn't contemplated doing in a long time. And he shouldn't be thinking of it now, in a cemetery, with a woman who was nothing but trouble.

The dry shirt twisted below her armpit. As he reached forward and yanked on the fabric, his fingers brushed against an unusual shape. It had been forever since he'd touched a woman's breast, but not so long that he'd forgotten what parts went where. Unless Blondie had a third nipple, she was concealing something. The unexpected jolt he felt from his knuckles skating down her rib cage took him by surprise. When their hands met near the waistband of her jeans, she turned his way. Apprehension was evident in the way she bit her bottom lip and pulled her fingers away from his.

"Did you design the logo, as well?" She was making small talk as he reached for a shred of sanity to keep his hands to himself.

"Depends."

"On what?"

"On whether a wrong answer will make you punch me again." The comment earned him a partial smile as she combed strands of wet hair away from her face. The cut near her eye started bleeding again and her actions smeared the blood across her forehead.

"Hold still a sec." He grasped her chin, then reached into the glove compartment for some paper napkins. He applied pressure against the wound.

"I'm okay, really." She pried the napkins from his fingers.

"Humor me and keep pressing."

"I'm out of humor."

"And yet still full of sarcasm." He flipped on the map light for a better view and transferred the cooler to her lap. "Drink something."

She opened the lid and eyed the contents. "How can your company stay in business if you give all this stuff away?"

"Advertising expense."

"Yeah, but do hunters really need all these things?" She gestured to the cooler and then plucked at her T-shirt. "And since when do they wear purple?"

"People love getting something for nothing. Hunters may not need it, but it builds customer loyalty and name recognition. Usually." Or maybe she had a valid point.

"Tell me how he died." She removed the wad of napkins from her face before dropping them into a cup holder.

That was certainly an attempt at directness. And since she'd already asked once, he didn't see the point in delaying the inevitable. "Josh had been missing a week before his car was found in a ravine forty miles from Denver. The highway patrol ruled it an accident, but I hired a private investigator to dig through all the reports, anyway. I'm curious why the PI didn't find anything about your marriage."

"He's not very good?" she said, before swallowing half the water in her bottle.

"He's the best." Dalton couldn't quite get a read on her. First demanding, then hostile, followed by defeated, compliant, accepting, and now, withholding something. He'd always been good at judging first impressions, but she was challenging everything he'd thought he knew.

She yanked a hooded sweatshirt over her head with another muffled remark.

Vagueness was not his forte. Dalton preferred getting to the point by the most direct route and with the least amount of details. "How did you meet Josh?"

"The usual way." She shoved her knees up under the wide-as-a-tent sweatshirt before offering him the other one. It was obviously the smaller size—her size—and she knew it. He threw it into the backseat.

"Online dating?"

"I would never date someone I met online."

"Friend of a friend, then?" Dalton was trying to come up with a few more choices that didn't involve a drunken one-night stand.

"Nope. My wallet was stolen. Of course, they got my college identification card and bus pass." She stared out the window. "I was six miles from my dorm room and my roommate wasn't answering her phone."

"No money for a taxi?"

"If I had any money, I would have used it on the bus." Blondie's teeth chattered, kicking him into motion.

He started the Cadillac and turned on the heat. "Keep talking."

"I thought someone was following me, and I panicked. Ran into the first business that was still open at nine-thirty on a Sunday night."

Dalton put the car in gear and made a U-turn. "A church?"

"An art studio. I burst through the door and ran into

your brother. Literally. It took nearly a month to get all the paint out of my hair."

"You met Josh at an art studio?" Dalton had to admit she was going the distance with her story. "An art studio in Denver?"

"Why would I be in Denver?" Her neck cracked as she shifted in the seat until she was facing him.

"What's wrong with Denver?" Evidently something, by the way she was preparing to pounce.

"I've never been there," she insisted. "I went to the University of Missouri."

"Okay, you've never been to Denver." Dalton kept his eyes on the muddy road leading from the cemetery. Her reaction to the city's name was far from normal and he should probably push harder to find out why. But something in his gut was telling him to wait. Never mind the fact that he couldn't come up with a plausible reason for Josh to be in Missouri.

The click of her seat belt buckle announced that she was no longer focusing all her attention on him. As rain splattered against the windows, he swallowed the remaining questions and waited for her to make the next move. She was quiet so long that it was killing him not to look at her.

After five full minutes of driving in silence, he heard the tires finally connect with the highway asphalt. His passenger chose the same moment to speak.

"What will it take to convince you that Josh was my husband?"

During their brief drive Dalton had replayed the hours connecting them in this day, apparently, without end. The arguments in his mind centered around one simple fact. His brother was a liar. Had always been a liar. Which meant the logical thing for Dalton to do was give his sister-in-law the benefit of the doubt. And he wanted to make the decision without looking too closely for a motive.

"You want to convince me? Then tell me what you planned to do once you tracked down my brother."

Kira wanted to know the answer, too. "After all this time, maybe I haven't given up on him. I hoped Josh would have a reasonable explanation for everything and save the day."

She felt pathetic admitting she secretly wanted her miserable almost ex-husband to save the day. Now his brother knew.

Why didn't she have a better plan from the start? She'd had plenty of time to herself lately. Enough sleepless nights since her arrest that skipping bail to track down Josh had seemed like a good idea. The FBI refused to listen to any of her theories, and wishing the money in that Denver account was Josh's way of apologizing for all he'd put her through was a total waste of time. Instead, he was somehow connected to everything. The missing money and fraudulent documents kept looping back to Geoff Griffin. Except for that damn bank account.

Or bank accounts. The Feds produced sworn statements from the banking officials in the Cayman Islands, stating she'd opened an account with them. Kira had never realized there were so many liars in the world. At the arraignment, she'd been ordered to surrender her passport. After searching her apartment, she'd finally found it in a box of Brandon's baby clothes.

Clothes he'd never worn and a baby she'd never held. The death of a dream. That's what angered her most about Josh's abandonment. They should have weathered the storm together. And now, he'd left her not only once, but twice.

Josh was a first-rate liar and she'd loved him without conditions. In return, he'd ignored their marriage vows and caused her the worst pain of her life. Sympathy for him was out of the question.

She looked at Dalton and tried finding any resemblance between him and Josh. Wrong eye color, darker hair and she'd guess a good thirty pounds heavier than Josh, who had more of a runner's body.

"So you and he were always close?" The word *always* had a way of tripping people up. At least it did during an insurance investigation. It took tenacity to get to the bottom of a story and expose the scammers who earned a living by being dishonest. One bogus claim could cost Midwest Mutual tens of thousands of dollars and raise premiums for every client. If Dalton Matthews really was Josh's brother, then maybe he'd help her clear her name.

"We kept in touch. But getting the bachelor boy to the altar would've been monumental news in our family. Unlikely it would've slipped under the radar when he came to Christmas dinner last year."

*Another lie.* Kira noticed Dalton used *unlikely* instead of *impossible.* "So your family's into marriage?"

"Most of us." His eyes darkened and sadness etched his features. She knew the look very well, having loved and lost someone. She faced the mirror every morning wishing she'd find it gone. She also knew they were no longer speaking of Josh.

Dalton's emotions were barely concealed, much like hers. She could eventually give him a pass for the stunt he'd pulled at the cemetery. But if his outward appearance was the opposite of Josh's, did it automatically mean his motives were anything but selfish?

But a selfish man would have left her lying in that damn shed full of lumber. He would have immediately called the authorities and had her arrested for trespassing. Dalton hadn't. He could have let the thug kill her instead of trading punches with the man. And once he found the other man's phone, he should have called the police and reported everything. But he didn't do that, either.

He kept doing the opposite of what she expected. Or maybe the opposite of what she'd been trained to expect. And if for no other reason than to prove her dead husband wrong, she was going to expect more from his brother.

"My name's Kira." She offered her hand before she could change her mind.

His surprise was evident as they shook hands. "Dalton. I see you're a fellow member of the unusual-name club."

"The answer to the age-old question of Kimberly or Rachel equals Kira."

"Nice."

"And you?"

"My mom was a Dalton."

"Gotta love creative mothers." His touch was warm, much like the eyes working their magic on the rational part of her brain. She could tell he sensed the attraction between them and also wished it was absent. It would complicate matters, especially if he *was* her brother-in-law.

He released her hand, but not the hold he had on her common sense. She liked to think she could distinguish between lying eyes and simple infatuation. Josh had had lying eyes that sparkled mischievously. Dalton's eyes held a mixture of wisdom and determination.

"You really don't look anything like your brother." She couldn't hide the skepticism lacing her tone.

"Different as night and day since we were kids."

"A possible reason why you didn't know about me?"

"I said different, not estranged. I assure you, we have the same mother."

"You're very precise for someone who's been hiding out in the woods."

Dalton Matthews drove the car and didn't offer an explanation. Yeah, she could definitely extend him a bit more trust. As for Josh, how many lies had he told her? The entire time she'd been searching the internet for any sign of him, she'd been using Joshua Kincaid, when it appeared he'd been just as comfortable as a Matthews.

A twinge of guilt scurried up her spine.

Seeing proof of Josh's death didn't hurt as much as it should have, as it might have if she'd been a real wife grieving for a real husband. A real wife wouldn't have wished her husband dead and then tried to erase him from her memory.

Then again, a real husband wouldn't have hidden his wife from his family or purposely deceived her from the moment they'd met. A real husband wouldn't have blamed her for losing their baby and then disappeared before she could recover from the shock.

Tears filled Kira's eyes and she quickly swiped at them before they trickled down her cheeks. A real kick-ass heroine wouldn't shed a tear over a man who'd done her wrong. She'd work twice as hard to settle the score, regardless of the cost.

"Look, I can understand why you don't trust me." Her voice wobbled, but she quickly recovered. "I have proof at my apartment that Josh is my husband."

"I'm guessing your apartment isn't in *Denver*."

She picked up on his sarcasm and nailed her monotone response. "I live in Kansas City."

"Of course you do." His head bobbed up and down. "Why would anything be easy today?"

"You don't have to help me," she insisted. "Drop me off at the bus stop and I'll take care of myself."

"Yeah, you've done a stellar job so far," he muttered.

"Stellar?" She hadn't heard that word in forever. Stellar Studio was the place where she and Josh had met. The place he'd considered his second home. Had Dalton used the word as a test?

He glanced her way. "Yesterday's crossword puzzle. The clue was: exceptionally good. The answer, of course, is stellar."

"Right." Her mind latched on to the coincidence, but the turmoil in her belly insisted it was more. Then again, a scoop of granola for breakfast hadn't fueled her all day.

"We need gas and food." The way he switched topics confirmed she'd read too much into the word. "There's a convenience store down the road. We'll both think more clearly after a snack."

"Right." She shifted in her seat.

"Proof of your marriage would help, but I think it's more important to tell me who's trying to kill you and how that involves my family."

"I can tell you what I know. I need a few minutes to process everything that's happened." Kira leaned against the headrest and inhaled the scent of leather.

"Fair enough. You've got about fifteen minutes to *process*." Dalton tapped a knob on the dash and music flooded the car. He adjusted the volume. "And bashing my brother's memory isn't an option. I want to hear about your proof."

"After we get some food. I'm starving." That was the truth. Forming a sentence without saying anything negative about Josh would test her lying skills. Especially when she was beginning to suspect his connection to Griffin wasn't as innocent as she'd initially presumed. Not that it mattered, now that he was dead. He wouldn't be clearing anyone's name. She shifted the flash drive to a more comfortable position. She had some of the answers, just not all the right questions.

Brother or not, she wouldn't stop until she'd proved Josh's deliberate deception and confirmed that Geoff Griffin was behind framing her.

## Chapter 4

Dalton slowed as the lights from a convenience store grew closer. Kira sat there twisting her fists in the ridiculously long sweatshirt. The possibility that she would try to escape gnawed at the back of his mind. Why did he care? One less problem to think about if she did. Then again, she wouldn't get far barefoot.

"What size are you? You can't go in the store without shoes, so I'll go in first."

"Good point." She stared down at her mud-streaked arches before shifting one foot to the dash. "An eight."

"Be ready to talk when we leave here. If you want my help, I need answers." Dalton spared her a glance. "And I want to know why you were at my house."

"Sure." Her enthusiasm was underwhelming and her expression confirmed that another round of lying was brewing between her ears.

He maneuvered the car to the gas pump nearest the

building and yanked the keys from the ignition before she could protest. "Sit tight and I'll check on the footwear."

Dalton slammed the door and didn't look back. He needed a few minutes away from Josh's wife. If Dalton had nothing else to go on besides her reaction to the word *stellar*, it would be enough. She'd definitely known his brother.

What could be worse than Josh getting married and continuing to screw around? Their mother finding out. With the frame of mind she'd been in since Josh's death, she'd have Kira living in Josh's old bedroom as soon as she heard the news.

Then she'd rally the troops for another Team Josh fan club meeting. Drag out the baby pictures and baseball trophies. Hook up an ancient VCR and play nonstop videos of Josh doing everyday things, like breathing.

Dalton gave the door a healthy shove as he made his way into the convenience store. Head down and determined, he went directly to the novelty aisle. All the crap you didn't know you needed could be found here. Beer cozies, camouflage air fresheners for your truck, T-shirts advising you to Keep Calm and a rack full of neon-colored plastic shoes.

He went to work searching for Kira's size. The eights were all gone. A seven would be too tight, but if he got her some socks, a nine should fit. Ugly orange shoes and a package of glittery purple socks. Perfect.

Up the next aisle he grabbed a Gatorade and a bag of pretzels. Then back to the checkout in less than two minutes. He dropped the items on the counter and reached for his wallet. "These, and I'll be getting gas on pump six."

"The red car?"

"Yes." He nodded. Glancing toward the car, he spotted Kira's face pressed against the window. The determination in her eyes didn't surprise him. Maybe the fact she was sitting where he'd left her meant something? Yeah, it meant she was still working on her story.

"Anything else?"

"Yes. My, um, friend will be in. Charge me for whatever she needs."

The clerk handed him the card. "You're all set. Thank you."

Dalton shoved his wallet in his back pocket and grabbed the bag. He shouldered his way through the door, pausing long enough to hold it open for a woman clutching the hand of a little boy who insisted on stomping through each puddle of water, much to his mother's annoyance. Dalton couldn't help but smile at his antics, but when he looked up, he found Kira watching the scene with unguarded intensity. A moment of vulnerability she'd been fighting not to show.

His heart sank. What in the world had Josh done to her? Dalton hadn't considered the possibility of a child without a father.

He reined in the thoughts. Josh was irresponsible, but he wouldn't abandon his child. The way their mother had been begging for grandchildren, Josh would hold a parade if he'd managed to produce an heir.

Kira shifted in the seat and allowed herself two seconds to admire Dalton's swagger as he strode into the convenience store. She pressed her face against the chilled glass of her window, resisting the urge to drool. Watching him in the store was the first opportunity she'd had to really see him. Broad-shouldered and action-oriented, he'd greeted the ponytailed girl behind the counter and given her a high-wattage smile.

She was a goner.

He gestured toward the car and Kira yanked her face

away, leaving imprints of her forehead, nose, cheeks and chin on the window. Had it been too obvious, swiping her sweatshirt sleeve over the marks?

She rifled through the contents of the center console and retrieved a crumpled twenty dollar bill and a half stick of gum.

She shoved the bill in her pocket and tossed the gum in her mouth, realizing a tad too late it was old and rock hard. She chomped on it, anyway, needing an outlet for her sudden burst of nervous energy. There was an excellent reason she normally didn't handle field investigations.

Anxiety.

Enlisting Dalton's help was a risky plan. She had to remain strong and give him enough information to continue helping her. He didn't need all the details at one time, especially personal ones. If she could remain calm—big if—and not tell him everything, then he might not turn her over to the police.

What if the FBI rescinded their agreement when she couldn't produce her wayward husband to corroborate her story? Everything changed so fast. She needed time to think and get her head on straight again, but that wasn't going to happen before she cleared her own name.

Griffin had tried to kill her. He'd framed her for his crimes, likely because he somehow knew she'd been getting close to bringing him down. Had he used Josh, too? Was there a chance he'd killed Josh? The thought only cemented her resolve to bring the bastard down.

Swaying Dalton to her side meant trusting him with the entire story. He believed she was after a payday from his family and wouldn't assist her in any plan painting Josh in a negative light.

She stared as he held the door for a woman with a toddler. Kira's throat tightened in response. Not just because age-appropriate kids tended to tear her heart out, but because it was a respectful gesture. And one Josh had always deemed silly.

Kira jumped when Dalton's face appeared next to her window, holding a large brown sack in his arms. Yanking open the door, he dropped the bag in her lap.

"I'm going to gas up. Get whatever you need from the store. I told the clerk to charge my card."

She dug through the sack, fingered the shape of a shoe and pulled it to the top. The ugly orange plastic shoes came with a bonus. Glittery purple socks that tween girls adored. Kira's feet were freezing so there was no second-guessing her options.

She transferred the sack to the backseat before ripping the tags from the footwear. A minute later she exited the car.

"Less than five minutes, okay," he stated more than asked. The spark in his eyes left her struggling to breathe. "I'm holding on to your gun until you come back. Hate to see you in any more trouble. Once we're on the road, I want the whole story or we're heading to the cops."

Swinging the car door closed, she straightened her shoulders and refused to acknowledge him. He'd like nothing more than to pawn her off on the cops. That ticked her off, big-time. And really, how much more trouble could she get into? It grated, the way Dalton flaunted his power, thinking he was better than her.

Just like his brother.

She could get away. Right here, right now. Plead for help. Someone would have to believe her. Maybe the mom she'd seen?

Irrational or not, Kira didn't care. She could ditch him and get through this on her own. But the thirty feet to the store entrance seemed more like three hundred. She felt his eyes boring into her like a branding iron. Her plastic shoes made a squeaking sound as she trudged into the store and nodded at the cashier.

Her stomach rumbled as she passed the pizza slices and fountain pop. The ice maker squealed as another batch dropped into the holding tank. By the time she'd washed most of the mud off herself in the bathroom, she'd worked out some details in her head.

Thank him for his generosity. Apologize for the inconvenience she'd caused, and get back to Kansas City, where her bail had been revoked and a warrant issued for her arrest. Or she could trust Josh's brother, a plan that would probably lead her to jail, as well.

Or she could choose option number three: run and don't look back.

She grabbed a cloth tote bag from a nearby display and ducked into the health and beauty aisle. Band-Aids, hair ties, hand sanitizer, antibiotic ointment, aspirin, toothbrush and paste were added to the bag. She rounded the corner and hit the next aisle in a flurry, tossing in a flashlight, extra batteries, a lighter, disposable cell phone and car charger.

When she glanced to the front of the store, the clerk was finishing up with another customer. Kira nearly ran to the checkout stand, then hefted her bag onto the counter. "I'm with the man in the red car." She pointed toward the gas pumps, but the car was gone.

*He'd left her.*

That wasn't the plan. If anyone was leaving, it should have been her. Dread burned deeply in her stomach. Dalton was gone. What if he told the cops exactly where to find her?

"Don't worry. Your friend is putting air in the tires." The young woman gestured to the side of the building.

"Oh." Overwhelming relief left Kira sagging against the counter. Pressing a hand to her racing heart, she inhaled a deep breath through her nose. She'd grown so used to being alone that it was almost a shock that he hadn't left her.

"Did you get caught in the rain?" the girl asked while dragging each item from the bag and sliding it across the scanner.

"Um, yes," she replied. "I'll be right back." Kira returned to the rear of the store with another mission. Finding them some quality food and snacks. She would've enjoyed a slice of pizza, but no telling how long it had been rotating under the heat lamp. Now the stress was talking, because she never ate junk food.

Okay, before she'd been arrested she never ate junk food. If she had a dollar for every time a claim for heart surgery crossed her desk... Or diabetes. Fat and sugar were absolutely the worst toxins you could willingly pump into your body. Before she slipped further into a tangent, she found a couple semifresh apples and bananas and two soy granola bars. She used the oversize sweatshirt as an apron, piling everything into the front. She removed two bottles of orange juice from the cooler and reached for some veggie juice.

"Nice sweatshirt," a voice squeaked behind her, almost sending one of the bottles to the floor. She turned and stared at a lanky teenage boy, blatantly admiring her chest. She glanced down and noticed the Buckshot's logo was the source of his admiration and released a sigh.

"Um, thanks." She offered him a tight smile, one usually successful in ending further conversation.

"They were all gone by the time I saved up enough tokens," he continued.

Apparently she needed to be a bit ruder. She leaned to

the side and stared at the checkout, hoping the kid would get the idea that she was in a hurry.

"How many cups did you drink?" he asked.

So much for subtlety. "How many cups?" She glanced down at the logo and then to the teen. If this was some lame joke about bra cup sizes, she was about to make a scene.

"Of coffee." He gestured over his right shoulder to the beverage counter. "Moose Mountain is my favorite. What about you?"

"I don't drink coffee." She eyed the self-serve area suspiciously before her gaze caught the familiar logo slapped on the front of a shiny steel dispenser. Familiar because Josh had a shirt with the same design, or almost the same. Was it hunting supplies or coffee that went along with the bull's-eye logo? She was about to find out. "Dalton Matthews gave me this sweatshirt."

"The owner of Buckshot's? Cool."

Dalton was the *owner* of Buckshot's and not a marketing representative? The moment she'd convinced herself he was worthy of her trust, she'd found out he lied. The sweatshirt material was suddenly tight around her neck, her body heating with anger at the thought of another lie falling from the lips of another man.

"Want it?"

The kid's face lit up. She dumped the armful of healthy food on the nearest shelf and reached for the hem of the sweatshirt, dragging it over her head before handing it to the young man.

"For the record, coffee is *very* bad for you." Not that it mattered, because flavored coffees and energy drinks were everywhere. Why not drink water?

"My mom says so, too." He grinned, taking the garment from her outstretched hand.

"Moms are very smart," Kira agreed, yanking her shirt down to cover her exposed belly button.

"Is this a private show?" Dalton asked, slipping in next to the teen and crossing his arms in apparent judgment.

"No, *Dalton*." She reached for the bottled juices and granola bars, abandoning the fruit in a fight-or-flight response. "Just chatting with one of your many fans."

The tiniest of cracks appeared in his stern expression and she knew she'd struck a direct blow. She'd also given the teen the perfect opportunity to worship his idol. The look on Dalton's face insisted she shouldn't make a scene. It was too late for that. He should have told the truth at the cemetery. Kira stepped aside and tugged on the young man's arm.

"Tell Dalton how much you love *his* coffee."

"Thanks, lady. I mean, um, ma'am. Mr. Matthews, sir," he gushed in unabashed adulation. Clutching the sweatshirt in one hand, he extended the other to Dalton. "It's awesome to meet you."

Kira ignored Dalton on her way to the checkout, scanning the remainder of the store for a harmless-looking person who might be convinced to offer her a ride. She stomped down the voice in her head that insisted rides with strangers were completely out of the question. Desperation overrode common sense every time.

She set her items on the counter and waited for the clerk to print a couple lottery tickets for another patron. A woman who looked exceedingly normal and had ally potential written all over her, until she asked for a box of cigarettes. Kira nearly launched into a speech about the hazards of smoking. Couldn't the woman read? It was written on the side of the box.

When the woman stepped aside, the clerk reached for the bottles. "Is this everything for you?"

It wasn't Kira's fault that the mini doughnuts were the featured item of the week. They were loaded with preservatives and a slew of additives no one could pronounce. And she needed them, especially since there'd be no escaping Dalton. She pushed two packages of the sugary treats across the counter. "And these, too, please."

"Nice try." Dalton materialized at her left shoulder. His tone was intimidating as he placed a hand at her waist. "Grab your bag. We're leaving."

His palm was hot, in contrast to her chilled skin, and it took effort not to lean into his touch. She turned her head slightly to flash him a saccharine smile. "Wait for me in the car."

"You've got five seconds before I drag you out of this store." His warm fingers inched higher on her back, eliciting a shiver and momentarily distracting her.

"Somehow I doubt that. Probably wouldn't be good press for Buckshot's *Coffee*, now would it?" She reached for two more packages of doughnuts and shoved them toward the clerk.

"I'm not kidding." He insinuated himself between her and the counter and yanked them out of the clerk's hand. "We've already paid."

Kira dug the crumpled bill from her pocket. "I'll pay for my own snacks, then." She could have survived without the doughnuts, but there was no way she was letting him dictate her purchases. Especially now, when she knew he'd been hiding his wealth.

"Let's go." He grabbed her wrist and reached for the tote bag.

"I *need* a box of tampons," she announced, loudly enough for other patrons to hear her request. It was an absolute lie, but she wanted to see him speechless and uncomfortable.

His eyes glittered in mock appreciation and she celebrated the triumph. What sane man wanted to argue with
a woman over feminine hygiene products?

"Can you grab those for me, honey?" Kira wanted him
to refuse, so she could return to the health and beauty aisle
and bankrupt him with another tote full of "necessities."

The coffee king pulled her into his arms and pressed his
lips against hers. She was startled and off balance, which
should have meant the attack on her senses was also un-
welcomed. Instead, her lips parted beneath his, allowing
his probing tongue entrance. Her traitorous hands moved
to his shoulders. Her breasts flattened against the solid
breadth of his chest, her nostrils filling with the scent of
damp sawdust. One of his hands cupped the back of her
head while his other arm encircled her waist and drew her
closer to his hard chest.

Her skin tingled in awareness; a sudden heat fired in
her belly with every stroke from his wicked tongue. She
hadn't felt a connection to anyone in so long. Hadn't allowed desire to rule anything but her work ethic.

"Anything for you, Blondie." He winked and released
her.

Kira steadied herself with one hand against the counter
and watched him stride away.

Oh, crap. She'd unwisely pushed him too far. And her
tingling lips were proof of who held the upper hand.

The clerk gave her a conspiratorial wink and slid the
doughnuts back in the bag while Kira resisted the urge to
locate Dalton in the store.

"I need a pack of Camels," he said, sliding the tampon
box in front of her. The clerk retrieved the cigarettes and
scanned both items.

"Anything else, sir?"

"Just these."

Kira choked as he dropped a large box of condoms in front of her.

A second later, he grabbed her ass.

## Chapter 5

"Time's up. Why is someone trying to kill you?" Dalton asked, adjusting the windshield wipers to match the steady rain. "If I'm going to put my butt on the line keeping you safe, I'd like to know what I'm up against."

"What do you mean?" Kira retrieved the other sweatshirt from the backseat and tugged it over her head. She waited another heartbeat before addressing what they'd done in the store. "And where do you get off, kissing me like that?"

He spared her a glance, almost daring her to continue with the line of questioning. She'd tossed out the implication that she hadn't enjoyed their kiss, and he knew she was a liar.

"I didn't tell anyone I was tracking down Josh. I don't know anyone who'd care." The last thing she needed was Dalton turning her over to the cops before she had enough evidence to clear her name.

"Maybe I'm asking the wrong question." He set the cruise control and acted as if they were discussing fabric softener sheets. "Why were you trying to *track down* my brother—as you put it—at the cabin? And why the heck did it take you so long to look? Did someone finally question his absence? Like your family?"

"Nope. My foster homes didn't want to be kept up-to-date on my life." Truthfully, she'd done nothing but work and had no friends. Josh had insisted they keep a low profile. She'd been left more times than she could count. She'd never known her father and could barely remember her mother. Forgetting every foster home she'd bounced through was a bit tougher.

Was it any wonder she'd bought into Josh's version of love? What in the world did Kira have to compare it to? It might be petty and wrong, because he was dead, but she wanted to see him pay.

"If you want my help, I need answers." Dalton glanced her way. "Why were you at my house?"

It was time to admit she couldn't find the information on her own.

"I was hoping to find Josh or search the house for any hiding spaces. He may have left something behind."

"There's nothing there. I've gutted every room and didn't come across anything worth hiding. Tell me what you're looking for." Again Dalton drummed his long fingers on the dashboard.

She hesitated and he saw it. He probably wouldn't believe anything she said now. Be it truth or fiction.

"You don't want to share? Okay. I'm giving you two choices." Dalton flipped on the map light and she shielded her eyes.

"We can drive to the police station and you can tell your story. I'll confirm the parts I witnessed. I'm sure they'll keep you safe until the admirer cuffed to my bathtub is in custody."

It was a simple and to-the-point answer for what should be done after a criminal offense. You tell the good guys and they take care of the bad guys. *As if that really worked.*

"What's option number two?"

"Level with me about why you were looking for Josh. What did he do to you?"

"Why do you assume he did anything?" The unease in Kira's stomach grew. Dalton's question felt as if he wanted confirmation of Josh's bad behavior.

"You can imagine my skepticism when someone I've never met shows up after he's gone."

"When I prove my marriage to Josh, then what? You won't turn me over to the police?" If Dalton turned her over to anyone with a badge, she'd be wearing an orange jumpsuit back to Kansas City.

"I want to make sure his name isn't connected with anything illegal."

"We can't always get what we want." She flipped the map light off. It reminded her of the bright lights at the police station when she'd been confronted with all the damning evidence. "Is there any way for me to take a look at Josh's stuff?"

Dalton tapped the brake pedal. "I see another car behind us." He slowed the Caddy to a few miles an hour over the speed limit. "I almost hope it's law enforcement."

Kira choked at his comment. It couldn't end like this, on the side of a road somewhere in Wyoming, without any real evidence to clear her name. "I can't go to jail."

"Probably the safest place you could be right now." The car was still moving, but it felt like slow motion.

"You don't understand." Kira grabbed his arm. "I'm sort of wanted."

"Why are you telling me this now?" Dalton's voice exploded in volume. "So I can be your accomplice?"

"No, I wouldn't—"

"You wouldn't what, break the law?" He stomped on the gas and the Caddy surged forward.

Her eyes focused on the outside mirror. If she saw flashing lights, what would she do? Asking Dalton to evade the police didn't sound like a reasonable solution.

The car in question gained on them before they reached the next curve in the road. She raised her head far enough to peer around the seat. "The police?"

"Afraid not," Dalton answered, taking the curve at eighty and increasing the speed to well over a hundred on the straightaway. "Your friend has managed to track you down."

Her feet bounced with the adrenaline coursing through her veins. She braced them against the floorboard and looked behind them. "If it's really him, why didn't he run us down at the store?"

The sound of gunfire replaced the remaining questions in her head.

"Stay down!" Dalton said, as the rear window shattered, spraying multicolored bits of glass everywhere.

She released her seat belt, dropped to the floor and began searching beneath the seats, certain he must have placed at least one of the guns there when they'd fled the remains of his home.

Bracing a hand on his thigh, she groped between his booted feet. Her head dipped very close to his knee, a distraction she didn't need. Looking up at the fierce expression on Dalton's face made her catch her breath. Her fingers finally came in contact with a weapon and curled around it as renewed anger coursed through her veins.

She wasn't a fabulous shot, but could certainly fire a few rounds toward the car pursuing them.

One of Dalton's hands pressed her toward the floorboards. "I'm not telling you again to stay down!"

"Stop bossing me around." She shoved him away and got to her knees in her seat.

"Can we outrun him?" she asked, after removing the cartridge and checking the remaining bullets.

"Maybe."

Kira braced herself and eyed the vehicle behind them above the headrest. She'd shoot only if it got close enough for her to have a snowball's chance in hell of hitting it with the few remaining bullets. The road curved and then straightened again.

The gap between the cars grew. Dalton was doing his part to distance them from the other vehicle, when it suddenly cut the space in half.

"Crap, crap, crap." She had to shoot, no way around it. She gripped the gun with both hands, balanced it on the headrest and aimed for a headlight. She fired two quick shots before Dalton swerved, bouncing her against the door. The gun dropped to the floor in the backseat.

"You could have warned me to hang on."

"We almost had a deer on the dash."

The Caddy surged forward again and Kira dropped her butt onto the seat.

"I need you to take over the wheel. Trade places with me," Dalton said. "I can't drive and shoot."

"What?" She watched as the space between him and the steering wheel grew. "Are you sure about this?"

"Slide your foot over to the gas pedal and get your hands on the wheel." It wasn't as easy as it sounded, but eventually they traded places. Dalton leaned across the seat, picked up his gun and fired. "Stay in the middle of the road."

There were several more shots and Kira worked at keeping the car steady and the speedometer near eighty. She'd never driven so recklessly, and the feeling in her gut was anything but excitement.

In the mirror, she saw the exact moment one of Dalton's shots connected with a tire. The other car kicked up gravel onto the shoulder, before heading into the opposite ditch and skirting the fence line.

Sparks flew as the barbed wire caught the undercarriage, slowing the vehicle's progression before it flipped onto its top and skidded to a halt. Kira stopped in the middle of the highway. Dalton threw open his door, shaking off a sprinkling of glass.

"Are you all right?" he asked, scanning the roadway and keeping the gun pointed toward the wrecked car.

She nodded, glancing from him to the bullet lodged in the dash. The highway behind them was dark and quiet, except for a tire spinning on the wrecked vehicle. He yanked the phone from his pocket and dropped it. After giving it two good stomps, he hurried to the driver's side and motioned for Kira to move.

"Do you think he's okay?" she asked. "I know I shouldn't care, but…"

Dalton scoffed and threw the car into gear. "For your sake, I hope he's dead."

Dalton would admit that Kira had done a good job. They were both alive because she'd followed most of his instructions. She was also a damn good kisser, which was disconcerting, because he'd just been trying to teach her a lesson and it had backfired, big-time.

Her bravery under fire could not influence how he handled the situation. As the wind whistled through the rear window, he hoped the man in the ditch was dead.

What was he thinking? Was he actually relieved at taking another life? This was pure insanity. "The cell could have been tracked to find us. That's not cheap or easy to do. Just who is after you?"

Kira had been noticeably quiet, staring straight ahead with her chin propped against her knees, her feet in those ridiculous purple socks and orange shoes planted firmly on the dashboard. He'd expected her to have plenty to say after the latest pursuer failed to kill them.

"There is no us." She turned her head to look at him. "Where are you taking me? And why didn't you tell me about the coffee thing?"

"Don't you think the guy back there may be a little higher priority? Plus, we need another car."

"A businessman like yourself should be able to multitask."

"Fine, I sell coffee."

"Not hunting supplies?"

He knew she wouldn't let it drop. "No."

"And the reason you couldn't tell me this was?" She snapped her fingers. "Oh, because your family has lots of money and I fit the money-hungry bitch profile, right?"

"So what if you're right? I did think you were after something else. Happy now?"

"Thrilled." She yanked the tote bag onto her lap with a thud. It easily weighed ten pounds and the contents cost one hundred and seventy-three dollars. She dug through the purchases—which hopefully didn't include any pepper spray or knives.

"What are you doing?"

"Finding some good drugs." Her hands were shaking so badly that it took several minutes for her to break all the safety seals. She downed four tablets before offering him the bottle.

"No, thanks."

"It figures," she mumbled, replacing the cap and dropping it in her bag.

"What figures?" He had no intention of rising to the bait or setting her off again—it sort of happened enough on its own.

"You refusing a couple of aspirin while pumping your body full of caffeine."

He ground his molars together and tried ignoring her clucking tongue as she searched for something else in her bag. Before long she started munching on a sleeve of chocolate mini doughnuts. The same ones he'd insisted he wasn't buying.

"Did you read the label on those things? They're full of crap." He reached for the package and she smacked his hand.

"No, you may not have one." She grabbed a shiny object off the floor and tossed it in his lap. "Eat a tasty soy granola bar."

"I'm not hungry." A suitable answer if his stomach hadn't gurgled before the words left his mouth.

She snorted and munched on another doughnut. "Yeah, I can tell."

A soy granola bar wasn't gonna do the trick. Not when he'd rather lick the chocolate off her sweet lips than be on the receiving end of her sharp tongue. His mouth went dry thinking of their kiss at the convenience store. Of the moment he'd caught her tugging the sweatshirt over her head, giving an eyeful of curves to the besotted teenager. She may have thought the kid was impressed by his presence, but Dalton knew better. He'd been that kid…a lifetime ago.

Gripping the steering wheel tighter, he tried clearing

his mind of all thoughts, but she was there. Kira and her bag brimming with unnecessary items. "Why were you stocking up on anything you could fit in your bag?"

"I did exactly what you told me. I even chose a reusable tote bag that donates the proceeds to help bring clean water to underdeveloped countries."

So what if she was environmentally conscious? He donated to plenty of charities and he couldn't allow her to divert another conversation. "I told you to get what you *needed*. You were clearly abusing the privilege."

"Coming from the man who lied about his occupation and all the freebies in his trunk?"

"I never intended to lie. But you wouldn't be the first person to pounce when they smelled money in the air." Money she could inherit. If she was Josh's legal wife, or now widow, she'd get 10 percent of Buckshot's and a seat on the board. And since Josh wasn't alive to defend himself, Dalton needed to prevent her from taking advantage of the situation.

"That makes it okay, then? Because you didn't *intend* to lie, it just happened?"

"Says the poster girl for honesty? Have you been telling me the truth about anything?"

She dug the last doughnut from the package and threw it in her mouth before crinkling the wrapper and shoving it into her eco-friendly bag. Definitely stalling. Her actions made his lips twitch in response. He could feel the softness of her mouth beneath his, taste the chocolate scenting the air.

Where were his cigarettes? He patted his coat pockets in annoyance until locating the package and ripping it open with his teeth. He'd known the moment he'd planted his lips on hers he would need a distraction to keep from returning for more. And since he'd quit smoking the month before, it seemed like a reasonable crutch.

"You're not going to smoke in here, are you?" She wrinkled her nose.

He flipped open the ashtray and waited for the lighter to heat up. "Yes, I am."

"So you're addicted to caffeine and nicotine?"

"I'm not addicted to anything." The lighter popped and he quickly lit the cigarette before Kira could come up with another protest. The first shaky drag was even sweeter than he remembered, the smoke drifting down his throat and into his lungs. He held it for a moment and then slowly exhaled and lowered his window a crack.

"Thanks for the toxic cloud," she said and waved a hand in front of her face. "Smoking causes lung cancer, raises your blood pressure and shortens your life span." The missing rear window allowed air to rush inside and forced the scent in every direction. "Plus, insurance rates are nearly double for smokers versus nonsmokers."

"I've sacrificed a lot for you today. My house and car are ruined. Not to mention there's been a target on my back since you arrived." He pressed his lips to the cigarette and inhaled again. "Any chance you could suffer in silence?"

"Suit yourself." She sighed—a long-suffering, very *loud* sigh. "Why people do things they know are bad for them, I'll never understand."

The break in conversation led to more searching through the tote, more window adjustments on her side of the car and more mumbling. He'd never been around someone with such a mix of irritating and appealing behaviors. He crushed his cigarette in the ashtray.

"I think it's time to involve the police, don't you?"

*"No."* Her fingers tugged at the T-shirt she wore, making silent adjustments.

"No? Haven't you noticed how everyone wants to kill you?" Her lack of cooperation was more than annoying.

"I don't have enough proof yet." She was obviously stalling and no doubt withholding something important.

"Tell me about the proof you do have." This was her last chance to come clean with everything she knew.

"It's not that simple."

"Sure it is. Start with what you're hiding in your bra."

# Chapter 6

Oh, crap. Kira shifted closer to the door and, hopefully, out of his reach. "I don't know what you're talking about." The denial was spoken before she could give it a second thought.

"I'm not playing games, Blondie." His hand tunneled under her shirt and quickly grazed her breast. "What is this?"

Kira was so shocked that she forgot having his hand under her shirt was a bad thing. Momentarily forgot. "Stop. Get your hands off me." His fingers swiftly slid beneath the underwire bra holding all her secrets and found the flash drive.

"This is the proof you've been harping about and you weren't going to show it to me." He grasped the tiny gadget and pulled the car off the highway.

"Give that back to me!" She leaned over the console separating them and used both of her hands to try to open his fist. "I won't let you take it."

The car slowed to a stop behind a grove of trees and he put it in Park. "You won't let me? In case you haven't noticed, there's been a shift in power." He pressed her back in her seat. "Lesson number one, Blondie. Tell the truth. If you had, none of this would've been necessary."

Kira's heart raced as air sawed in and out of her lungs. She couldn't let him keep the flash drive. "Looks like you've borrowed a play from your brother's book." This was not the time to release any more ugly truths about her marriage. About her struggles to survive as a teenager without an ally. About her struggles to survive life, period.

"Enough of your cryptic comments about Josh. He was my brother and family takes care of—" Dalton stopped suddenly, the anger in his eyes replaced with compassion.

She didn't want his sympathy. She didn't want the pain weighing down her heart. But most of all, she didn't want to remember Josh and his betrayal. Her throat clogged with tears and she needed to lash out at someone. "Finish your sentence, Dalton. Family takes care of…family."

He made a point of turning the ignition off, probably to avoid looking at her.

"Aren't you going to tell me what you really think of me? Bet you've got a hundred words floating around in your head, so go ahead, spit them out so the world will know how loyal you are to *your* sainted brother and *your* family." It was more than bitterness; it was the knowledge that she had nothing left to lose.

"Tell me what's on here." He kept his fist tightly closed, not offering any glimpse of the prize he held.

"How did you know?" Kira pointed to his hand.

"I felt something when I helped you change shirts at the cemetery." His voice dipped to something more intimate and her skin warmed at the thought of his hands on her again.

"When you got so angry at the store, I needed to make sure you hadn't moved it somewhere else." The logic of his actions didn't mesh with the thorough way he'd kissed her.

Heat suffused her cheeks. He'd used the kiss as a way to distract her. And he'd prolonged the activity, kept her wrapped in his arms, only because he didn't have a choice.

"Doesn't matter. I'm the only one who can decrypt it. Without me, it's worthless." She took a small measure of pride in seeing him frustrated. He was a fixer. One of those guys who was used to solving problems.

"You're lying." He stared at the two-inch rectangular gadget and then at her. "I can count on one hand the number of things you've been truthful about. Bet I could find out all your secrets in less than five minutes."

"I doubt you care quite that much."

"You'd be wrong." He transferred the flash drive to his other hand and reached for the tote bag. The wind shook the car in a satisfying way that made her think Mother Nature was on her side. Now what?

She watched him pull the phone and the charger from the bag and toss them in her lap. "Open those for me."

It was sort of like prepping the electric chair for your execution. She knew what would happen next, but she was helpless to stop it. Opening the plastic packaging gave her a marginal reprieve. Dalton finally whipped out a pocket-knife and cut through the layers with barely any effort while she still worked on releasing the charger.

Her brain slipped to autopilot. She was somehow able to focus all her attention on the task with the pretense of normalcy. Phones were harmless. Phone chargers were never there when you needed them. Like Josh. And now Kira's whole world was crumbling and her greatest wish was to forget she'd married a lying, cheating bastard. Forget about the son who deserved to be buried in a family cemetery instead of an unmarked grave. And forget about clearing her name from a lengthy list of trumped-up charges.

"Ready to tell me the truth?" His question knocked her back to reality. She needed a moment to gather the words in her head so they made sense. She couldn't blurt out the facts or he might not give her a chance to explain her actions. After opening the prepackaged phone, she plugged it in, wondering where to begin. Was there any part of the story that didn't make her sound like a psycho nut?

"I work, I mean worked, for Midwest Mutual Insurance in Kansas City. I've been building a case for almost three years that one of my superiors knows nothing about." *Please don't ask why, please don't ask why.* "I didn't have enough evidence yet, but I knew I was close. Apparently I wasn't the only one, because I received a threat to back off. I didn't. Then five weeks ago I was arrested. The FBI traced some missing money, millions actually, to foreign accounts in my name."

"Are you guilty?"

"What?" Kira hadn't expected Dalton to jump to the end of the story.

"Simple question. You either did it or you didn't."

"There is nothing *simple* about this story. Simple would be an expired parking meter and a five-dollar fine."

"You're stalling."

"No, you're being rude. Why'd you even ask me for the truth if you've already made up your mind?"

"First reaction is usually the most honest." He gave a careless shrug.

"Have you ever been arrested, Dalton?"

"No." His tone implied the idea was beyond the realm of possibility. Good. Let him continue to believe he was out of reach.

"I have evidence on the flash drive."

"Like what?"

"Besides the forged bank statements, I have copies of fake death certificates and payments to nonexistent doctors, supposedly approved by me."

"With all that evidence, why haven't the Feds taken a second look?" Dalton sounded skeptical and unconvinced.

"Someone inside my office is working to exaggerate my guilt." Even saying the word *guilt* left an unpleasant taste in her mouth. "It's the only thing that makes sense. Every idea I've had to prove my innocence has been a dead end."

"How does Josh fit into all of this and why did you come looking for him?"

"I briefly shared a bank account with Josh. There was never more than a few hundred dollars in it. The account was closed shortly after we were married—by Josh—and only he can confirm that. Josh could help clear my name. But the way he died, under the circumstances you outlined, I know there's more to it now. I'm afraid it all has to do with Geoff Griffin."

"And you think he's trying to kill you." Dalton wiped his free hand against his jeans and her eyes followed. The simple gesture had her reliving the few times his body had pressed against hers. It was completely unacceptable how she slipped from extreme annoyance to utter attraction in a millisecond.

"I didn't know he wanted me dead or I wouldn't have involved you. Dalton, you've got to believe me." Her hand was on top of his—which was still on top of his jeans. A bolt of lightning lit up the car through the broken rear window. A reminder of how close they'd come to dying.

"You can't take the flash drive. It's all I have left." She *wanted* to tell him more. She was tired of facing it all alone. But this was Josh's brother. She definitely couldn't trust him to choose her over Josh, even the memory of Josh.

Wind gusted through the broken window, swaying the car from side to side. The light rain switched to a torrent, delaying any conversation. The trees helped, but the rain poured into the backseat. Dalton grumbled something and then retrieved the tote bag from between her legs.

He tossed a couple items aside before latching on to the bottle of painkillers and prying open the top. After shaking a few tablets into his palm, he downed some Gatorade.

A flash of lightning temporarily blinded Kira and she jumped. Forceful blasts of cold rain shot through the broken window. Dalton tugged on the cord to the phone and flipped it open.

"Who are you calling?"

He punched a few numbers, looked up. His lips moved but she couldn't decipher the words. What if he was calling 911? Probably the easiest way to get her out of his hair. The confining seat belt made it impossible to get an abundance of oxygen to her lungs. Raindrops thumped against the roof of the car, creating a deafening drumbeat.

It was like the moment she'd awakened and Josh had told her about the baby. She'd loved her child since the day she'd learned of the pregnancy. She'd read all the baby books on the library shelves, avoided sugar and caffeine. Every kick to her ribs was a blessing. Proof of the tiny person she and Josh had created.

Josh's enthusiasm had grown significantly when he'd learned they were having a son, and she thought things would turn out okay. Then, in an instant, everything was gone. She hadn't fought hard enough and she'd lost every single thing that mattered to her. She couldn't sit here and pretend she was okay. She had to get out of this cramped space, where panic was fighting to take over.

Dalton was calling the police or the sheriff or whoever was the law in this part of the state. He'd likely do everything in his power to see Josh's name cleared, and she'd be the only one to blame. He had the money to make it happen. Griffin provided the evidence.

Panic won.

She snatched the keys from the ignition and threw her shoulder against the door, but it didn't budge. Yanking at the handle was more successful, landing her on her butt in the muddy gravel of an unlit road. Oh, Lord, what had she done?

Forcing herself to move, she scrambled to her knees on the rough stones and then her feet, losing one of her shoes in the process. The rocks cut the sole of her stockinged foot and she stumbled sideways, kicking off the other shoe. She fisted the keys and ran down the ditch, a stream of frigid water quickly numbing the pain. Clamoring up the other side of the embankment, she blinked against the rain blinding her vision.

Kira had no idea which way to head, only certain of her determination to keep going. She heard Dalton's voice, ignored it and ran. It was pure madness to continue through icy rain strong enough to blow a car from the road. She couldn't see the holes in the ground, or the trees ahead, but this was her last opportunity to avoid jail.

Lightning splintered the sky briefly, guiding her into the cover of a nearby grove. The scent of pine filled her nostrils as cones crunched beneath her feet. She had to keep moving. Her lungs ached with the effort of drawing breath, and she cursed her own lack of endurance.

She swerved to the left, dodged one large limb and smacked her shoulder on another low-hanging branch. The keys flew from her hand and disappeared. She'd never find them without a light. Or if she did try to search, Dalton would find her.

Stumbling forward, Kira continued through the darkness. Failure was not an option. Almost belatedly she noticed the rain was tolerable beneath the towering pines. She shoved her hair away from her eyes, spared a glance over her shoulder and ducked behind the largest tree trunk.

Her fingers were already numb from the cold. Her shoulders shook with the effort it took to stifle a cough. She couldn't outrun Dalton, so she'd keep quiet until she was certain he either gave up his pursuit or made his way beyond her hiding spot.

"Kira!" His angry voice echoed through the canopied forest.

She stayed silent, cupping her chilly hands over her lips and releasing a breath. She closed her eyes and remembered Kansas City in July. The steam pouring off the sidewalks, the rattle of her sometimes temperamental window air conditioner and the scent of cocoa butter sunscreen.

"Kira! We're in the middle of nowhere. Get back in the car."

Why the demand seemed especially amusing, she had no idea, but she swallowed the hysterical laughter bubbling up her throat. *Be quiet.*

"Aren't your feet sore without your shoes?"

*Of course they were.*

"I don't think you meant to jump out of the car. You left your bag. How are you going to survive without all your essentials?" he yelled, getting closer.

Cute. She could do it. She was a survivor. Weeks of scorn and years of abandonment toughened you up. The wilderness during a lightning storm was a cakewalk.

"I'm leaving and I'm pressing charges for every single stunt you've pulled."

She laughed and the sound carried straight up the tree trunk and reverberated through the branches. It was funny only because everything transpiring between them amounted to the *least* of her illegal activities. And he had no way of leaving.

The few seconds she'd allowed her mind to wander equaled a complete loss of focus. Where had he gone? Had he actually walked away or was he simply waiting for her to reveal her location? She couldn't believe he cared enough to waste another moment of a stormy night in a dark forest.

She was so cold. So alone and wishing for another outcome. As she sought warmth for her frozen hands, her fingers longed for the reassurance of the flash drive. How much time had passed? When would it be safe to move around and where would she go? She sank to the ground and shoved her muddied purple socks beneath a layer of pine needles. Dalton was right about one thing: she needed a plan.

A river of water raced down Dalton's spine. Every inch of his body was wet and cold since Kira had fled what was left of his car. But his Coast Guard training prepared him for far worse than this night. All those drills at 0300 hours were more than enough practice for him to survive a few hours of being wet on dry land.

He could still smell the salt of the ocean. Feel the waves knocking him out of the safety zone. Being the fastest swimmer in his high school mattered less when the pool was replaced by the unpredictability of an angry ocean. And being the first one to make it to the wall meant you'd endured twelve hours of survival swimming.

Blondie had caught him off guard twice in less than six hours. He shoved his wet hands into equally wet pockets. Did she really believe stealing his keys meant she'd won?

Not a chance he'd allow her to scurry to the car and race away without him.

Not happening.

But how much longer would she continue this farce? He checked his pocket again, verifying that the flash drive was still there. He ought to be home in bed, where it was nice and dry. Oh, right, his home was destroyed. After months of tearing down walls and replacing windows, he'd found the place was starting to feel like a home.

He scanned the area for movement, yanked the cell phone from his pocket, guarding it as best he could from the rain. He doubted the cheap thing was waterproof, and it still had no reception. He would have gladly shared that information with Kira if she'd given him a chance.

The troublesome woman didn't deserve any consideration. Armed, she'd shown up and ruined months of his hard work. The lady had more enemies than he could count and she also refused to follow the simplest of commands.

*Commands?* Was he training a dog? Dalton would admit his people skills were a bit rusty. Training a dog might be easier than getting one desperate woman to follow a few simple suggestions. He refused to think of himself as a bully. He could be nice when a situation called for it. This situation didn't.

Crazy woman. Josh's wife? A woman without common sense or simply one who chose to ignore the simple solutions?

A sneeze. She was definitely nearby, approximately fifty feet from him, jogging in the opposite direction. He almost yelled her name. Almost returned to his worthless car in relief. But he'd hauled her damn bag, full of everything except an umbrella, this far. She was getting it back. He ran at an angle, hoping to cut her off before she reached the fence in the distance.

"Where did the fool woman go now?" He stopped and stared at the last place he'd seen her, thinking she'd somehow reappear. She didn't. Was it another one of her stunts? Had she known he was nearby?

The wind increased. Pellet-sized hail pounded him from every angle. He sheltered his eyes from the assault, trudging through the knee-high grass.

He ducked back under a tree, blocking some of the white pellets now covering the ground. His Caddy would be ruined. Who was he kidding? The car had already been shot up.

Kira Kincaid's emerald eyes burned in his memory, along with the look of utter surprise on her face when he'd kissed her. The softness of her lips when she'd fallen into his arms and returned his kiss. He couldn't be attracted to Blondie. The pull toward this enigma proved how long it had been since he'd been with a woman. He'd forgotten how good they smelled.

A therapist would probably tell him it was a breakthrough in his healing process. What a load of crap. He wanted his keys. The anticipation was all about wanting to get out of here. Nothing more.

From somewhere behind him, the unmistakable sound of hail striking metal reached his ears. Could he be imagining hail hitting a roof? No, there was a certain rhythmic pounding.

Behind him sat a decades-old trailer, similar to one he'd stayed in while trout fishing a few years ago. This one had seen better days.

Distance and darkness improved its appearance. And there was Kira. For a split second, something akin to relief left Dalton immobile. He argued against the thought, his mind choosing sides in an attempt to keep the proverbial rowboat from tipping. Was it relief that he was finished with her or relief at seeing her again? With a large rock in her hand, she methodically pounded a padlock attached to the only door. He slid down the incline without making too much noise.

"Need some help, cupcake?" He easily avoided the rock she tossed.

"Dalton." She swiped her muddy hands against her equally muddy jeans and shoved her hair from her face, leaving a dark streak. "I don't have your keys."

Why had he thought she'd be just as relieved to see him? Shoot, he was relieved he'd found her. *Idiot is my middle name.* He took a step toward her and she flattened against the trailer. "No keys? Am I going to have to strip-search you for them?"

"I'd like to see you try."

He gave the weakened padlock a solid yank, breaking it from the door. Shining a nearly useless Buckshot's penlight into the interior, he took Kira's arm, ignoring the desire to pull her closer. Her skin was like ice, covered in goose bumps. Her dirty feet must be frigid, as well.

Once inside, he slid the barrel bolt. Although the outside of the trailer was dented and rusty, the interior was surprisingly clean. Clean until he and his muddy companion arrived.

The trailer was six by twelve feet. Half the space was devoted to a kitchen with a tiny stovetop, a table and two benches, the other half to a bed. Someone had left a plastic container with sheets and blankets on the short Formica counter. Dalton bent to untie his wet leather boots and dropped her bag of necessities on the floor.

"Get undressed." Why had he lugged that thing with him? *Because she might actually need something from it.*

"If you really think... Not a chance." Her teeth chattered as she protested.

"If you'd stayed in the car, this wouldn't be necessary."

He forced himself to open cabinets. No food. No flashlight. "Stop stalling and give me your clothes."

"I won't be giving you anything."

"Wanna bet?" Through with playing games, he pulled her shirt and sweatshirt roughly over her head and tossed them to the floor. For once in his life, he wished he was wrong. But the bra hiding beneath the layers of clothing was definitely a front hook, and the cleavage he'd glimpsed before was even more tempting.

Bully or commander, he was in charge, and it was time she figured it out. "Strip."

A gleam of defiance returned as she threw her shoulders back, thrusting the contents of that lacy bra in his face. Her fingers dropped to her slim hips and released the snap at her waist. The zipper slid south, along with his full attention as she shimmied and shoved the wet denim down her legs. Nice legs. Great legs. The penlight shook in his hand.

A pair of hot-pink panties, high cut and plastered to her silky skin, taunted him. She kicked the jeans to his feet and propped her hands on her hips.

"Satisfied?"

Talk about a loaded question. Long dormant parts of his anatomy sprang to life, reminding him of everything he missed. He caught himself staring at the scraps of material covering her breasts and choked on his initial response.

Remembering how she'd run through the rainy darkness hardened his resolve. She didn't deserve any sympathy from him. He tossed her a flowery sheet to cover up with. Even the *bully* wouldn't allow him to neglect her completely.

"Get in bed." It was the safest place to confine Kira without worries of her escaping again. It wouldn't surprise him to find her scampering in her skimpy underwear back to the car.

He searched the pockets of her jeans, then angrily tossed the muddy mess into a high cupboard. He left her sweat-shirt on the floor. "Where the hell are my keys?"

Her reply included mostly four-letter words. Good. Let her be even half as pissed as he'd been, standing in the rain waiting for her.

"Keys?" he bellowed, holding out his hand. But instead of climbing into bed as he'd instructed, she stood ramrod straight with the sheet tossed behind her on the bed. His itchy fingers were nearly close enough to touch her. If he leaned forward a bit more, he could snap open the bra and watch her breasts spill into his hands.

"Do you think I'm hiding them under these?" Her fingers slid to her hips and she shoved the panties down to her ankles and stepped out of them.

His mouth went dry and his arousal throbbed in his tightening jeans. He was in so much trouble. Dalton couldn't pull his eyes away. She was beautiful. Where did he expect her to have those keys, now that she'd stripped? And the damn penlight left nearly everything for his imagination.

Luckily, the bright material of her bra seemed to glow in the darkness. Almost reminded him of a flotation device, except this time, he was the one drowning. A wise man wouldn't play along. A wise man would focus his attention over her right shoulder and feign disinterest. A wise man would also stop fantasizing about the creamy skin surrounding the peaked nipples clearly visible through the clingy fabric.

After unhooking the bra's front clasp, she peeled the wet fabric away from her damp skin as he watched. She slowly bent and retrieved the underwear before launching both items of lingerie at his chest.

"Honey, can you hang those up for me?" It was the same

tone she'd used at the convenience store. She should have learned her lesson the first time.

"Anything for you, cupcake." He opened the door and tossed the items into the rain, wishing he could force himself to follow. It would take more than a cold shower to get his starving libido under control.

She wrung some of the water from her hair and then used the sheet to dry off the rest of her body before wiping the mud from her feet. When she bent to retrieve something from that dang bag of hers, Dalton thought he was going to pop his zipper.

Why should he be forced to remain in wet jeans for the rest of the night so Cupcake could be high and dry in the only bed? He removed his shirt, tossing the soaking mass at her feet.

Her attention shifted from the tote bag to him.

He was mesmerized by the intensity of her gaze. Logic told him to stop. Desire wouldn't let him. He dropped his pants to his ankles.

She took a step backward and waited. The worthless penlight had already burned through its battery, leaving only a few bolts of lightning to break through their darkened cocoon. He was left to wonder if her retreat meant exactly what it looked like. Kicking his jeans aside, he reached for her.

Slipping one hand beneath the nape of her neck, he urged her forward as his lips found hers in the darkness. She tasted like chocolate with a hint of something fruity. Her chilly hands pressed against his chest. She was cold and wet, and the combination did nothing to lessen his desire.

Her frigid fingers wound around his neck and tugged him closer, almost as if she was trying to climb beneath his overheated skin. Beyond the way she melted against him, there was something primal about their connection.

Before, he'd wanted words to explain her actions. Now he just wanted to take whatever she offered.

After her deliberate striptease, he could visualize every curve of her naked body pressed to his. His hands brushed against her rib cage, slid to her hips and paused. Shoulds and should-nots battled in his mind as she moved closer, pressing her breasts against his chest and practically climbing under his skin.

His hands slipped lower, encompassing the perfect roundness of the bottom he'd first noticed in his shed. Her lips pressed against his collarbone.

"You're freezing." Reality made a brief appearance as he yanked the blanket from the plastic tub and wrapped it around her shoulders.

"So warm me up." She insinuated one leg between his and adjusted her slim arms around his neck, trembling. From the cold or desire, he wasn't sure which.

He'd told enough lies in his life that he probably could have volleyed something back. But he needed to finish what they'd started at the convenience store. Her lips were chilly, the inner recesses warm as his tongue flicked against her teeth, vying for entrance. Her fingers skated up and down his spine as her hips gyrated against his.

He shifted, struggling to reach the edge of the bed, before pulling her down on top of him. The simple foam mattress sank at least four inches under their weight, and for a brief moment he thought the trailer might tip.

The chill of her body was a relief to his overheated skin. And when she straddled his hips, he nearly lost control. A low moan escaped her throat and she tossed her head backward, allowing him greater access to the fullness of her breasts. Her nipples were erect and begged to be tasted.

He rose to his elbows, leaned forward a few inches and licked one tight bud.

# *Chapter 7*

A rush of adrenaline fired through Kira's veins, drowning out the doubts skirting the edge of her subconscious. Pleasure was a luxury she hadn't enjoyed in a very long time, and ignoring the consequences was far from her usual style. She could feel Dalton's reluctance, knew he would stop again if she gave the slightest hesitation.

She wouldn't.

She also wouldn't compare the Matthews brothers and wish the circumstances were different. Dalton hadn't given up on finding her. Instead, he'd followed her into the rainy night, carrying her bag of ill-gotten goods. He didn't have to help her. He could have searched for his keys and walked away.

Kira wanted him and she didn't care what his reasons were for staying with her. Let it be about generating heat and preventing a bout of pneumonia. Let it be about sex. Let it be about forgetting everything else for a few hours.

She pressed his shoulders into the mattress. He obliged and she followed him down, his mouth slipping from her breast and gliding up her neck to her mouth. The smell of rain still clung to his lips, mixing with a masculine scent she would forever link with Dalton.

Her eyes slid shut as she absorbed the sensations of his damp hair beneath her fingertips, razor stubble grazing her breast and his warm mouth tugging at her nipple. Her greedy hands longed to touch him. Trace the muscles running across his shoulders.

Heat radiated from his body, warming her chilled flesh. His hands glided to her bottom and adjusted her position so she lay directly on top of him and then the itchy blanket covered her again. Sensation swamped her.

She ground her hips against his arousal and reveled in awareness of his muscled arm pressing against her, holding her firmly in place. He was wonderfully warm, and his capable fingers lingered on her most sensitive parts.

He turned them both sideways and tucked her arm behind her, his teeth nipping at her shoulder. There wasn't a comparison she could've made or any words beyond clichés to describe how thoroughly he explored her mouth.

His hand slid between them and cupped her core, his fingers teasing light circles against her most sensitive spot. Her hips thrust upward to increase the contact and her body heat jumped off the charts. His chin grazed her breast and then his tongue traced around her areola.

Slow, sweet torture. Kira didn't want it to end, but she couldn't deny her release as she crested the first wave of pleasure.

His hand halted in midmotion.

"Don't stop," she murmured, thrusting her hips upward in an effort to brush against his fingers. But he anticipated the move and pulled away.

"I can't hear you," he whispered.

"Please don't stop."

His hand returned and, without deliberation, stroked across her core in unhurried confidence. Her pleasure mounted to an uncontrollable level, throwing her off the ledge she'd been standing on.

She'd cried his name and compared him to at least two gods before he jumped off the bed, stumbling to the other side of the trailer. She grew chilled as soon as he left her.

"Dalton?"

"Give me a minute."

"What's wrong?" she asked, dreading the answer. He'd changed his mind and didn't want her, after all. Embarrassment heated her cheeks.

"I'm sure I brought everything from the car, but I can't find the box of condoms."

She sat up and yanked the blanket to her chest. "I, um, might have thrown them in the backseat." When they were in the store, she knew he'd added condoms to the list to make her uncomfortable. The same way she'd done by requesting the tampons.

"I'm sorry." The apology was for more than the misplaced box. Kira trembled, wanting more of his touch, but she should have said the words sooner.

He collected his clothes and reached for the door.

"Where are you going?"

He finally looked her way. "I need some air. Cold rain is better than what my body is insisting I do to yours—condom or no condom."

"You don't have to—"

"Yes. I. Do." He shoved his legs into the pants and stumbled outside.

A second later her bra landed on the counter with a wet thud and the door slammed again. Kira wanted to cry through her frustration at his noble deed. She'd been on the verge of discovering what chemistry between two people meant. But she'd never been in any sort of relationship where her feelings were considered.

And as desperate as she'd felt about having another child, she didn't want it like this...through deceit. There had been enough dishonesty in her life. She wanted and needed Dalton's help finding Griffin, but it was worth the cost.

She stumbled from the bed and grabbed the tote bag he'd left in the small kitchenette, with her items scattered across the floor. One by one she picked up the pieces, much as she had done numerous times since Josh's betrayal. She located the bottle of pain reliever, pried open the cap and shook a couple more tablets into her hand.

She hunted for anything to wash the pills down, latched on to a bottle of juice and took two hefty gulps. By now her feet had grown chilly. She clutched the bag to her chest and fell onto the bed, wrapping the blanket firmly around her.

She knew she couldn't sleep and she refused to cry. The musty camper deflected the pelting rain, but the wind howled through the cracks around the windows. She scooted into one corner of the small bed and huddled in a ball. Alone again.

Silent tears burned her cheeks. Maybe she'd allow herself five minutes for a pity party. The day was a total loss. She'd failed to find her husband. She'd involved another innocent person in her dilemma. And she'd dredged up even more of the emotions she'd kept buried for so long. The bag slid to the floor.

No matter what it took, she had to make sure she used everything she'd collected to prove her innocence. Dalton had presented another roadblock when he'd taken the flash drive. But he wouldn't succeed in covering for Josh.

Kira had learned her lessons the hard way. And as much as she didn't want to hurt Dalton, in the end, it was all about clearing her name.

Dalton didn't get a moment's rest for the remainder of the stormy night, most of which he'd spent outside, pacing in the darkness. He'd searched for Kira's panties, but they were nowhere to be found. Knowing she wasn't wearing any would drive him insane.

He'd waited in the freezing rain for over an hour. Plenty of time for him to think. He'd almost bedded a woman he hardly knew. A woman who could be on her way to jail. The lack of condoms was a sign that things were moving too fast.

When she finally fell asleep, he'd sneaked into the trailer and sorted through the contents of Kira's bag. He hadn't paid too much attention when he'd been hauling it through the woods. Most of the items needed a good drying out, but he was happy to find a flashlight at the bottom. Once he installed the batteries, he was able to make a thorough search of the camper.

He munched on a soy granola bar, pulled a handful of items from the bag and lined them up on the table. Bandages and pain relievers, a sleeve of doughnuts, Band-Aids, hair ties, hand sanitizer, antibiotic ointment, lip gloss, toothbrush and paste and the tampons. Now he knew she'd been bluffing about needing them.

At the very bottom of the bag, he found a lighter. Bingo. There was a kerosene heater hidden beneath a bench, but he couldn't find any matches. Five minutes later the heater was running and he peeled off his clothing, laying his jeans and T-shirt over the plastic tub to dry.

As the rain continued to pound against the trailer, Dalton discovered another plastic tub beneath a bench on the opposite side of the table. Inside he found two pairs of thick socks, T-shirts and sweatpants. He yanked one of the shirts over his head and pulled on dry socks.

The other clothing was too small, but there was also a first aid kit, a roll of toilet paper and a compass. The last item could get them to the road. Returning to the Caddy might not be very safe. If the man following them located the vehicle, he could be searching for them right now.

Dalton spent the remainder of the night seated in the kitchen area, listening to Kira talk in her sleep. Yep, she was quite the chatterbox. She hated gravy, lost her favorite pair of sunglasses and believed her mug shot was flattering. She apologized too much and to everyone, almost as if she was reading from a phone book.

As daylight glowed on the horizon, he shoved her few belongings back into her bag. They needed to get moving soon and, for safety's sake, in another direction. Maybe somewhere he could pick up a cell tower and make a call. Get them back to civilization and find a computer, so he could learn what was stored on the flash drive.

Kira stirred. He quickly dressed, shoving the compass and phone into his jeans pockets as he waited. He should stop considering her feelings and wake her without preamble.

Circumstances had brought them together. Poor judgment had caused him to drop his guard. And raw need summed up the rest. He was disappointed in himself. Disappointed and feeling more than a little guilty for enjoying what they'd shared.

In the early light of dawn he tried convincing himself she was nothing special. Right. He'd almost slept with a woman he barely knew. A woman who said she'd been married to Josh and who had done everything in her power to make their situation as difficult as possible.

Her eyes fluttered and then slipped open while she stretched and yawned. Her blond hair was flattened on one side of her head and he noticed a few touches of greenery tucked between the strands.

"What time is it?"

"Six-thirty."

She nodded. "Can I have my clothes?" She covered her nose with one hand and sneezed twice. "And a Kleenex."

He retrieved the toilet paper and tossed it onto the bed.

She blew her nose and looked around the trailer. "Is there a bathroom in here?"

"Afraid not."

"I need to use the…facilities." She held up the toilet paper for emphasis.

He sat back and crossed his arms. Maybe she did and maybe she didn't. From this point forward he wouldn't take a word she uttered at face value.

"First we talk."

She started to object and then quickly pursed her lips together. Now that he had her attention, what should he say?

"About what?" She was well versed in appearing unaffected by his comments.

"Why did you run from the car last night?"

She shrugged. "I thought you were calling the police. Dying in the woods seemed better than going to prison."

"Why didn't you ask?"

"Because we—" she gestured between them "—aren't friends. I'm causing you all sorts of trouble. I could tell you'd had enough."

"Are you psychic or something?" If he hadn't decided which way to turn, how could she possibly know that he was done helping her?

She tugged the sheet a bit higher and leaned against the trailer's wall. "Dalton, you took me to a cemetery and showed me a whole lot of graves. You care about family, and Josh was your brother. It makes no sense for you to help me."

"My life hasn't made sense for a while." Everything she said was true. Family mattered to him, and getting mixed up with her had been twelve solid hours of insanity. But he'd also let her think that Josh wasn't capable of the kind of deception she described.

"Then give me my clothes so I can leave."

"Don't you mean so *we* can leave? Together?"

"Of course."

Last night he would have turned her over without a second thought. The stunt with the keys and then the game of cat and mouse in the rain earned her zero loyalty from him. And then he'd sat a few feet away and listened to her nightmares. He knew the kind of inescapable pain that tormented dreams. He'd hammered a few nails at three o'clock in the morning to avoid sleep. On the anniversary of Lauren's death, he'd used a sledgehammer and knocked down an old shed. At nightfall, he'd lit a match to the pile of boards and sat for hours watching them burn.

Running from the truth wouldn't solve anything.

He looked at Kira, her eyes swollen and her nose red from crying, and felt her defeat. He, of all people, knew what happened when someone was cornered. Their despair became palpable. Their facade for the world started to slip and they saw no way out. *Like Lauren.*

"Dalton?"

His attention refocused and he noticed Kira had slipped to the edge of the bed and dropped her bare legs over the side. Her skin was streaked with mud and covered in scrapes and bruises.

"Clothes."

He tossed her the stack he'd gotten from the plastic tub. "Put these on."

"Why can't I have *my* clothes?"

He tossed her the bra. She waited.

"And my underwear?"

"Gone." He shrugged, not caring whether she believed him or not.

"Do you mind?" She gestured for him to turn around.

"I've already seen every inch of you, so drop the act." The memory was imprinted on his brain and replaying itself in vivid detail. Her taste on his lips, her hips thrusting against his hand, the urgency in her touch as she neared release.

"I was wrong about the Matthews charm." She threw the sheet aside and reached for her bra. "Your mother must be so proud."

"Yours must be hugely disappointed." As soon as the words were spoken, he wanted them back. She'd baited him and he couldn't do the easy thing and let the remark pass, even knowing she'd grown up in a system not known for creating warm feelings. She turned, leaving him staring at her back. Watching her dress was nearly as bad as watching her undress had been the night before. He was torturing himself by rationalizing that he couldn't trust her. His fingers burned while he tried shutting down all his emotions.

He stared at the floor until her bare feet were covered by the dry socks he'd offered to her. As his gaze moved upward, he took in the baggy sweatpants that were much too big for her. He'd forgotten about a shirt and she trumped his error by taking her sweet time adjusting the bra's clasp between her breasts.

Breasts he had held and tasted.

He turned away from her and reached for the second pair of sweatpants.

Desperate times, desperate measures. He ripped the crotch out of the pants, turned to Kira and jerked the garment over her head.

"What are you doing?"

"Making a sweatshirt for you. Shove your arms up through the pant legs."

Her hands never moved from her hips.

"Let me help you." So what if he enjoyed seeing her spine straighten in annoyance? Also not his fault that he had to physically force her arms through the openings, which involved a lot more contact with everything from her arms to her abdomen. And those breasts.

"You can't be serious." She glanced down at the two mismatched pieces of clothing and then collected her unruly hair into some kind of messy bun at the base of her neck.

It was gawd-awful.

"You'll be toasty warm now." If the color lighting her cheeks was any indication, body temperature wasn't an issue. Plus, he'd have no trouble keeping track of her, because she'd definitely stand out in a crowd.

"In case you've forgotten, I'm missing shoes."

He had forgotten. But then he remembered the summer his foot had been in a cast. Every other night his mother had wrapped a plastic garbage bag around his cast and attached rubber bands to keep it in place, just so he could shower.

There must be trash bags somewhere in the trailer. A thorough search uncovered a few small plastic grocery bags. He inspected them for any rips and then gestured for Kira to extend her foot.

She leaned against the edge of the bed and crossed her

arms over her chest. Raising her foot slightly off the floor, he double bagged it, tying a secure knot a few inches above her ankle.

Pure genius. He copied the routine for her other foot and admired his handiwork.

Kira seemed less than impressed. "Wipe the smile off your face."

"Not a chance." He stood and patted her knee. "Payback, cupcake."

She sighed. "Are we going to the car?"

"Only if you have the keys." There was no point in returning to the disabled vehicle.

Blessed silence. She took a sudden interest in her new attire, tugging at the "neckline" in earnest. He waited until she finally looked up at him.

She shrugged. "Okay, I lost the keys last night."

"You should have stayed in the car," Dalton insisted.

"I wasn't thinking straight yesterday. You took the flash drive and I panicked."

"No plan?" he asked, goading her. It was much too easy for him to read her.

"I used to be a great planner. Not so much lately." She chewed her bottom lip and stared at him. "Where is it?"

"It's safe." She was visibly relieved. "But we can't stay here."

"I know, I know," Kira agreed.

"The men who are after you might have already found the car. We need to get moving." Evidently, it was enough motivation to bring her to her feet, the plastic bags rustling as she shuffled to the door.

"Are you hungry?" He reached for the chocolate doughnuts, offering them to her.

"I'm starved." She plucked the package from his outstretched hand.

Dalton shouldered the door open, then scribbled a note, leaving it with several twenty-dollar bills to make up for imposing on the trailer the previous night. He stepped outside, where the ground was soggy but the air was crisp and inviting. Turning slightly, he offered Kira his arm. She retrieved a handful of toilet paper, shoving it beneath the sweatshirt, then followed him outside. After securing the door as best he could, he led her west.

They'd been headed north last night, so he had to believe that if they traveled west, they'd eventually find another highway. Or at least get to an area where he could use the phone.

Kira walked next to him, eagerly munching on doughnuts. Maybe that was the key to gaining her silence, an unending food supply. He let another minute pass before he asked the question that had kept him awake all night. The question he almost didn't want answered.

"Who is Griffin?"

# Chapter 8

Kira clutched the tote bag beneath her elbow, securing it to her side. Breathe in, breathe out. It would take effort to make the tone of her voice believable, since she had no way to escape or evade his question. She tossed the last doughnut into her mouth as a delay tactic. "It's complicated and it might not make any sense to you."

"Excuse me? I own the biggest coffee company on the planet."

"No offense." She shaded her eyes from the sun's glare. "Insurance stuff is too dry for most people."

"I'm not most people."

Kira was thinking exactly the same thing. Most people wouldn't have given her multiple chances. They would have dialed 911 at the convenience store and watched as she'd been arrested. Definitely would have ditched her after a car chase and bullets flying. Never would have followed her into a lightning storm at night. Or found a way to warm her. She owed him some sort of explanation.

"The government is bleeding money due to fraudulent Medicare claims. It's too easy for someone to buy a medical degree from a little-known college in another country. They start a business, comb the obituaries for anyone over seventy and submit claims for treatment prior to their death."

"Isn't there a system in place to thwart it?"

"Of course, but the same people work both sides. They produce the security software for insurance companies and turn around and sell the bypass software to anyone willing to pay."

"And the government can't do anything to reduce the number of claims?" Dalton asked. "Do they have boots on the ground in the states with the highest numbers for insurance fraud cases?"

"They aren't sitting on their hands, if that's what you're asking. But, like most things, cutbacks mean less oversight and more opportunity for corruption."

The two of them walked in silence. Or relative silence, as she continued on her quest to get every morsel from the doughnut package. Kira wished she had something to wash the taste from her mouth.

"If you work for an insurance company, then why are you on the wrong side of the law?"

Kira wiped her mouth and shoved the trash in the tote bag. "I'm very good at my job."

"Who said you weren't?"

"I've investigated at least a hundred different doctors' offices. We've brought charges against eighty-two individuals posing as doctors and recovered sixty-eight million dollars in fraudulent claims, strictly for Midwest Mutual. Medicare fraud costs taxpayers over twenty billion dollars a year."

"What aren't you telling me?"

"I was closing in on Griffin, okay? In my spare time, because I have no life, I lived and breathed to bring him down." *Also because I missed Josh.* She shook off the thought. "Remember that threat I told you about? I think Griffin is framing me, for at least some of his handiwork."

"Your proof—those payments to nonexistent doctors you mentioned, approved by you—"

"*Supposedly* approved by me. His operation must be even bigger than I thought. I'd never seen those claims before, yet I have plenty of other fraudulent claims I can link to Griffin." She may have shared a bit too much information. The thought distracted her enough that she slipped on the wet grass, fell and landed on her butt.

Dalton did a very poor job of fighting his laughter. "What I wouldn't give for a camera. You look like a redneck clown."

"That's not very nice." She tsked a couple times. And really, was it necessary to make fun of any clothing choices, when he was the one who had dressed her? Plus, she needed a bathroom.

"I'll help you up." He extended his hand.

Kira glared at him for a second, then reached up to take his hand.

A shotgun blast broke through the humor of their situation, and Dalton quickly joined her on the ground. She couldn't breathe, couldn't turn her head to see anything but sunshine through the knee-high grass. "Is someone shooting at us?"

Dalton's palm covered her mouth. "I think it's hunters. Deer season." She nodded and he removed his hand.

"Let's ask them for a ride," she whispered.

"Stay still a couple more minutes."

Kira had dealt with more than enough guns and bullets in the past twenty-four hours, so it didn't take any convincing to keep her pressed to the wet ground. She heard voices of at least three people, maybe four.

Dalton stared down at her, held a finger to his lips and crawled forward several feet, apparently for a better view. She listened but couldn't decipher any of the words exchanged. Her skin started to chill and she tried thinking warm thoughts again. Started thinking of all the things she'd do when this was over.

When she was cleared of the charges, she was taking a trip somewhere warm. She'd always wanted to visit Hawaii, but her fear of flying meant she was limited to traveling by bus or train. She'd probably be banned from ever renting another vehicle.

*When this was over.* It had to end soon, right? She was not cut out to play hide-and-seek with bad guys or good guys or all the other guys in between.

A whistle pierced the air. "I know I hit him. How far do you think he went?"

Kira grabbed Dalton's leg, praying he'd give her some kind of signal if the hunters were headed their way. When his hand covered hers, she bit her tongue, closed her eyes and listened. Maybe they *should* ask the hunters for help. Would they offer them a ride to the nearest town? Then again, they did have guns and might think they were deer covered in mud.

"Okay, they're out of sight. It's safe to get up." Dalton rose and pulled her to her feet.

"Which way did they go?" She stood and slipped the tote bag over her shoulder, briefly checking the ground for anything that may have fallen out.

"To the south, but I'm wondering if they left a vehicle parked somewhere nearby. Two of them were noticeably overweight and probably not used to walking a long distance."

Yeah, and they probably had high blood pressure, too.

Dalton tugged on her hand and they jogged across to the tree line. He was in much better shape than she was, as evidenced by the fact he wasn't even breathing hard when they reached their destination.

"Here's the plan." He reached for her shoulders and turned her to face him. "I want you walking on my left side. Your sweatshirt is bright enough to draw attention and we need to blend in a little longer. Understand?"

Was it her imagination or did he stress the fact that he had a plan?

"Kira?"

"Yes, I understand."

He hooked an arm around her waist and they stepped into a patch of orange and brown leaves covering the ground. A few more leaves were gently falling in the light breeze, and her feet crunched on twigs mixed in with the leaves. Dalton kept her from tripping more than once as the terrain dipped and sloped.

The shelter of the woods also kept the sun from reaching them, and Kira grew chilly again. Was she ever going to be warm? Dumb question. It immediately had her pondering the brief time she'd spent in Dalton's arms. She inched closer to his body as they walked. Then she stepped on a sharp twig that cut right through her makeshift footwear, and she yelped in pain.

He jerked to a stop and raised her foot for inspection. "I really wish you hadn't lost your shoes."

"My fault. Tell me we're getting close to civilization. Can you see anything?"

He glanced behind them, mumbled something she couldn't decipher and tugged her onto his back. "I haven't done this in forever."

"Dalton, I can walk. Honestly, you're going to hurt your-self, and Lord knows I can't carry you anywhere."

He laughed. "You'd try." His strides easily doubled hers and she realized he'd been letting her set the pace earlier. "I used to do this all the time in basic training, eons ago."

"You were in the army?"

"Coast Guard."

Her legs were wrapped around his waist, her chest pressed against his spine and absorbing the heat he radi-ated. "I can't picture the connection between coffee and the Coast Guard."

"I had a buddy who could talk me into anything. Two cocky kids fresh out of high school and ready to save the world. Found out pretty quick you can't save everyone."

Who hadn't he saved, this man who protected her from her attackers, from herself and the elements? It was diffi-cult picturing him failing at anything. He was hauling her around as if she weighed nothing. He wasn't even breath-ing hard or breaking a sweat.

But last night he had been. His breath skating across her naked body. His hands touching every sensitive place, fill-ing a need she hadn't acknowledged in a very long time.

"I'm sorry I dragged you into this mess," Kira mur-mured. "It's not your responsibility."

"You're sorry a lot. Hell, you even apologize in your sleep."

"I do not." She cringed at the thought of babbling for hours. If she'd talked about Griffin, was there a chance she'd mentioned Brandon?

"How would you know? You're asleep." He turned his head to make eye contact with her. "I have a pretty good memory. Want me to cover the high points?"

Oh, crap, times a dozen. Was there even a good answer

to that question? At the very least she had to tell him something to divert the conversation.

"The FBI wants me because they think I embezzled eleven million dollars. They found eight hundred thousand dollars in a bank account in Denver. An account Josh told me he'd closed right after we were married."

Dalton's shoulders stiffened. Perhaps she'd struck a nerve?

"Or maybe he was diversifying his accounts so all his money wasn't tied up at the same time."

"All his money?" She scoffed. "I never saw any money."

"We can't be talking about the same person."

"Josh was completely focused on his painting. My job paid the bills." Even though Kira tried keeping her anger in check, the bitterness managed to find its way out.

"Painting was just a hobby." Dalton navigated over a fallen tree. "Josh majored in computer science."

"Wait a second. Are you saying he'd already graduated and could have been working somewhere?" Kira loosened her hold and leaned forward to see Dalton's face.

"Yes, he graduated. Studied art in Paris for nearly a year. Dividends from Buckshot's stock funded his adventures."

"And how much were these dividend checks that he spent on himself?" she demanded. Or a better question, why was she dwelling on Josh's behavior, when it wouldn't bring him back to face the music?

"You're describing a self-centered person. What in the world led you into marriage?"

"Um, he was very charming." Why hadn't she kept her mouth shut? There was no way she could confess the truth about her unplanned pregnancy and Josh's eventual abandonment, at least not while she was clinging to Dalton and wearing plastic sacks on her feet. But she had to be truthful with herself. Having unprotected sex not once, but almost twice, with brothers, was too embarrassing to admit out loud.

"Not only were you married to my brother for almost four years, the entire time you lived mainly in poverty while he pursued a love of painting?"

"It was actually only—"

Dalton shushed her before she could admit they'd been together for only eight months. He loosened his grip and she slid from his back, scanning the area to try to figure out exactly what he had seen. She nearly jumped for joy when she spotted the full-size pickup truck parked less than a hundred feet in front of them.

"Stay here." He gestured for her to squat down out of sight.

She nodded and moved into position, which quickly had her bladder sending out distress signals. She fished the toilet paper out of her bra and waited impatiently for Dalton to give the all-clear signal. Several minutes later he waved her forward as he popped the hood on the truck.

Kira hurriedly took care of business and carefully trekked to Dalton's side.

"What are you doing?"

"Disabling the GPS. If the owner reports it stolen, it will take more than five minutes to find us."

"Right."

"Climb inside and buckle up." Dalton dropped the hood and slipped behind the wheel.

Kira had no trouble opening the door and setting the tote bag on the floorboard, but it took two tries to balance on the running board before climbing inside. She scanned the interior as he started the engine.

"Did they really leave the keys in it?"

"Nope, unlocked. The spare key was in the wheel well."

He reversed the truck and made a quick turn to point them in the opposite direction. The rutted track had seen better days, the low areas holding murky rainwater in various sized puddles.

Dalton fished a compass from his pocket and laid it on the console between them. Then he pulled the phone from his other pocket and handed it to her. "Tell me when we have enough bars to make a call."

"Who are you going to call?"

"Watch the phone, please."

"Fine." She yanked at the material around her neck and sighed. "I need something to drink." She twisted in her seat and glanced to the seat behind her. Nothing. She checked the phone as Dalton pulled onto a roadway. No bars.

"Where are we going?" She punched the button on the dashboard for heat and adjusted the vents to blow on her.

"I'm thinking."

The early-morning sun was shining in her face, and Kira flipped the visor closer to the passenger window to block some of its rays. She checked a lidded compartment in the console.

"Anything?"

"I found an iPod and a bag of sunflower seeds."

"On the phone?"

"Oh, yeah, sorry." She dropped the items in the console and closed the lid, retrieved the phone from her lap and checked the screen. "I can't tell what's flashing."

"Let me see." He plucked the device from her grasp and squinted at it before punching in a string of numbers. "See if you can find a map somewhere."

Kira checked the compartment in her door and then the glove box in front of her. Besides the usual folder with the vehicle registration and proof of insurance card, she found a birthday card and a pen. She unhooked her seat belt and reached beneath the seat, retrieving an empty plastic soda bottle and an ice scraper.

"Hey, it's Dalton."

Kira's ears perked up. The phone was obviously working, but who had he called? He glanced her way and she shook her head. No map. He nodded, switched the phone to his other ear.

"Yeah, it has been a while." The lines bracketing his mouth spoke louder than the voice she heard echoing through the phone. He'd had no choice but to call the person on the other end.

Because of her.

"The phone I'm using doesn't have GPS and I need some directions. Sure, I can wait." He motioned for Kira to find something to write on.

She pulled the birthday card and pen from the glove box and waited.

"I'm headed north on Highway 77, trying to get to Casper."

They were going to Casper now? And then what?

Dalton snapped his fingers to get Kira's attention. "The road is closed at 487. Okay, what's an alternate route?"

She wrote down the information and caught bits and pieces of what the other person said. What if Josh had other siblings? Kira probably should have asked the question sooner. Right now, her mind was wandering way too much.

Dalton slammed on the brakes and made a sharp right turn onto a gravel road.

"Ouch!" Her head smacked against the window. "Give me a little warning next time."

He raised his eyebrows in annoyance at her outburst and released a heavy sigh. "I'm helping out a friend."

She doubted he considered her a friend, but what did it

matter? Except that Dalton was noticeably uncomfortable with the phone conversation.

Interesting.

Kira turned in the seat, giving him her full attention. He concentrated on driving, with a single-mindedness she'd expect from someone who owned a globally known company. He got things done. His answers switched to yes and no, with an occasional grunt.

The call ended. Dalton dropped the phone into his lap, avoiding her gaze. She was getting the feeling that maybe the conversation had stirred up unpleasant memories.

"What's our plan?"

"Going to Casper." He punched the button for the radio and scanned through a couple stations.

"And then what?" Maybe they should talk about what happened next.

"First we get you out of harm's way. Then we put a stop to all this insanity."

# Chapter 9

"Problem?" Dalton questioned, turning off the ignition and silencing the radio racket. They sat in the last row of long-term parking at the Casper, Wyoming, airport.

"I don't fly." She shook her head. Even saying the words made her nauseous.

"Don't be ridiculous. Flying is a hell of a lot safer than driving cross-country. Alone."

"You'll never convince me it's safer ten thousand feet above the earth. I like my feet planted on solid ground."

"Cruising altitude is actually thirty thousand feet."

"Not helping." She gripped the seat belt tighter. "I'm staying in the truck."

Dalton reached over and pulled part of a leaf from her hair. "You may want to shake out your clothes and hair."

"Why?"

"With all the marching through the woods, you could have picked up a tick or two." He tugged on her makeshift sweatshirt. "Want me to check?"

Kira slapped his hand. "No, I don't want you to check." Having Dalton's hands on her was a distraction she didn't need. She had to get the flash drive back.

"Who knows what might have dropped from the trees and into your hair."

Her scalp immediately itched. He knew exactly what buttons to push with her. A dozen different parts of her body responded to the implication of creepy-crawly things under her clothing.

She shook her hair free from the messy bun, jerking her fingers through it to check for anything foreign. A small leaf crunched beneath her fingers, sending tiny brown pieces onto her lap. A few pine needles followed, along with something looking suspiciously like the leg of a spider.

Kira bailed from the truck's cab. As soon as her plastic-covered feet hit the pavement she was bending at the waist, frantically shaking her head upside down in hopes of dislodging anything else not permanently attached to her head. Only after giving her hair a thorough finger combing did she stand upright again.

The motion made her dizzy and she steadied herself on the open door of the pickup.

Dalton was sliding out of his seat, so she allowed herself five seconds to admire his cute butt as he exited the truck, before diving across the console to double-check that he hadn't dropped her flash drive.

"What are you looking for?" he asked.

"Um, nothing." She adjusted her mismatched sweat-shirt and pants before climbing out of the truck on his side.

"So you have no interest in this?" He held the flash drive in his hand.

She lunged forward and tried to swipe it from his grasp.

He easily avoided her hand and shoved the plastic memory stick into his front pocket.

"You shouldn't have taken it from me in the first place." Kira wished she were brazen enough to shove a hand in his pocket and retrieve what was hers. She'd missed a prime opportunity to get it when she'd been clinging to his back.

"No, you shouldn't have lied about it in the first place. Plus, we both know it's safer with me."

"So why'd you let me crawl all over the front seat if you knew what I was looking for?" She rounded the truck, grabbed the tote bag and slammed her door for emphasis.

"It was a nice view." He winked at her.

Kira slowly counted to ten. "You are such a jerk."

He followed her around the vehicle and grabbed her upper arm, pressing her against the door. "Or I'm the jerk who's saving your life. If you'd rather be introduced to airport security, say the word."

She'd come too far to merely turn herself in, and he knew it. "Where are we going? I already told you that I don't fly. And I'm not getting on any plane until I hear your plan."

"I'm taking you somewhere that Griffin can't find you." Dalton scanned the parking lot and hurried her up an empty aisle. "I want to get to the bottom of this as much as you do."

"How are we going to get through security without my identification?"

"You only need ID for commercial flights." He nodded toward the silver metal building. "We're taking a private plane."

She added two and two together. "The call you made?"

"You got it. The same call I was going to make last night, before you took off." Dalton flipped through his billfold and removed some kind of access card he swiped to gain them entry to the field.

Kira knew her behavior last night had complicated things even more. She'd never been in a situation like this before, having someone chasing her and wishing her harm. Her alliance with Dalton was the only thing she had in her favor.

He pulled her through the gate and secured it again. "Once we're airborne you can relax. We'll be landing on private property."

Relax? Probably not. Picturing a small two-seater plane with a little shake, rattle and roll thrown in for good measure was not reassuring. She might have been okay on something carrying, say, two hundred other people. If it crashed, at least she would have company and maybe a chance at survival. A tiny plane, not so much.

Nevertheless, even though she didn't relish the concept of flying, it would be good to stop looking over her shoulder for a while.

They approached the first building, which had the letter *H* over the entrance, and Dalton used the keypad to enter a number. He helped her inside and softly closed the door behind them.

Lights automatically came on, maybe linked to the alarm system. She shaded her eyes until they adjusted.

She'd attended a few ball games at Kauffman Stadium in Kansas City, and the area laid out in front of her was roughly three-quarters the size. She stared up at the ceiling, trying to count the halogen lights, which certainly could have lit up a stadium.

He tugged on her arm and she followed him to the opposite side of the building. The plane he stopped in front of made her chin drop.

"Holy moly." It definitely wasn't a puddle jumper or

one of those experimental planes thrown together with a kit. It was a…jet? It couldn't be his plane. Could it? But there was the Buckshot's logo plastered on the side, a giant bull's-eye with an arrow in the center. And the tagline If You've Got One Shot, Make it Buckshot's.

Well, at least she wouldn't have to worry about having her fingernails pressed into the dash as they made their escape to whatever secret location he'd decided.

She glanced to the rear of the plane and then the nose as he walked around the other side and opened a panel. She followed, walking underneath the plane. It was the only benefit to being short. He flipped a recessed handle and lowered a flight of steps in front of her.

"Go on inside while I check a couple things."

"But I've never been on a plane before."

"Up the stairs and turn right. It will take you to a private bathroom, where you can freshen up. You probably have about ten minutes before you need to find a seat and buckle up.

Kira bolted up the stairs. It smelled a hundred times better than she would have expected. A mixture of new carpet, leather furniture and varnished hardwoods. She made a quick right, then ripped the plastic bags and over-size socks from her feet and sighed as her toes sank into the plush gray carpeting. She almost dropped to the floor and rolled, but felt too dirty and disgusting.

With the tote bag over her shoulder, she hustled down the dimly lit hallway, following it past a kitchen area and through some double doors to a bedroom suite. Wow, the man knew how to travel. And really, would you even care where you were going?

She headed straight for the bathroom. The stainless steel door was ajar and she flipped the light switch on before stepping inside and securing the lock. The cherrywood vanity was topped in black granite, with brushed-nickel faucets.

Her reflection in the mirror was even worse than she expected. Myriad scrapes and bruises marred her face and arms. A basket of mixed toiletries sat near the sink and she rifled through it and removed a toothbrush and a small box of toothpaste. She ripped the latter open, applied a glob to the brush and scrubbed the daylights out of her fuzzy teeth.

She hurried to use the toilet and then quickly washed her hands and face. A sudden surge of optimism raced through her veins. Dalton insisted they would be safe once the plane was in the air. Dare she believe him?

She stepped from the bathroom into the bedroom. She hadn't heard any sort of announcement, so she did the next logical thing. She checked the cabinets for any clothing and discovered bras, panties, T-shirts and nightgowns. All from the same famous lingerie company.

Kira didn't have to think twice; she sorted through a drawer until finding her sizes. After stripping off the sweatpants and bra, she changed into a fresh set of matching undergarments. There were also several pink shirts in various sizes. She pulled one over her head and it fell to her knees. Obviously a nightshirt. She kept it on, anyway, and kept looking. The remaining items were all bikini swimwear. She left her old sweatpants on the bed and went in search of Dalton.

No, she wasn't happy that he'd taken the thumb drive or that he'd placed himself in charge of the situation. But maybe she should thank her lucky stars that he'd followed her into the rainy night. Without his help, the thugs chasing her would certainly have caught up with her.

And she'd be dead.

Shrugging off the chill racing up her spine, Kira hurried through the doorway and down the hall to the main entry area. Four groupings of double, oversize seats were arranged on both sides of the plane. She chose a spot near a window.

"Are you buckled in?" Dalton asked, as he dropped into the scat next to her.

"Yes."

"I'll let you know when it's okay to move around."

"I thought you were flying? Is there another pilot on board, too?"

"Yes, there's another pilot, who doesn't need any help from me. You, on the other hand, might need someone to share some basic information on airplanes. I'm your man."

*Dalton is my man?* Kira was certain he didn't mean it that way. He was just offering to sit next to her and distract her with plane talk. He didn't have to do that. But arguing with him was like yelling at drywall.

She watched as the plane rolled out of the hangar and taxied toward a runway. Allowing herself another moment to relax, Kira closed her eyes and slowly inhaled and exhaled. The thought of flying always terrified her. But now she really was at the end of the road. Nowhere to go but up. Even on a flight riddled with uncertainty.

"How are you feeling?" Dalton pulled a blanket from beneath another seat and offered it to her.

"Fine." She responded after drawing two more deep breaths and opening her eyes. She took the blanket from Dalton's hand and spread it over her legs.

If the initial scents of new carpeting and varnished wood hadn't been enough to convince her that the plane was brand-spanking new, the plastic wrap intact on the seat across from her would have done the trick.

"Where are you taking me?"

"To the family ranch in Texas." He reached under the

blanket and held her hand. "There's nothing for you to worry about."

No worries? Yeah, right. How about the fact that she enjoyed Dalton's attention? Any physical contact with him left her heart pounding and her pulse racing. She had to get this under control.

"That seems like a long way and I don't want to inconvenience you any further." The short burst of energy she'd received a couple hours ago from the package of doughnuts was long gone, and the quiet hum from the jet's engines was the only sound filling the cabin.

"You and I are sort of a team now," Dalton said. "We're safer together."

She didn't quite have the energy to argue with his logic.

"Let's get some rest while we can, okay?" He pressed a button on her seat and it reclined to a more comfortable position. The oversize leather chair was easily large enough to hold two people. And before she could protest, Dalton pulled her into his arms and covered them both with the blanket. It should have meant an easy glide into sleep, but her mind continued firing an endless frame-by-frame recap of the past twenty-four hours.

The moment she'd driven around the bend in the road and noticed all the renovations to the cabin, she should have known she was intruding. Okay, she knew she was intruding, which is why she'd stopped the truck and proceeded on foot. It had been surreal to be back in a place that held such good memories. She could stay in that inner happy place only as long as she avoided interacting with anyone. Pretend she was safe. Pretend she had a future. Pretend that anyone cared about her enough to help.

Her days at the cabin with Josh had been the last time she'd been truly happy. He had showered her with his undivided attention. They'd had a whirlwind romance and she hadn't been smart enough to suspect he was toying with her from the start. It was probably a good thing he was already dead, because she was having all sorts of ideas about how to cause him as much pain as he'd caused her.

Dalton's right arm had fallen asleep thirty minutes ago, but Kira looked so peaceful in his arms he didn't want to move her. He also couldn't communicate with the pilot about the sporadic turbulence that bounced the plane from side to side.

It reminded him of Lauren and the way she'd planned out her tours to the last detail. She'd said that flying so much meant she'd eventually be involved in a crash. Her answer: a tour bus to use on most of her concert dates in the United States. She'd believed that the key to safety was mixing up the way she traveled and whom she traveled with.

It was a superstitious ritual, but one that provided another level of comfort to Lauren whenever she was away from home.

"Who is Lauren?"

Dalton's head jerked up at the sound of Kira's voice. She was staring at him as though he'd been rambling for a while. Her cheeks were flushed an enticing shade of pink, which matched the T-shirt barely covering her hips. Her hair billowed around her shoulders with angelic ease, the golden-blond strands reflecting the light.

"My wife." He couldn't remember anyone ever asking him the question.

Everyone knew Lauren.

Knew about her sudden rise to fame, knew about her tragic death.

"You're married?" The color drained from Kira's skin.

He shook his head in denial. "No, I *was* married."

"So you're divorced?"

He didn't want to talk about it, but her borderline mortification at the prospect of him being married meant he needed to set the record straight.

"My wife committed suicide eighteen months ago." There, he'd managed to say it without any long pauses or cracks in his voice.

"Oh, Dalton, I'm so sorry." Kira patted his leg before placing a hand on his knee.

Her green-eyed gaze turned somber and her eyes filled with tears. And then there was silence between them. She was waiting for him to change the subject or to provide more details. He wasn't sure if he could do either.

Covering her hand with his, he rubbed his thumb across her bruised knuckles, and she flipped her hand over to entwine their fingers. His heart tightened in his chest as he willed the painful memories to their rightful place in the far recesses of his mind.

"I'm listening."

He chuckled, certain she didn't know how simply she'd released the tension in his body. "It sounds like you're talking."

She sighed. "You know what I meant. I'll listen if you want to tell me about it."

What could he say about Lauren without adding more emotion to their day?

Kira pulled her hand from his grasp. "Don't feel obligated to share anything with me. Jeez, we hardly know each other."

Not completely true. They'd both lost spouses and neither one of them was certain what had gone wrong. But maybe now wasn't the best time to dredge up everything he'd shared with Lauren.

"I hope it was all right that I cleaned up. I found a T-shirt in one of the dressers."

He took a good long look at Kira. Her face was freshly scrubbed, revealing a hint of bruising along her jawline, and a fresh bandage was on her forehead. An intoxicating mix of jasmine and musk floated around her. The T-shirt was actually from a famous lingerie company and he had no doubt what she was wearing beneath it.

Someone had been using the corporate jet for more than business. Someone who dated several lingerie models, so it wasn't a surprise they'd left some items on the plane. Leave it to an old friend to provide items barely qualifying as clothing.

"I couldn't find any pants, so I'll have to wear those ugly sweats again."

He stared down at her bare legs and resisted the urge to touch her. Having her half-dressed and seated next to him brought all sorts of unwanted images to mind.

"Do you want me to wear something else?" Her innocent question sent desire arcing between them in the span of two heartbeats. He allowed it to simmer for another few seconds before standing and stepping away from the temptation of her warm body.

It wasn't enough. Her eyes sparkled mischievously and he shoved his itchy fingers into his front pockets, latching on to the thumb drive and steeling his resolve to keep her at a kiss-stance, or distance.

He was losing it.

He retreated from her and the secret smile painting her lips. A little devil. She had designs on getting the thumb drive with seductive distraction. Underestimating Kira or her determination to regain the driver's seat was unwise.

He grasped at the first, apparently safe, topic jumping into his head. "The clothes must belong to Tate. We were best friends growing up." Past tense. And although he never intended the implied *we aren't friends anymore*, it hung in the air.

"Something happened to change your relationship?" Kira tugged the blanket from the seat and wrapped it around her shoulders.

Dalton knew she already sensed the truth. "Lauren was his sister."

Kira stared at him for another moment. "Everybody grieves differently." The blanket drifted to her waist, and she secured it there before crossing her arms over her chest in a knowing manner. "Time is supposed to make it easier to deal with losing someone we've loved."

"When?" The sarcasm in his tone was much harsher than he intended, and he immediately felt contrite for taking his frustration out on her. But before he could retract the statement, some abrupt turbulence knocked Kira out of her double seat. His arms wrapped securely around her before the two of them tumbled to the floor.

The plane hit more turbulence and Kira was immediately on alert. So was Dalton. He tensed, perked an ear toward his pilot. The surrounding fluffy clouds had been replaced with gray denseness. Water dribbled across the outside of the window.

"Mr. Matthews?" a voice inquired over the intercom.

"On my way," he said loudly over his shoulder, before turning back to Kira. "You should buckle up."

She did as instructed and waited. Dalton would surely tell her if they were in trouble, right? Her stomach danced, either from the sound of his voice or from the movement of the plane.

"Kira, are you okay?" The intercom crackled as he spoke over it ten minutes later while the plane continued to shake from side to side.

"I'm fine." Which was the biggest lie ever told, because she was anything but all right, being on a plane in obvious distress.

"The storm we tried to miss turned into a blizzard. Hang tight until we get on the ground."

"Dalton?" When he didn't respond, she tightened her seat belt and prayed. None of this was his fault. Okay, almost none of it was his fault. If only he'd walked away at the convenience store, he wouldn't be risking his life for her. Again.

An early-autumn storm dropped visibility to zero, causing Dalton and his copilot to change course from his family's ranch near Waco to his ski chalet. The secluded retreat had its own runway and Dalton got them on the ground before the heavier snow started falling.

Kira added a few essential toiletries to her tote bag while Dalton wielded a cardboard box filled with rations from the plane's kitchen and then led her and the copilot down a paved path toward their final destination.

The soft gray blanket from the plane was wrapped around her shoulders. Unfortunately, she had to wear the temporary shoes Dalton had made for her, causing her to shuffle along the sidewalk leading to the chalet's wide front porch.

Spotting the for-sale sign in the front yard, she paused a moment, glancing around the area. She couldn't see a road from here, so who would be able to see the sign?

"Do you own this house, too?"

"Yes." His clipped response put a stop to any other questions she may have wanted to ask.

He stomped up the front steps while she gingerly placed one foot in front of the other and reached for the railing.

Dalton balanced the box on his shoulder and reached for the alarm keypad. The door flew open.

Somebody was already here? Kira made her way onto the porch, uncertain what she should do or say. Maybe the Realtor rented the property while it was on the market? If so, where else could they go?

The man who opened the door was about Dalton's height, but with short jet-black hair. "I thought you were dead."

"More like you wish I was dead," Dalton responded.

"They said your house exploded."

"The house didn't explode. It was my truck," Kira offered.

"Hello there, Gene. Good to see you again." The man appeared to know both Dalton and the copilot.

"Nice to see you again, Mr. Wilson."

The dark-haired man leaned to one side, making eye contact with her. "I don't believe we've met."

"Make yourself useful and carry this to the kitchen." Dalton shoved the box against the man's chest and then turned to help Kira navigate the final steps. When he tugged her inside and shoved the door shut after they'd all entered, she noticed Mr. Wilson was nearby, watching them.

"Gene, can you get a fire started? And I'll have that ride for you in a bit." Dalton cleared his throat. "Kira, this is Tate Wilson. Tate, this is Kira."

Dalton reached for one of her feet and removed the bags and sock, dropping them onto the tiled entryway.

"I'm sorry for showing up—" she began.

"Stop apologizing," he interrupted. "It's *my* house." He reached for her other foot, yanked off the sacks and sock. Kira leaned against the wall and watched while Dalton next removed his boots. She was afraid to do or say anything else that might cause more tension.

"What bedroom are you using?"

"The one off the kitchen," Tate replied. "Need to turn up the other furnace if you're staying upstairs."

"Fine. Kira can shower down here." Dalton grabbed her hand and led her past Tate, down a hallway and through the kitchen. They rounded a corner and entered a bedroom, then Dalton steered her through to the adjoining bath.

The counter was lined with cans and bottles. Shaving cream, moisturizer, hair mousse and gel stood next to a bottle of mouthwash, toothpaste and teeth whitening strips. Okay, wow. All the pieces were coming together.

"Is he gay?" Kira whispered.

"You'd think so, right?" Dalton shook his head in disgust. "No, he's not gay. Vain, yes. Gay, no." He checked the cabinet beneath the sink and pulled out two towels and a washcloth, stacking them on the counter. "There should be soap and shampoo in the shower. Take one of those extra long showers that women love and I'll find something for you to wear."

"I don't want to cause any more trouble for you."

"Then take a bath." He checked his watch. "I need at least an hour to get rid of Tate."

"You can't kick him out because of me. Dalton, there's a storm coming and he was here first." She was prepared to list more reasons why it was wrong, but Dalton's glare sent her in a completely different direction. "I'm taking a really long bath now."

He slipped off his wristwatch and pressed a couple buttons before laying it on the counter. "Don't come out until the alarm sounds."

She pointed to the watch. "Is it waterproof?"

"It's water resistant. Why?"

She plucked it from the counter and slipped it on her wrist, then frowned, shaking her head. "No telling how much trouble I can get into. Alone. In a bathroom." She gestured to the sink. "With man stuff everywhere."

She was disappointed when Dalton didn't continue the conversation. He sighed, locked the doorknob and pulled the door shut behind him.

# Chapter 10

If Tate could do nothing else right, at least he'd stocked the pantry. The women he normally surrounded himself with were more the fashionista variety. Tate was a gourmet chef with thousands of recipes stored in his giant brain. Dalton preferred simple meals that were immediately recognizable and just as good served left over.

He headed to the kitchen and poured himself a cup of coffee. Seeing Tate Wilson for the first time in over a year brought old emotions to the surface.

"Tell me about your new friend." Tate dropped an armful of clothing on the counter and crossed his arms over his chest.

"This doesn't concern you." Dalton dumped two teaspoons of sugar into the muck Tate called coffee and stirred so hard the spoon clanked against the mug.

"Maybe not, but I want to get all my facts straight before you try throwing me out."

"There aren't any facts, just speculation."

"About what?" Digging for any nugget of information was Tate's main character flaw. He could never let an argument end because he never forgot anything. Ever.

Dalton switched gears. "How did you know about the explosion?"

"The sheriff's office called. Sounded like more than a truck caught fire. It surprised me to be listed as your emergency contact." Tate poured himself a cup of black tar and slurped. "Good thing you showed up. My next call was going to be to your mother."

"I'm fine." Truthfully, his mother had checked in with him three times a day in the months following Lauren's death. Dalton had managed to stretch the calls to once a week on Wednesday nights. One thing was in his favor: it wasn't Wednesday.

"You're fine?" Tate banged the mug on the counter. "Nothing has dragged you out of the woods for months. Then boom—literally—you're playing with explosives and running around with a woman who obviously has issues, but no shoes."

"Your opinion means nothing to me." Dalton didn't need to justify a thing. Not to the man who'd sold him out. "Is this how it's going to be?"

Tate leaned on the fridge, then impatiently shifted forward again, the coffee forgotten.

"How many times have you visited her grave?" Dalton demanded.

Tate stared blankly, then shrugged.

"From the guy who never forgets a single damn detail." Dalton emptied the pot and his mug's contents down the drain. The black swill didn't deserve to be deemed coffee. He searched the cabinets for some Buckshot's, leaving the next move to Tate. They used to be best friends. But they hadn't been civil to each other since the funeral.

Tate cleared his throat, braced his arms on the counter and dropped his head. "Seventeen."

"You went to her grave seventeen times?" Dalton's stomach churned as he measured ground coffee into the machine and pressed the start button.

Tate slapped the granite counter. "She was my baby sister."

"We were like brothers, man. You think I killed your sister, my wife. You told the press that I must have been involved."

They were suddenly toe to toe, both men's fists clenched. Dalton wanted to swing. He wanted to knock his brother-in-law's block off. Then Tate relaxed. He shoved his hands into his pockets and his shoulders dropped.

"I didn't leak it, but I was wrong not to deny it." He was too calm and relaxed, almost depressed.

Dalton couldn't believe the bad luck that had forced them to land. And then more rotten luck that Tate would be here, right where it all had happened. "Why are you here, Tate?"

"I can be alone. No one comes here. You abandoned it."

"And it was Lauren's favorite place."

"Yeah." He pushed away from the counter and clapped his hands, faking a smile from ear to ear. "I need a drink."

"I need you sober."

"Now, that proposition doesn't sound nearly as inviting as getting sloshed and enjoying your interesting friend." Tate crossed to the refrigerator and pulled out a bottle of water. He guzzled half the contents before setting it on the counter.

"She's not that kind of friend." Dalton needed real caffeine to steady his nerves. "But thanks for finding her some clothes."

"You're welcome. If you need anything else, let me know."

His ex-best friend made him feel like a guest in his own home, but it wasn't worth arguing about.

"No matter what state our relationship is in, Tate, I need your help. I've got something I need to get to my techs."

"So how did Kira become your problem?"

"Who said there was a problem?" Dalton shrugged and willed the coffeemaker to brew faster. No coffee, no cigarettes and no patience left for the inquisition that was sure to come. Perfect.

"There's definitely a problem, buddy. I've seen it with my own eyes." Tate made an hourglass figure in the air and nodded knowingly.

The very last thing Dalton needed was juvenile prodding from his old friend. Maybe he should have given a bit more consideration before asking for help. But Tate always had his back. Or used to. But still, he had extensive knowledge of security, guns and jets. Added bonus that he was a doctor.

"Come on, what's this favor?"

Tate fed off all this adventure crap. He needed the constant adrenaline rush and tended to take risks without thinking a situation through to a safer conclusion.

"There was a time when you could have talked me into anything, probably because you had a way of selling every idea with a stack of attractive adjectives," Dalton murmured. "Nothing was ever just an adventure. It was an unbelievable opportunity. You can change ordinary events into ten-point earthquakes."

"Got it. I'm a leader and Dalton is a sheep. Your mother blamed me when you passed up the scholarship to Stanford and followed me into the Coast Guard. You still mad that I ended with a higher rank? Or that I got through school quicker?"

That age-old crack Dalton could ignore. He'd never been jealous of Tate seeking dangerous assignments patrolling the Gulf Coast in pursuit of drug runners from Central America. He wanted to slug Tate's arm for the joke. For a second, he almost did. But he saw the change in Tate's face, as his old friend was suddenly overcome with grief. Dalton recognized the look. He saw it too often in the mirror. They couldn't forget what had happened. They both knew Tate was right to blame him for his sister's death.

"Do you expect us to talk about the good old days and forget the last two years?" Tate asked.

"No. But you're right. Kira's in trouble. You don't need details. And if you can't deliver this—" he removed the flash drive from his pocket "—to my tech guys, she might end up in jail or worse."

Tate grabbed the drive and shoved it in his own pocket. "I better get going before the storm hits for real. This should be an exciting drive." He tugged his jacket off the back of a chair and headed toward the garage.

"Take Gene with you, please."

"I'll pull around front. Wouldn't want the boss not to have privacy. Text me where to drop it off."

Dalton should thank him. He needed Tate's help and probably would have called him if they'd made it to Denver. Providence? Luck? Whatever it was, Tate was here, and as much as he hated Dalton, he'd help. So instead of following, he told Gene he had a ride and then took the clothes for Kira to the first-floor bedroom.

Dalton quickly realized most of them were from a well-known lingerie company. Tate obviously entertained more than one of their models here. That wasn't utmost in Dalton's mind. Knowing Kira was a few feet away, enjoying a steamy bath, was the distraction. Picturing her wearing any of the items sent his mind exactly where he didn't want it to be. There was no way he'd be able to keep his hands off her.

He opened a dresser drawer and yanked out an orange Buckshot's T-shirt. Nothing remotely sexy about it and it would clash with her eyes. He paired it with flannel pajama bottoms from Tate's drawer. Then Dalton bolted from the room before his aching body could change his mind to join her.

Straight up the stairs and into the bedroom he and Lauren had shared. He turned to his old dresser and yanked out jeans, underwear and socks. Then he stormed through the doorway and slammed the door behind him.

Every bedroom had its own bath. A cold shower was exactly what he needed. A distraction to clear his foggy brain.

Icy pinpricks numbed his back, cut into his scalp. He could handle the freezing water against his skin. It was telling Kira that her evidence was headed down the mountain with Tate that sent a chill up Dalton's spine. She'd be safe here, and hopefully, she trusted him to keep her that way.

But he needed to know what was on that flash drive. She didn't want him to know about it, didn't want him involved. Thought she could go it alone. But it was becoming clear to him that this Griffin guy was willing to kill for the evidence she claimed to have. Well, now Dalton had it. He was in charge of the game. She'd have to play by his rules. Then why was he standing under ice water instead of facing her fury?

"Are you sure you aren't hungry?" Dalton asked, as he joined Kira on the couch.

Of course she was hungry, but not quite hungry enough

to eat two of her least favorite foods. Her stomach growled as he shoved a Fig Newton in his mouth. Steam danced along the rim of his coffee mug and he smiled at her before washing down the cookie with a swallow of the stinky brew.

"I adjusted the thermostats on the furnace and water heater. We should have some heat and more hot water in the next hour. Then you can stay in any of the bedrooms."

"Good." She loved the fire. Watching the flames dance was slightly hypnotic.

"Are you warm enough?" He leaned toward her and slid a hand underneath the blankets, finding her foot and gliding his thumb across the arch, causing a shiver to race up her spine.

"I'm okay."

"Willing to share some heat with a coffee lover?"

"Maybe."

His palm skated past her ankle and lingered on her calf. She shouldn't be encouraging him at all, and still a smile tugged at her lips.

"Body heat might be the only thing saving us from freezing to death."

"What about the furnace?"

"It's sometimes temperamental." He set the coffee mug aside and pulled her onto his lap.

She shouldn't have gone so willingly, but rationalized that getting closer to Dalton meant a better chance at retrieving what was hers. He must have had a similar idea because he trapped her hands between their chests and tucked the blankets around her, creating a snug cocoon.

"Comfy?" His voice hummed across her skin, and Kira found she was enjoying their proximity far too much.

She nodded, thinking what it might be like to have his strength keeping her safe beyond the scope of a few hours. The possibility left her grasping for a quick change in subjects.

"Do you ski?" she asked.

"No, I fall. A lot. Never quite got the hang of it."

"So you haven't been here for a while?"

He glanced toward the ceiling and shifted her against him, his quick exhalation of breath tickling her earlobe. "No."

A single word holding a million different meanings. No, he hadn't been here in a while. No, he wasn't answering any more questions about his personal life. No, he didn't want to think about his wife.

Silence wedged its way between them, creating a type of dual solitude. Tension eased from her body in measured increments, along with a giant sigh, which summed everything up.

"You're safe here."

"If you say so."

"Even if someone figures out we're together, this is the last place they'd look. Trust me."

Trust him? She shouldn't have involved him at all, wouldn't have gone to Wyoming in search of Josh if she'd known Griffin was keeping close tabs on her. "What if Griffin's men somehow track us here? Then what?"

"We're miles away from the nearest town and the alarm system is virtually impenetrable. Plus, with the storm approaching, there's no way for anyone to reach us."

*There is always a way.* A muscle in Kira's cheek danced nervously. Never a good sign, since the same tic had preceded her unplanned pregnancy, her elopement and Brandon's arrival into an unfriendly world.

"You sound so sure, but I don't think Griffin will give up easily."

"I didn't say anyone would give up. They'll just have to dig a whole lot deeper to track you here."

"I need to have a plan in place. And before you tell me not to worry, save your breath. I got here because I underestimated what someone else was capable of. I won't make the mistake a second time."

"I won't let anything happen to you," Dalton promised.

She pulled away from him and settled herself at the other end of the sofa, securely wrapping the blanket around her body. "I would rather err on the side of caution. Tell me about the layout of the house and the security system you use."

He took a sip of coffee before answering. "The house is five thousand square feet, with six bedrooms and private baths upstairs. Downstairs there's an additional bedroom, two more bathrooms, a library, dining room, kitchen and game room, as well as this living room. There's also a four-car attached garage."

"Sounds like a lot of empty rooms for someone to hide in."

"No one is here." Dalton shifted his feet to the coffee table and Kira lost her battle against a smile.

"Nice socks." They were gray, heavy-duty work socks, but the heels and toes were orange, the same color as the ugly shoes she'd briefly worn.

"Bet my feet are warmer than yours."

She couldn't allow him to sidetrack her. She had to steer the conversation to their safety within the house. "I want you to show me how to work the alarm."

"Okay." He quickly polished off his coffee and exchanged it for the cup he'd previously offered her.

"Um…" She paused until he glanced her way. "Could we do it now?"

"Why don't you sit tight for another fifteen minutes,

give the furnace a chance to catch up, and then I'll show you the alarms and the downstairs?"

She nodded and surreptitiously tried to see beyond the dimly lit room. What if they lost power?

"Is there a generator somewhere?"

Dalton nodded. "Out in the garage. Plus, there are plenty of flashlights around the house and a cupboard full of candles."

She didn't like the unfamiliar surroundings, especially since she already felt at a disadvantage. Of course, Dalton had to pick that very moment to renew the questioning.

"I need to know what's on the thumb drive."

"No." She was such an idiot. Why hadn't she fought harder on the plane to retrieve what was hers?

"This isn't a negotiation, Kira. You're in trouble here and you need to tell me exactly what proof you have and where it came from."

"That's what you think I need. You had no right to take it from me in the first place. I want it back."

"Possession is nine-tens of the law."

"And theft is *against* the law." She jumped off the couch, tightly wrapping her blanket around her body.

"So is trespassing. Do you really want to compare which one of us has broken the most laws?"

The chill left Kira's body, replaced with sudden warmth from the anger racing through her. Why was it so difficult to accept his help graciously? Was it merely because she suspected his only motivation was keeping his family's name out of the news? Did it matter? Blood was always thicker than water.

"If I tell you what's on the flash drive, will you give it to me?"

"It's in a safe place."

Kira's breath clogged her lungs. What had he done with it?

"But it's here, right?" Her gaze swept the room and landed on him.

His lips pressed against the coffee mug, unhurriedly taking another sip.

Had he already gotten rid of it? She glanced to the window, watching the snow steadily increase. Maybe it was on the plane? Then another piece clicked into place.

"Tell me you didn't," she demanded, already knowing the answer. "That's why you got rid of the pilot and your friend. It had nothing to do with wanting to be alone with me. You sent the flash drive away with Tate. To where?"

"Denver."

# Chapter 11

Kira counted to fifty and then started over again. Why had she gotten so angry with Dalton, when in reality she was angry at herself?

She should have demanded that he return the flash drive. But no, she hadn't done anything after he'd threatened her with security at the airport. She'd never imagined in her wildest dreams that he would have sent the drive to his tech department. "For safety," he'd said.

More likely it was because he didn't trust her. He demanded trust *from* her, but he definitely didn't trust her. She stopped counting. It was useless to try to fall asleep, especially while replaying Dalton's expression when she'd told him she'd encrypted the flash drive.

She wouldn't allow another man to take charge of her life and railroad her into settling for less than she deserved. She'd allowed Josh to treat her badly, without standing up for herself. Allowed one hasty decision to determine her future.

She snuggled deeper into the soft flannel sheets of the queen-size bed and made a promise to herself. No matter what it took, she would see Griffin behind bars. Dalton had merely muddied the waters by removing the flash drive. But he was right, the evidence was safer away from her. If only she had a computer. She could access her online Dropbox and pull a few of the documents she'd collected. It wasn't as complete as everything she'd stored on the flash drive, but maybe she could gather enough to prove to Dalton she was telling the truth about Josh.

She could still see doubt in his eyes. Whether it was directed at Josh or her, she didn't know. But she could prove that they'd been married and that Josh had worked for at least two of Griffin's companies. There was definitely a link and perhaps it would be enough to buy Dalton's continued assistance.

An hour later, Kira tossed off the covers. She slipped her now toasty bare feet onto the plush bedroom carpet and exhaled in acceptance. Her mind was too full to get any rest, and hiding from Dalton seemed like the chicken's way out. *Cluck, cluck, cluck.*

She moved the window drapery to one side and watched the wind whip the heavily falling snow in every direction. The quiet emptiness of the house surrounded her as she opened the bedroom door a crack and peered into the hallway. No sound met her ears. It was almost as if she was alone in the house. A dim light beckoned her to move toward it.

The gourmet kitchen was straight from the pages of *Architectural Digest*. Gleaming stainless steel appliances and dark granite counters circled the room, which boasted a restaurant-style cappuccino machine and an array of glass coffee canisters.

What was so great about coffee, anyway? Stinky, bitter tasting and too expensive for her budget. If she was going to spend five dollars on anything covered in whipped cream, it would definitely be hot chocolate.

Buckshot's probably didn't even offer anything aimed at non-coffee drinkers. Kira stomped to the cupboard above the coffee canisters and climbed on the counter. There had to be a tea bag somewhere up here.

"What are you grumbling about?" Dalton asked.

It wasn't really her fault the counter was slick or that she jerked sideways and toppled toward the floor in a very unladylike fashion. But instead of landing on the hard ceramic tile, she found herself pressed against Dalton's broad chest as he broke their fall.

It was very wrong to enjoy having her hands on him again.

Very, very wrong to sigh when she inhaled his scent.

And far worse to forget why she was in the kitchen in the first place.

"Do you notice that when we're together, there's a lot of falling involved?" he asked, both arms wrapped around her as he stared up from his vantage point.

"I've noticed," she responded, her voice barely audible. She moved to the left, attempting to slide off him, but he held her tighter.

"Where are you going?"

"I'm getting up and off the cold, hard floor." Honestly, her body wasn't touching any part of the floor. But being pressed against the warmth of Dalton's hard frame was a hundred times more uncomfortable. Damn him for making her feel alive again. Was she ready to be that optimistic person with her whole life in front of her?

His arms fit snugly around her waist, then one large hand slid lower, to cup her butt and stop the squirming. "I want to talk to you."

"Yeah? How about we wait until we're vertical again?"

"Because I'm not chasing you all over the house. I've got your attention, so why delay?"

He had more than her attention. Tingles of awareness crept over her skin while she tried slowing the gallop of her unsteady heart. Surely he could feel the thumping against his chest. She squelched the desire to squirm beneath his hands as well as his gaze and forced herself to relax.

"Okay."

"Kira, I need for you to trust me on this." His previously playful tone turned to stoic seriousness.

"Well, my definition of trust doesn't include someone else controlling my life. Or making me feel confined."

"I'm not."

"It sure seems like it. Can't you give a little?"

He started to smile.

"Not a sexual innuendo, buddy." If her arms weren't trapped between them, she might have pointed an accusing finger in his face. She settled for raising her knee against his obvious arousal and holding it there long enough for him to receive her message.

"Whatever you say," he said, loosening his hold.

She shouldn't have smiled or given him any encouragement at all, but she was pressed against all his interesting parts and not putting up much of a fight.

"You have the most kissable mouth."

Whenever he said the word *kiss*, her lips were ready to comply, even though her brain was chanting *absolutely no kissing*.

"No kissing," she insisted, sounding as if she'd be willing to do way more than touch her lips to his. The proximity threw her off-kilter. She had to get out of his arms and up off the floor before hormones prevailed.

Dalton didn't seem to have the same dilemma. "Not a very convincing protest. Try again."

"Do you treat all your guests this way?"

"You are so good at dodging a topic. Who'd you learn the delay tactic from?"

"Let me up," she demanded.

He released her and rolled the opposite direction, then jumped to his feet. Retrieving a chair from the nearby dinette set, he placed it beside her. "Then let's get you—what was the word you used?—*vertical*."

She smiled, in spite of the chill currently numbing her toes, and allowed Dalton to raise her onto the padded seat. For the first time she noticed his appearance. He was wearing a pair of gray flannel pajama bottoms and a bright orange Denver Broncos T-shirt. He could have diverted traffic through a road construction zone or maybe taught a hunters' safety class.

"Promise me something." She licked her lips and glanced up at Dalton's face.

"I hesitate to say I'll promise you anything. Who knows what your wicked mind is cooking up?"

"Wicked, huh?" Her brain did a quick rewind to their time in the camper and her toes immediately warmed. "Promise me when all this is over, we're torching every orange T-shirt you own and having a giant bonfire with s'mores."

"Bad?"

"The lighting isn't helping." She squinted for emphasis and then released a sigh. "I only wanted a cup of tea."

He crossed the room and filled a teakettle with water before placing it on the stove. The *click, click, click* of the gas burner coming to life was a welcoming sound. It felt like home, like a lazy Sunday afternoon when she'd settle into her recliner with a cup of Earl Grey and a good book.

"I hope you aren't a purist." He leaned against the center island and shot her a high-wattage smile.

Kira shrugged her shoulders.

"So you won't reject a mere tea bag instead of the traditional teapot and loose-leaf brewing method?"

She shook her head again, more than a little surprised at his interest in anything unrelated to coffee. "Are you implying I'm some kind of snob?"

"Well, you don't like coffee and you hate my favorite color."

She laughed then, adjusting herself on the chair with added flourish. "And how long have you had this unhealthy attachment to orange?"

"Since I was a kid and my first baseball team was the Giants. We had orange shirts and it's stuck with me ever since."

"I see. Bet you're a Broncos fan, too." She was surprised Dalton was willing to move beyond questioning her.

"Of course. Gotta root for the home team."

By this time he'd collected two mugs, spoons and honey, lining them up on the counter as he waited for the kettle to whistle.

"What's your favorite color?" he asked.

"Red."

"Red is a power color, you know." He smiled across the counter at her. "That's why Santa wears it." Dalton winked.

"Really? I did not know that."

"It's in the Buckshot's logo because the ad agency said a splash of red would cement our brand. I'm a little surprised you've never heard of us."

"I don't drink coffee."

"Yeah, you've said so about a dozen times. But didn't you ever see a billboard with our logo? A Super Bowl commercial?"

"I don't remember any billboards, and I hardly ever watch football."

The teakettle whistled and he turned the burner off before filling both their mugs with the steaming water. "Can I add anything to yours?"

"Plain is good for me."

"Let's move out to the living room and find you a more comfortable chair." He returned the kettle to the stove and then picked up both mugs. He headed through the doorway and on to the far side of the room, near the fireplace and a giant TV.

Kira sat a moment longer and then stood, stretching the knot from her shoulder. The stress from the past thirty-six hours had her wishing for a magic wand. For now she'd settle for a hot cup of tea, a cozy blanket and the man in the next room.

What did he want? He hadn't made any demands. She knew he was curious, but he hadn't pushed her to reveal anything after telling her Tate had her flash drive.

Kira dropped onto the couch, yanked a blanket up to her waist and reached for the cup of tea on the coffee table.

Dalton turned the television on and scrolled through a few channels. "It'd be nice to get a clear picture without climbing on the roof and adjusting the satellite dish." His comments quickly turned to a stream of four-letter words and suggestions for satellite providers to shove things in truly inappropriate areas.

"Now who's got the potty mouth?"

He glared at her over his shoulder. "I'm sure you've heard worse."

True. But it was amusing to watch his patience evaporate. She sipped her tea and mentally cataloged the broad shoulders in the ugly shirt and the first-class butt her fingers were itching to touch. Now she wanted to touch him? *After* she'd blown a perfectly good opportunity in the kitchen?

"One decent channel. Am I asking too much?" Dalton glanced at her for confirmation.

"Are you pouting?" she asked.

"No, I'm not pouting. I'm frustrated the TV isn't working and we have no idea how long this storm is going to last."

"You're definitely pouting."

"Drink your tea."

Kira dropped her gaze to the cup in her lap and lazily circled the rim with one finger. She decided some quiet muttering to herself wouldn't hurt anyone, so took a sip of the ginger peach tea and switched her rambling to Italian. She'd worked in a pizza place during college where the owner was notorious for berating the staff. Besides receiving some nice tips, she'd learned a few ways to say idiot in Italian and Portuguese.

*"Idiota."*

"I don't believe it." Dalton's voice interrupted her mumbled recitation of classic Italian.

"I'm not talking about you," she lied, lifting her innocent eyes to his. Only he wasn't looking at her. His attention was glued to the television, where he'd successfully located one clear channel.

Kira squinted at the image on the screen. "Oh, you've got to be kidding me." She slammed her cup on the table and stumbled to Dalton's side as the blanket tangled around her feet. "What are they saying?"

"Give me a second." He punched a few buttons on the remote and the speakers behind her boomed in response.

"The suspect is seen here in a 2012 DMV photo, and in this convenience store footage from yesterday."

The only thing missing was a bowl of popcorn. The reporters had somehow managed to splice together the images of her removing the Buckshot's sweatshirt and then her lip-lock with Dalton, so it resembled a low-budget porn flick. The camera didn't do him justice. He was much sexier in person.

"Investigators have learned Mrs. Kincaid is also believed to have siphoned millions of dollars from her employer, Midwest Mutual Insurance, out of Kansas City, Missouri," the announcer reported.

"We are fully cooperating with the FBI's investigation and have surrendered all of Mrs. Kincaid's files for review." Her weasel-nosed boss, Evan Daniels, garnered his own fifteen seconds of fame.

"I don't think he likes you," Dalton commented.

"He was never my biggest fan," Kira admitted. Her being arrested at Midwest Mutual during Friday's taco buffet probably hadn't helped.

"Are these the same charges you were talking about earlier?" Dalton squeezed her shoulder and she leaned into his touch.

"Okay, yes, but it doesn't make it any easier to swallow. They're calling me a criminal on national television." Kira had nothing left to lose. Things had been so publicized in the press she already felt at a disadvantage.

"Then, when all this is over, we'll hire the best publicity firm in the country to restore your squeaky-clean reputation."

Kira bit her tongue to keep from objecting. She shouldn't be happy that Dalton felt responsible for her, right? It had been so long since she'd depended on anyone else. The warmth spreading through her chest was proof of nothing.

Damn. She would definitely lose her job and probably spend years in prison. Of course he was making light of the situation, trying to make her think all the damage could be undone with the wave of a hand. But the next image on the screen guaranteed it couldn't.

She knew the exact second Dalton realized it. His hand dropped from her shoulder and he took a step closer to the TV.

"I'll be damned."

"Mrs. Kincaid was previously married to Joshua Kincaid Matthews, pictured in this wedding photo taken in 2011. The two never officially divorced. Matthews was killed in a fiery car crash near Denver in August of this year. An anonymous tip to Crime Stoppers has investigators working to reopen the accidental-death case and link it to Mrs. Kincaid. Local police are attempting to connect evidence from the scene to DNA taken from the suspect's home."

This could not be happening. "They took pictures from my apartment and rummaged through my things. They think I killed Josh." Kira dropped to the floor as numbness crept through her limbs.

The wedding picture shrank to a box in the corner of the screen and a reporter from News Channel 9 was shown in the beam of several spotlights.

"You'll see a few live embers remain, but not much else, at the home of Dalton Matthews, Buckshot's Coffee CEO. An explosion destroyed the home, and reportedly, the authorities located one body within the debris. Although Mr. Matthews has managed to avoid the limelight for months, I'm sure you'll all remember the tragic loss of Lauren Lee, his wife, and pop music's brightest star. As you can see from the crime scene tape behind me, this investigation is currently under way, and we have Sheriff Lyle Watkins to give us an update."

"Your house is gone?" Kira asked. "Do you think that thug set a fire or something?"

Dalton shushed her.

"Thank you, Natalie. I want to assure the viewers of Benton County that there is no need to panic. This is an isolated incidence of arson, perpetrated, we believe, by the suspect you have shown. Additionally, this would be classified as a black-widow crime. If the evidence we have gathered remains consistent, we can reasonably assume this case is linked to the death of Joshua Matthews in August. Authorities in Missouri are working to verify that he was legally married to Kira Kincaid. As the widow, she stands to inherit a 10 percent share in Buckshot's Coffee. Those shares would sell for upward of ten million dollars, and to me, it sounds like strong motivation for murder."

*They think I murdered him?* As much as she'd wanted Josh to suffer, Kira had never really wanted him dead. Hadn't even known he was dead.

"As soon as an autopsy is performed on the body inside, we expect to confirm the identity."

"Sheriff, can you predict with any accuracy if the body is indeed Dalton Matthews?" the reporter asked.

"I'm not much for speculation, Natalie, but my twenty-seven years in law enforcement and the mounting evidence we've collected is very telling. Your savvy viewers can draw their own conclusions."

"Yeah, right, that's all speculation," Kira said to the television.

"Thank you, Sheriff. We'll keep you apprised of changes in the scope of the investigation. As earlier reported, Kira Kincaid is armed and dangerous. Anyone with information about her whereabouts is asked to call 800-CRIMETIP or 911."

Dalton muted the television and turned to stare at her.

"If they found a body, it's got to be the guy I left cuffed to the tub."

"Maybe it was an accident," Kira said.

"Yeah, right. I seem to be an accident magnet." He tapped the remote against his palm. "Tell me why your last name isn't Matthews."

"My last name isn't Matthews because when I knew your brother, his name was Joshua Kincaid."

Dalton yanked her off the floor. "Did you have any involvement in Josh's death?"

"Yes, if wishing him dead counted as involvement."

Dalton stared at her as if he was seeing her for the first time. "What did you do to my brother?"

"I prayed he'd suffer half as much pain as I did."

"If you hated him so much, why'd you marry him in the first place?"

"I married for love. I married because I wanted a future with your brother. But most of all, I married him because I was pregnant."

## Chapter 12

Kira watched Dalton's anger dip to annoyance, then denial, then shock. Neither of them spoke a word. The seconds turned into a minute, then two, while Dalton processed her confession.

"Josh has a child?"

She nodded, uncertain if she'd be able to explain the circumstances, now that she'd blurted a fact few people knew.

"Boy or girl?"

"A son, Brandon."

Dalton sighed. "You're saying my brother walked away from his responsibility to his child? Where is he? Why did you leave him?"

"No, I'm saying he walked away from his responsibility to me. To our marriage."

"You lost me." Dalton stared down at her. "Wasn't he paying child support?"

"No, it wasn't like that."

"Then what was it like? You're not making any sense."

Her trembling fingers rose to cover her mouth. Kira couldn't cry, but she didn't know how to keep the tears at bay. Emotion clogged her throat as she stood mutely in front of him.

"Tell me." The request was tempered with empathy, the same kind she'd emitted at the cemetery when she'd realized he'd lost someone close to him.

"Our son was stillborn." Oh, sweet heaven, she hadn't allowed herself to say it out loud before. Ever. Her vision narrowed as her mind replayed the moment Josh had told her the news. She hugged herself, trying to keep the grief from enveloping her. "I lost them. I lost them both."

Dalton pulled her close and she collapsed against him. Somehow they ended up on the couch, her face pressed against his neck as years of pain overwhelmed her. The words were a scattered mixture of daily prayers for another chance and devastating acceptance of the unfairness of life. Kira cried until her eyes burned and her lungs ached. She cried until there were no more tears left and Dalton's shirt was soaked.

Her sobs turned to hiccups and he held her tightly. He rolled to his back and pulled her on top of him, then covered them with a blanket. His fingers slid through her hair as he pressed his lips to her forehead.

"I'd known Lauren since we were kids." His voice broke and he cleared his throat. "Tate and I used to run wild in the neighborhood from sunup to well past dark."

Kira could picture a miniature Dalton, with an angelic face and innocent brown eyes filled with mischief.

"Lauren was always the baby, you know? Tagging along and trying to copy every stupid prank we pulled. And we couldn't leave her out, because then she'd tell her mom and get us all grounded for a month."

The smile in Dalton's voice told Kira they'd probably deserved every ounce of punishment they'd been dealt.

"She was a kid when we headed off to the Coast Guard, but she'd grown up a lot by the time we were out and I went to college. She used to sing the national anthem before all the baseball games, so everyone in town knew she had the talent to break into music. She said she never had the desire."

"Dalton, you don't have to do this."

"I can't remember a time when Lauren wasn't a part of my life." He'd be lying if he said Kira didn't remind him of Lauren. Her bright nail polish and petite stature were two things he could name. But where Kira was daring and sometimes bold, Lauren had been reserved and anxious.

"She never expected the fame."

No one expected the fame.

"'Left Alone' was a fluke, until she performed it at the Colorado State Fair. And suddenly, there was no turning back. She couldn't refuse the recording contract. She'd composed that song the night of her senior prom, when Joey McCracken stood her up."

"I remember that song."

"Along with millions of fans. Who could have guessed her words would resonate with teenage girls all over the globe?" It gave Dalton chills to recall the arenas packed with screaming fans. "Once things got rolling, there was no stepping in front of that speeding train."

"She had an amazing voice," Kira agreed.

"Everyone played a role in keeping Lauren safe. Tate had extensive training from his time in the Guard, so for a while he became her chief of security. Her mother traveled with her to every location, waiting in the wings while she performed, offering all the support she sensed Lauren needed."

"She was very lucky to be surrounded by people who obviously loved her."

Dalton nodded. "Then the letters started. We shrugged them off. What big-name stars didn't get their share of nutty fan mail?"

"I'm sure a lot of celebrities deal with the same thing."

"But then the creep switched to email, breaking into Lauren's account and posting her private thoughts to the public domain." Dalton reached for one of Kira's hands and intertwined their fingers.

"She was crushed. If I hadn't benefited from the stunt, I would've been first in line to drag the man to justice. But the emails were about me." A smile tugged at Dalton's lips. "She had a crush on me for a while and questioned what it would take to get my attention."

"Those were very personal feelings to have posted for the world to read. She must have been mortified." Kira shook her head. "I would have been."

"She was, at first. And then when everything died down, I called to clear the air. We talked and then made plans for dinner." He smiled again. "It was simple. We had a lot in common, so there was already a foundation in place, something for us to build on.

"I had just taken over for my father as CEO for Buckshot's Coffee, and she was trying to balance her singing career with family time. Somehow we made it work.

"Six months later we were engaged. Another six months and we were married." Dalton's thoughts slipped to their wedding day. Lauren had been just as excited about having an outdoor wedding as she was to win the Grammy for Best New Artist. "She would have given it all up to stay at home and start a family. But touring and promoting were part of the music business, and she had to finish out her contract."

"Plenty of pressure," Kira murmured. "Did she regret recording the first song?"

"I don't think she regretted it, exactly. But family was a big part of Lauren's life and she lost the freedom to see everyone whenever she wanted." Dalton frowned. "She never wanted the music world to be her life."

"How long were you married?"

"Three years."

There was a moment of silence between them before Kira shifted so she could see his face. "I'm sorry, Dalton. I know how tough it is to lose someone you love."

"I should have seen the writing on the wall and stopped the tour. But Lauren was always worried about the crew being out of work and suffering because of her decisions. She didn't need all the responsibility."

Dalton released a huge sigh. "She came to me at Christmas and said she was ready to quit. Why didn't I listen to what she'd really been saying? She was telling me— point-blank—that she was finished with life. I should have done something."

"She made choices, Dalton. When someone is depressed it skews their interpretation of everything around them."

"You aren't hearing me, Kira. I should have known what she was thinking. Our lives were always connected. Why didn't I know what was going on inside her head?"

"So you're saying her parents and Tate, plus all the friends she had—they all knew what she was thinking?" Kira's hand brushed across his shoulder. "Ridiculous. You can't believe a word of that."

"It wasn't their responsibility. It was mine." And speaking of responsibility, he had tangible proof that Josh and Kira were married. Dalton needed to make sure she was safe and get his team of attorneys busy clearing her name. Tomorrow. Tonight she needed him, right here. He wondered how his mother would feel when she saw him taking Kira's side of the argument…

The silence extended as Dalton sat there, lost in thought. Kira's body gradually relaxed, until her calm breathing told him she'd fallen asleep.

Kira woke the next morning alone on the couch. Her eyes were gritty from crying, but her body was relaxed. Dalton must have stayed with her for a while. She slid off the couch and stretched.

Slowly, she made her way down the hallway. Dalton's voice echoed from behind a closed door. She continued to the shower, found some fresh clothes and went to the kitchen. Dalton was waiting.

"I want to show you a few things."

She spent thirty minutes learning how to start the generator, where the flashlights, candles and matches were kept and how to use the security keypad. Dalton even entrusted her with the secret code, which she chanted in her head until the lure of that closed door in the hallway broke into her thoughts.

Dalton had been inside the room it led to earlier, making business calls. She tested the knob, found it unlocked and inched the door open to peek inside.

Cool air rushed at her, causing a shiver to race up her spine. Shelves lined the walls directly opposite the door and a sparkling statue on the top ledge caught her eye. It looked like… Wait a minute, it couldn't be. Opening the door completely, she stepped into the frigid room and spared a final glance over her shoulder. Dalton had gone outside to adjust the satellite dish, so she should have a few minutes of uninterrupted snooping time.

Walking past the desk, she moved closer as utter amazement clogged her throat. There were four Grammy awards, coated in a layer of dust.

She set down her tea and pulled a chair over to the shelf, a niggling of doubt bubbling in her stomach. One quick look and she'd scurry out of the room. She climbed atop the chair and read the shiny gold plaque on the first award: Best New Artist 2008, Lauren Lee.

As she hastily scanned the remaining shelves, Kira spotted a picture prominently displayed at eye level, of Dalton posing with Lauren on the red carpet at some important shindig. No doubt about it, the man cleaned up well. The cut of the tuxedo jacket accentuated his broad shoulders and he appeared larger than life itself.

Kira's hormones shifted into overdrive. Which had to be wrong, right?

Lauren was doing her best to play to the camera in a tight-fitting red gown, showcasing her assets, along with a dazzling diamond necklace circling her throat. But the best accessory, by far, was Dalton standing by her side.

Kira hopped to the floor. Leaning forward for further scrutiny of the picture, she immediately read the look of apprehension in Lauren's eyes. The smile painting her lips was forced and meant to appease the paparazzi, which had probably been lined up for blocks to get a glimpse of the latest singing sensation to hit the pop charts.

Dalton was beaming, holding Lauren's hand as if they were two high school sweethearts on their way to the prom. That's what love should look like.

Kira would have remembered being on the receiving end of such a look. She stared at the picture on the bookshelf as her eyes filled with tears. For the first time in her life, jealousy settled across her skin. Jealous of a dead woman. Could she sink any lower?

Good Lord, what was she doing? She couldn't sit around and wait for Dalton to make anything happen. It wasn't his fault she'd cornered Griffin. Wasn't his fault she was in danger. Dalton was using his money and resources to help her. No one had ever done such a thing for her. Even Josh, the man who'd pledged his love to her, hadn't helped her when she'd needed the most support. She may have loved and hated Josh, but Kira couldn't live with herself if something happened to Dalton.

She squared her shoulders and slid the chair to the desk, only then noticing the laptop hiding under a pile of un-opened mail. She immediately lifted the lid, but since it was an older model, it took a minute or two to boot up. There was a shaky connection to the internet, judging by the icon in the bottom right corner of the screen blinking on and off.

Kira raised the window blind and looked outside, trying to see the mountain range. She checked the screen again and the icon disappeared. After picking up the laptop, she hurried to the open doorway, pausing long enough to make sure Dalton hadn't returned inside.

The long, oak stairway was infrequently used. Several layers of dust had accumulated on both sides of the carpet runner. The swirling snow was visible, courtesy of a rect-angular window midway up the steps. When she reached the top, she checked the computer screen again and found the icon flashing once more. The internet router must be in one of the rooms she hadn't explored.

She made her way to the end of the hall, silently eased open the door there and peeked inside. The room smelled faintly of lilies and lavender, but mostly of stale air and emptiness. Heavy draperies hung from oversize curtain rods spanning a width of a dozen or so feet. The walls were painted a pale yellow meant to be soothing, but because of the stale air, the space felt more institutional than homey.

Kira glanced over her shoulder and listened. The house was quiet, so she stepped into the room and checked every outlet, without locating the router. Finally, she opened the first panel of draperies covering the floor-to-ceiling windows. A large window seat was revealed, along with the elusive router. The glare from the fallen snow blinded her for a moment before she slid onto the brocade-patterned cushion and allowed the draperies to drop into place.

It was quite a bit colder near the dusty windows, but that was a fair exchange for the wireless connection icon blinking green on the computer's screen. She quickly tapped the keys and reached her email home page before entering her name and password. Seconds later she was scrolling through her emails and downloading several of the documents she'd sent herself from her work email account.

She typed in the address for an online document storage site. A few months ago, in a moment of semibrilliance, she'd uploaded several more files on Griffin obtained during her investigation. Her top-secret-after-hours-cure-for-insomnia quest to stop the flow of money into his pockets. There were original documents showing four of his bank accounts in the Cayman Islands, Belize and the Netherlands. Now she just needed to find a way to link them to the eleven million dollars *she'd* supposedly embezzled.

But as her fingers hovered over the keyboard, she absently tapped the space bar and the box prefilled another username. She paused, read the name and then hit the tab key, successfully inserting the password, which had already been saved. A few seconds later, Lauren Lee's name appeared on the screen.

Kira stared blankly at it, uncertain if she should log out right away. Her eyes refocused and she scanned the page, noting the documents were all in folders labeled with the month and year. She scrolled to the bottom, tapped on the first folder and opened the document listed. It was Lauren's journal and Kira knew immediately she shouldn't read any further. Her eyes skimmed the page, anyway. She smiled briefly as Lauren described how she'd come up with the melody for "Secrets" while mixing up a batch of chili for a party she was hosting with a few of her friends.

She'd accidently purchased ranch-style beans instead of the usual chili beans, and the chili had been a new favorite for the small gathering of people. Everyone had quizzed her about her "secret recipe" and she'd been proud to have something in her life she didn't have to share with the world.

Kira closed the file and chose a different month, acutely interested in Lauren's life on stage. She'd posted several times while in Europe, logging all the sights and sounds of the huge arenas, and the devoted fans who'd camped out for days in the winter weather to get tickets. Beyond all the lights, glamour and world travel, Lauren had been a regular woman who'd had an extraordinary gift. Her voice was uniquely sweet and a bit sultry.

Bits of conversations she had with Dalton were mixed in with Lauren's notes. It seemed odd to Kira that if the woman had been depressed enough to take her own life, more of these records didn't tell of her true feelings. Did Dalton even know about this site? Had he read any of Lauren's entries?

Kira clicked out and was ready to exit when she noticed an untitled folder mixed in with the others. It was probably nothing, but snooping through one more file seemed minor compared to all her other transgressions of the past few weeks.

The first sentence of Lauren's entry had Kira's skin rising in goose bumps.

*Dalton canceled our weekend plans at the last minute, but I'd already driven up to the chalet. I decided to work on ideas for next year's tour. The world will have to survive without me, because I'm only doing thirty shows, all in the good ol' US of A.*

Didn't quite sound like a woman wanting to give up on her music.

Kira closed the file and chose another.

*The Buckshot's jet is being serviced and Dalton couldn't get a flight out of Atlanta today. I told him not to worry, I'd be fine. Then Josh calls and it turns out he's in Kansas City. We had dinner in his room, and evidently the wine was stronger than I'm used to, because I was too tired to make it to my hotel. Josh let me have his bed while he slept on the couch. Always the gentleman.*

Kira snorted, scrutinized the date on the entry and nearly fell off the window seat. It was October, and she'd been studying for a midterm while Josh was supposedly getting extra studio time with some mentor in the art world. He was such a liar. Lauren Lee was his sister-in-law, and he'd never said a word about it.

A slew of crazy possibilities took shape in Kira's mind. What if the person harassing Lauren had been in her circle of trust? After everything Josh had put Kira through, she'd peg him as more than capable of twisting circumstances to fit his own agenda.

She lost track of time as she scrolled from file to file, scanning for Josh's name. It popped up more than anyone else's. In fact, he had an uncanny knack for being nearby each time Dalton and Lauren were unable to connect.

"Kira?" Dalton's voice called to her from down the hallway.

She froze for a moment, uncertain if she should remain quiet or show herself and face his disapproval. Staring down at the message on the screen, Kira quickly tapped a few more keys and saved the folder directly to the computer's hard drive. She had to share the information with Dalton. He had every right to know what game Josh had been playing with Lauren during the months before her death. Josh had obviously felt nothing for the people he considered family. How could he betray Dalton?

Closing the lid on the computer, Kira left the window seat and hurried toward the doorway, hoping to catch Dalton before he realized how far she'd intruded in the room he'd obviously shared with Lauren.

He'd already crossed the threshold when his eyes locked on to hers, and there was absolutely nothing she could say to defend her actions. She'd trespassed, and the guilt must be clearly written on her face.

"What are you doing up here?"

She noticed his attention was completely focused on her, as though he was avoiding even a cursory glance at the rest of the room.

Honesty seemed the best course of action. "I thought I could get a better internet connection from up here. I wanted to access a few files on my private email account."

He stared at the computer clutched in her hands. "Where did you find Lauren's laptop?"

"It was buried under a bunch of papers in the office downstairs."

His hands fisted at his sides. "I wish you hadn't touched it."

Kira nodded. "I assumed it must have been hers, after I logged in. I'm truly sorry if I've upset you, but I think you need to read what I've found."

"Put it away." He turned and gestured her toward the open door.

"Dalton, it's very important you read this." Kira extended the laptop toward him.

"No. I want you out of this room."

"Please, Dalton, I know losing Lauren was devastating, but—"

"It's more than losing Lauren," he interrupted. "We fought that night and I wasn't here when she needed me."

"Here?" Kira's head spun with the announcement. "Please tell me you don't mean right here, in this house."

"I haven't been back since."

When he didn't say more she started pacing and throwing out a litany of Italian dirty words. "You wouldn't be here *now* if it weren't for me. This is my fault." She ran to the windows, yanked the draperies out of the way and stared at the blizzard raging outside before turning to face him. "How long before we can leave?"

"Probably a couple more days."

"Dalton, you shouldn't have brought me here. You should have asked me first. Why doesn't anyone think to ask me what I might want to do?" She probably would have thrown something his way if there'd been anything handy.

"Do you think this was my first choice?" He stared at her and shrugged.

"I would never, ever have asked you to do this." Her voice trembled as she tried keeping the tears at bay. She shoved the computer into his arms on her way out the door. "If you believe nothing else about me, I hope you believe that."

## Chapter 13

Dalton couldn't think with the overwhelming silence filling every inch of the bedroom he'd once shared with Lauren. It was also her favorite place to gather her thoughts
and release her creativity. Her laptop sat next to him and
he'd calmed down enough to at least consider Kira's plea
for him to read something important she'd found.

She shouldn't have touched it. She shouldn't have even
ventured to this part of the house. But as much as he'd
like to blame everything on Kira, he was the one who'd
brought her here in the first place.

He had two clear choices. He could wallow in grief for
the next few hours or he could do something to lessen the
pain. He stared at the light pink computer case and rubbed
his thumb across Lauren's initials, etched in the lower left
corner. Her journal had been something she had loved,
and if he allowed himself the chance, he might be able to
understand her reasons for giving up.

Or he might have proof that her unhappiness was linked to him. That was an obstacle he had to overcome, the fear he needed to reach beyond. He opened the laptop and waited impatiently for the programs to load. His fingers were almost numb from his trip outside in the cold, plus the shock of finding Kira here. He had to snap out of it.

He clicked the recent-history button and tried connecting to the last website Kira had viewed. Nothing. He checked for any downloaded files and saw rows of folders brimming with entries. Lauren always wanted to keep things fresh for the fans, so he'd expected to find a couple half-finished songs or maybe some ideas for future tours.

He scrolled to the center of the list and opened one, feeling a strong connection to Lauren, along with an uncertainty that he had any right to view whatever she'd written, perhaps things she felt so important that she couldn't share them with him. He released a breath as he read through an entry from two years ago, when she'd been on a break from touring.

*I know my music is a gift, but it's starting to feel like an obligation. Dalton reminds me I'm committed and I have to fulfill my contract, but Josh says I shouldn't care about the money. If I had my way, I'd donate it all to music programs in the schools or maybe sponsor some kind of festival in Denver for aspiring songwriters.*

This was the Lauren he remembered, the one who was always happiest helping someone else. He checked the date—six months before Lauren's death—and tried remembering if they'd been together or apart. He wasn't sure, and it bothered him immensely that he'd forgotten the day-to-day life they'd shared. Her on the road. Him stuck in corporate meetings.

He opened another folder and continued reading about Lauren's life. Parts made his heart ache; other parts made him smile. It was a great compilation of the true Lauren. She loved performing, but sometimes she had to force the enthusiasm for all the extra music promotions.

The common thread in almost everything he read was the mention of Josh's name. He'd spent more time with Lauren than either one of them had ever let on.

His brother and his wife had had an affair.

Dalton read until the low-battery light flashed on the screen. The charger was in the office, and he intended to read all of Lauren's entries before he turned in for the night. He inhaled another whiff of the air that still seemed to hold her favorite perfume.

The weight in his chest lifted. He felt relief. Lauren had been having an affair.

There was nothing to be gained by sharing the truth about her deception with anyone else. Kira already knew, but beyond the two of them, this secret would remain buried at the Matthews family cemetery. He would be a bit more direct with Tate, to find out how much he knew.

But Dalton had to let it go. Lauren wasn't in this room or roaming the house like a ghost. She lived inside his heart and she'd always be with him.

Downstairs there was another woman who'd suffered more than her share of pain. Because of Josh's deception and abandonment, Kira had never been allowed to grieve. She'd carried the blame for the failure of her marriage and the loss of her child.

What Josh had done was unforgivable.

Kira was feisty and proud and determined to prove her self-worth to the world. Her reaction to finding Lauren's journal proved she was caring and understanding, and because of her, Dalton had found closure in the truth.

He flipped the laptop closed and made his way to the door. Glancing over his shoulder, Dalton swallowed the painful memories associated with this room. Nothing would ever erase Lauren from his mind, but it was his choice which memories he would cherish and which he would discard.

Kira hid in the bedroom until the afternoon turned to night. She passed the time alternately berating herself for dredging up more pain for Dalton, and congratulating herself for her computer-savvy abilities, which had led to the discovery of Lauren's journal.

Eventually Kira took a bath. She could stay in the tub until her skin resembled a prune, and it wouldn't matter to anyone. It also meant she was a bigger chicken than she'd ever imagined herself to be.

Dalton needed more time to himself. He had every right to grieve for the beautiful and talented wife he'd lost. He also had every right to be angry with Kira for trespassing in Lauren's room.

Enough wallowing in regret. Kira dried herself off and unlocked the door leading to the bedroom. Her mood would improve if only there was something to sleep in besides bright orange Buckshot's T-shirts in size XXL.

No luck. She grudgingly yanked one of the ugly shirts over her head, then pulled open a dresser drawer, retrieved a pair of socks and put them on before her feet could get chilly.

Her reflection in the mirror above the dresser was a disaster. She'd shoved her hair into a very messy bun on top of her head and her face was flushed from the heat of the bathroom. A myriad of scratches and bruises covered her arms.

Her stomach grumbled again. If she didn't eat something, she'd certainly wake up with a headache. Unlocking the bedroom door, she peeked out into the hallway and listened for any activity in the rest of the house. All was quiet.

She really wasn't up for another confrontation with Dalton. A quick in and out and she'd be in bed. Her plan went straight to hell as soon as she walked into the kitchen.

Only a few night-lights lit the room and Kira made out Dalton's dark figure seated at the dining table with a bottle of liquor. Vodka, Scotch or bourbon; she'd never taken the time to learn the difference. What she did notice was the bottle was less than half full.

He poured another glass and gave her a mock salute as she entered the room. "To cheating brothers everywhere." He was drinking because of her, because of what she'd discovered and dredged to the surface for him. Her feet were frozen to the floor, but her heart was melting inside her chest.

"I'm sorry. I'll be out of your sight in a minute." She forced her legs to move, taking one step, then another, stopping when she reached the refrigerator. She yanked on the handle, scanned the shelves and retrieved a small block of cheese and an open bottle of wine. It really didn't matter what kind, because she probably wasn't going to taste it, anyway. She set the items on the counter and dug through the box of rations from the plane until she located a sleeve of crackers.

"What is it about you?" Dalton asked.

Kira laughed. "I'm a magnet for trouble. I have horrible judgment and my expectations are too high." She stared at the wine, debating whether or not to search for a glass or drink straight from the bottle.

"I see something else entirely." The chair legs scraped across the tile.

She didn't want to converse with him and absolutely didn't want to see the loathing in his eyes.

He continued talking. "I see a woman who fights to protect her name."

She felt Dalton's eyes on her as she pulled a wineglass from the cupboard, yanked the cork out with her teeth and poured.

She gulped half the contents, refilled her glass and finally met his gaze. One part of him appeared shattered and needy, the other half brooding and sexy. He could reach right through her armor and capture her emotions before she could hide them. She stood transfixed, wineglass in hand and refusing to break the silence.

"Desperate enough for clothing you'd wear one of these ugly-ass orange shirts?" Dalton plucked at the material covering his chest and laughed before taking another hefty swallow from the glass in his hand. His voice was slightly brittle, his actions unmeasured.

She should say something, anything, to deplete the tension in the air.

When he absently peeled the label from the bottle while keeping his attention focused on her, she swallowed another gulp of wine for fortification. It wasn't enough, so she finished the glass and poured herself another, wondering why she felt the need to continue the charade of not wanting him.

Was the wine supposed to give her the strength to resist him or a reason not to?

They had more in common than he appreciated. Both of them were touched by tragedy and betrayal, both of them wanted to get beyond it and both of them were failing miserably. He finished the liquor in his glass and shoved the bottle to the center of the table.

The wine was slowly warming her body and loosening her mind. Kira needed to eat something. Her eyes darted to his and she couldn't move a muscle. He was giving her a chance to retreat, to lock herself in her room, and she should take it. But there was something about this man and this moment keeping her in place.

She carefully set the glass on the counter, and when she glanced up again, he'd already eliminated the distance between them. Stark need reflected in the depths of his eyes.

When his heated hands framed her face, she shivered. And then he kissed her as if he meant it. The taste of malted liquor clung to his lips and when his tongue invaded her mouth, she slipped her arms underneath his shirt. His skin was warm to the touch as her fingernails skated up his rib cage, eliciting a growl of desire from him.

Dalton lifted her onto the counter, and her legs circled his waist when he reached beneath her shirt, humming his approval when he comprehended she was naked underneath. Their mouths separated long enough for him to yank the shirt from her body, causing a shiver when her bare bottom connected with the cold granite counter. She groaned and reached for the drawstring on his pants. At some point she lost the power to form sentences, every thought became fractured and the sensations washing over her became an incessant wave.

The wine loosened her beyond her normal boundaries. Sex on a kitchen counter? Add it to the list of things she'd never pictured herself doing. Somehow she'd become a woman with the courage to let it all go.

Words were few in their exchange. It was a melding of desire and emotion. Kira's head drifted back as her legs tightened around his waist. His mouth was at the base of her throat, sinking lower with each kiss he planted on her skin.

She slipped her hands to the waistband of his pants and slid one inside, to run her fingers along his shaft. He groaned in response and then dropped his mouth and captured her breast. Kira arched, pulling his head firmly against her and moaning in appreciation of his efforts.

He stopped long enough to yank the shirt over his head, then pulled her face to his. She dived inside his mouth and was excited when he met her kiss for kiss. His mouth was warm and drugging, the kind where you could get lost and forget about anything else.

Soon his pants joined the orange shirts at his feet. He pressed his lips against the inside of her knee and kissed his way up her thigh. She stiffened beneath his touch, feeling more than a little out of her element. She couldn't let him, could she? Then his eyes sought hers, the minutest of pauses. This had quickly gone from a mere coupling of bodies to an unspoken request for her to trust him.

She wasn't sure if it was the belief he would have stopped that was giving her the courage to continue, or finally understanding what it meant to make love with a man who was putting her needs above his own.

"Don't stop."

His breath skated across the most sensitive part of her body and a shiver raced through her. He paused before starting with her other knee, giving the same treatment to every inch of her skin. By the time he reached the apex of her thighs, every nerve felt centered on her core.

When his tongue finally touched her she pulled away from his mouth. He tugged her forward again with one strong arm and continued the decimation of any remaining defenses. She squirmed on the countertop, unconsciously moving her hips toward him as she fell back on her elbows.

Had she known he was capable of wringing so much pleasure from her body, she might have sat naked on the counter all night. His wicked tongue glided up and down in a lazy effort, keeping her right on the brink of ecstasy.

Somebody was doing a lot of moaning, and when she

realized it was her, she quickly bit her tongue to silence the sounds. Dalton's assault moved to high gear and she was lost in a high-pitched climax of epic proportions.

The heavy breathing was all her. Flat on her back against the cold granite? Her again. It couldn't get any better than this, could it?

Dalton replied, "Sounds like a challenge," before scooping her up and striding to the bedroom.

She'd said that aloud. But who was she to complain?

The room was blessedly warm and he quickly deposited her between the sheets and tossed a blanket over her. "Don't move."

Oh, sweet mercy, she sure hoped he was planning to finish what he'd started. Admiring his naked butt was a bonus, and Kira took an extra second to scoot to the middle of the bed so he could slide right in when he returned.

She heard him swearing a blue streak and then it sounded as if he was dumping out drawers in another room. What in the world was he doing? "Dalton? Is everything okay?"

She switched on the bedside lamp and turned to her side, straining her neck to see down the hallway. He came barreling through the doorway.

"Remind me to thank Tate for being the condom king." Dalton ripped a single packet from the box in his hand. "And scoot over."

"Only because you said please."

"I think you said it enough for both of us."

Kira blushed all the way to her toes. There was no way to argue against the truth, and he'd probably never let her live it down.

"We could try everything all over again," he offered, placing the packet in her hand and then kissing her soundly. "Lady's choice."

He was way too smug. Kira intentionally crawled over

him to turn off the lamp and then planted her naked body on top of his as she slowly tore the package open with her teeth. She straddled him, relishing his quick intake of breath. She sat up long enough to roll the condom into place. Slowly.

When the task was complete, he gripped her buttocks and flipped her beneath him, sliding one knee between her thighs and stealing her breath with an endless kiss. She bucked underneath his weight, trying to reposition him where she needed him the most. His lips trailed across her collarbone and she shivered in anticipation. He was going to make her say it again.

"Dalton."

"Hmm?" He murmured against her breast before pulling her nipple into his mouth.

"Please, now," she begged.

He moved again and filled her with one slow thrust after another, until her rocking hips forced him to pick up the pace, and the tremors turned to joint release.

# Chapter 14

Daring, demanding, sexy, sinful and surprising. Dalton had taken everything Kira offered, humbled by the new-found pleasure she'd experienced, evidently for the first time.

"What do you like?" he'd whispered against the shell of her ear.

"Everything."

"Narrow that down a little for me." He'd nibbled the column of her neck earnestly, awaiting a reply. When she'd remained silent, he'd asked, "What were you doing before?"

"I have no idea, but it wasn't anything like that." Her voice had wobbled over the statement, growing breathy on the last word.

Dalton must admit the black marks against his brother were entering the triple digits. The only way Kira wouldn't know what she liked was if his brother had done more taking than giving.

Last night had started out fast and a little daring and

had ended with the realization it wasn't just sex between them. Dalton had lain in bed for the past hour, staring at the ceiling and listening as Kira purred against his shoulder.

He heard a high-pitched beep and briefly thought it was the security alarm. A moment later he recognized the phone's ring. Must be the disposable cell he'd held on to, and Tate was the only one with the number. Dalton shoved his legs into his jeans and raced to find the phone.

"Hey." He shuffled to the kitchen counter to start a pot of coffee, clutching the phone to his ear.

"I reached out to a couple of mutual friends and they're headed your way with some supplies and manpower. Despite what you think about no one knowing your location, your friend has given plenty of motivation for her to be found."

"How soon?" During the night, the wind had picked up, and from the window over the sink it was hard to tell if more snow was falling or if what had already fallen was being tossed around by Mother Nature.

"By tonight. Promised Atkins he could fly the jet sometime, and offered him double, since you chose his least favorite climate."

"Driving up here is out of the question."

"Yeah, he knows. Even stressed the fact that he's the *expert*."

"Okay, what else?"

"I kept your secret and everyone thinks you died in a fire Kira started."

"Officially or unofficially?"

"CNN says it's a foregone conclusion."

"I'll mark them off the Christmas-card list." Dalton dumped a pot of water into the coffeemaker and turned it on.

"Oh, it gets better." Tate paused for some sort of dramatic effect. A high-pitched giggle on his end interrupted the update and Dalton dropped onto one of the stools in the kitchen.

When the sexual squeals continued, Dalton interjected, "Is your flavor of the week by chance a phone sex operator?"

He heard a few more bursts of laughter and then silence.

"As I was saying," Tate continued, "there was an emergency meeting of the Buckshot's board of directors and a decision was made to offer a two-hundred-and-fifty-thousand-dollar reward for any information leading to Kira's arrest."

Dalton whistled and pulled a mug from the cupboard. "Don't worry. I wouldn't turn her in for anything less than a million."

"Glad to know your loyalty is on the auction block."

"And since I'm in charge, what's another million?"

Dalton almost caught the mug before it fell against the granite and broke into pieces. "Excuse me? Who the hell put you in charge?"

"Our esteemed board felt I was best suited to manage the day-to-day activities until the crisis is resolved."

"Haven't you slept with half the board?"

"I was assured that fact didn't affect their vote."

"Bullshit." Dalton tossed the broken pieces into the trash and reached for another mug. "Enjoy the power while it lasts, and remember, I'm still capable of kicking your sorry ass."

Tate snickered. "From your ski chalet high in the Rockies? You've got me quaking in my boots."

It took an extreme amount of self-control for Dalton to keep from trading more barbs. Silence on his end of the line should have ended the conversation.

"Think on this," Tate stated. "By failing to kill Kira,

whoever died in the house fire back in Wyoming crossed the wrong person, someone powerful enough to frame her for the fire and *your* death. My guess is he's biding his time until she reappears." There was another dramatic pause. "Or, with resources like that, maybe he already knows where she is and he's headed your way."

Dalton scoffed. "The only way anyone knows where we are is if you told them."

"I wouldn't betray Kira." Tate's intentional omission of Dalton's name meant the conversation was over.

Stacie Jo Ripley ignored the horns of several annoyed drivers and sauntered across the street in her four-inch-heeled go-go boots. Her little red dress worked its magic once again and she was about to collect a tidy sum for her troubles.

She adjusted her store-bought breasts before stepping onto the opposite curb and digging a fresh stick of gum from the depths of her purse. October in Denver was a crapshoot. A day of sun. A day of rain. Maybe another snowstorm like they'd experienced the past two days.

No matter. After today, she'd have the means to relocate to a warmer climate. But definitely not to Florida. It was full of old people and she drew the line at sexing anyone over the age of forty-five.

Maybe South America. Didn't they love blondes down there? Hell, what was she thinking? She didn't have to be a whore for hire anymore. Starting tonight, she could buy some respectability. Land herself a wealthy boyfriend and maybe even go from a C to a D cup. She liked the sound of that.

"Nice ass."

She turned and parted her lips in a glossy smile. "No flattery necessary, honey. Just show me the money."

He pulled a wad of cash from his coat pocket, peeled off a couple bills and shoved them between her breasts. "Show me what I'm paying for."

"Of course, baby." He was hot enough she'd have done him for free in a heartbeat. But he'd come to her seeking information on her latest John. She pulled out her rhinestone-encrusted cell and scrolled to the newest number.

"He called this number a bunch of times." She sighed. "I don't think he likes this guy very much. Anyway, there's a girl with him named Kira." Stacy Jo held up one finger. "Um, at some fancy ski house in the mountains." She lifted a second finger and then a third. "And they think some guy's framing her for killing somebody else, I think in Wyoming." She giggled. "If you ask me, it sounds more like a soap opera than real life."

He plucked the phone from her outstretched hand and then leaned forward to whisper in her ear. "There's only one problem, babe. No one asked you."

A second later, he shoved her off the curb in front of a slow-moving semi. The truck did a good job shutting her up.


The smell of coffee penetrated Kira's senses and stirred her from several hours of much-needed sleep. Given how she felt about the brew, it might as well have been stench from a pig farm.

She rolled to the center of the bed and buried her face in one of the pillows, groaning in regret. Okay, maybe it wasn't regret. Just a realization she'd done one more thing she couldn't take back.

Had she ever been so bold before? Probably not, but it felt good and she planned on doing it again. Being bold, that is. She could get used to feeling empowered. And it was funny how Dalton didn't need to make her feel inferior in order to feed his ego. There was urgency, but there wasn't a rush.

She'd been married, but had never known the aching need Dalton aroused in her. Never knew intimacy meant being so intimate. Never knew what she'd been missing.

How could she pretend the experience hadn't changed her? If Josh had made half as much of an effort in the bedroom, she would have followed him around like a lost puppy.

But Josh hadn't needed her the same way she'd needed him. He'd been sneaking around with Lauren, undermining Dalton's marriage when he should have been focusing on his own. Why was Kira so susceptible to the charm of the Matthews men?

She needed a shower. A very hot shower and a thousand-calorie breakfast to put her in the right frame of mind. And then she'd be ready to face Dalton again.

Dalton stood in the kitchen listening to Kira's off-key rendition of a Sugarland tune. He needed to focus on what it would take to get her out of trouble and on the right side of the law.

It was time to call Ethan.

Dalton swung open his office door. Just in case he needed to take some notes, he wanted to be in a quiet spot where Kira wouldn't overhear. After punching in the Buckshot's number, he entered Ethan's extension, hoping it wouldn't go right to voice mail.

"Tech support, this is Ethan. May I have your employee number please?"

"One."

After a momentary pause, Ethan said, "Dalton?"

"Yep, it's me. And I'm not making contact from the other side."

"But it's all over the news you were killed by some crazy lady," the younger man said.

"Tate is the only one, other than you, who knows the truth. I need you to keep quiet."

"My lips are sealed."

"Now, did you get the flash drive decrypted?"

"Yes, I've been working on it. Tate didn't say it was from you." He tapped on his keyboard a few times. "Do you want the good news or the bad news?"

"I'll take the bad."

"Several of these files show a direct link to Josh."

How many other people had been harmed by Josh's deceptions? "And the good news?"

"I can probably erase his information without deleting any of the other files, if you want me to."

Dalton drummed his fingers on the desktop. "Bad, huh?"

"A few of the files had an embedded IP address leading right to Josh. I have a feeling whoever collected this information never figured out how to dig deep enough to prove the connection. There are some incriminating files related to Geoff Griffin and the owner-author, Kira Kincaid. Mostly shuffling of government payments through six or more companies before they disappear. Looks like insurance fraud and embezzlement."

"How much damage are we talking about here?"

"I don't see anything associating Buckshot's with Josh's actions. But in the last six months, the amount of money stolen has almost tripled. I can understand why the authorities are anxious to tie this all up with a nice neat bow."

Dalton frowned and doodled on a piece of scratch paper. Now what? "I didn't expect you'd really find anything about Josh." Dalton hated not having a definitive answer. "Give me a day or two to decide how to proceed on this."

"Sure, I can sit on the information as long as you want," Ethan replied. "Give me a phone number, in case something changes and I need to get in touch with you."

Dalton rattled off the number and then voiced what had been on his mind all night. "One more thing, Ethan."

"Name it."

"Track down a birth certificate for me. Not sure of the exact date, probably three to four years ago. But it should be in the Kansas City area, with the mother listed as Kira Kincaid."

"Anything else?"

"Yeah." It pained him to say the words. "There should be a death certificate, too. Same date as the birth." He absently tugged open one of the desk drawers and then slid it shut.

"Is Josh the father?" Ethan asked.

"The father?" Dalton echoed. His heart raced as his brain connected all the pieces. What if Lauren had been carrying Josh's child and not his own? Yesterday he would have laughed outright if anyone had voiced such a ludicrous theory.

"Dalton?"

"Let me know what you find out." He quickly disconnected the call and pocketed the cheap phone. Sliding the chair closer to the bookcase, he reached for the framed picture from their night at the Grammy Awards ceremony.

Lauren had been giddy with excitement, starstruck by the number of musicians who knew her name. Hitting double platinum with her first album had caught many people by surprise. But winning the Grammy for Best New Artist had cemented her as a celebrity.

Dalton searched his memory for more details, wondering now if Josh had been nearby. Was she thinking of him while she'd been clutching Dalton's hand?

This was torture and completely pointless. His wife and his brother were both gone, and disparaging their memory wouldn't make the situation bearable.

There would be a firestorm of crap as soon as the press got wind of Josh's involvement in Kira's investigation. Two months ago, when Josh was killed in a crash an hour outside of Denver, the news media had jumped at the opportunity to rehash every tragedy his family had faced over the past few years.

Dalton's dad and two of his uncles had died before reaching their forty-fifth birthdays, so the media had played up the supposed curse plaguing his family. And then Lauren's suicide was brought to the forefront, taking Dalton back to the day he'd discovered her body. He couldn't return there, wouldn't feel the numbing pain and overwhelming guilt again.

He placed the picture on the shelf, paused and then turned it facedown.

He valued family and loyalty above everything. But tarnishing Josh's memory might not be out of the question. Could Dalton do the right thing and clear Kira of some of the charges leveled against her? Or would he be the next man who let her down?

Griffin yanked the snowmobile's keys from the teenager's outstretched hand before climbing onto the machine. This was his last chance. If he didn't silence the woman and her champion today, then he'd be the one running for his life. He signaled for Rico to follow him. Instead, the arrogant son of a bitch revved the engine and took off before Griffin could even get his helmet in place and his snowmobile started.

Rico had been paired with Franklin in the past, and the cocky Mexican seemed unaffected by frigid temperatures and mountain air. The little bastard didn't know who Griffin really was. He'd introduced himself using the name Carson. It was time to clean up this mess himself.

He'd take care of her new savior and get rid of the bitch at her dead husband's grave in the family cemetery. Justice would be dealt today. Griffin's problems would disappear with the death of Kira Kincaid.

He stomped on the gas pedal and the snowmobile shot forward several yards, then died. He turned the key a second time and the engine restarted, but with a noticeable sputter. He glared over his shoulder at the kid who'd scored a wad of hundred-dollar bills in exchange for the snowmobiles and a promise to lock up shop for the day.

Oblivious to his annoyance, the tattooed teen was busy texting someone. Griffin turned his attention to the plume of snow Rico was leaving in his wake. No way was Griffin letting the guy take charge of this assignment or rob him of the pleasure of tying up loose ends.

Griffin gunned the motor and raced across the open field. He knew he wouldn't be able to catch Rico, let alone overtake him. Anger fueled his determination and he sped across the snow in pursuit. The snowmobile ran smoother when he reached fifty miles per hour, but he was only just able to keep Rico in his sights.

The temperature was in the teens, but his cold-weather gear kept Griffin plenty warm. They had twenty minutes of driving across a fairly open stretch of ground before a forest of pine trees appeared and forced them to slow the machines. He checked the GPS screen on his phone before tapping the wired mic system in his helmet and summoning Rico.

Rico reduced his speed to a crawl and Griffin was able to pull alongside him.

"The kid said there'd be some sort of path heading

southeast through the trees. Guessing it's been covered by all this snow, so keep your eyes peeled for it."

Rico grunted something in another language and Griffin's annoyance jumped again. Foreigners. If they were in the United States, then they needed to speak English.

"I'll take the lead now," Griffin instructed, flipping the shield over his face and then moving into position. Let the man inhale his exhaust and stare at his back for a while.

Griffin followed the tree line for the next twenty minutes, searching for any break wide enough for a snowmobile to get through. The wind grew stronger and the snow swirled in front of him, slowing their progress to a crawl. He consulted the GPS again, growing impatient with the time they were wasting.

Rico whistled into the mic and when Griffin looked over his shoulder, the man was gesturing to a small gap between the trees. No way was that big enough for them to get through. Before Griffin could voice his opinion, however, Rico steered his snowmobile into the space and carefully maneuvered around a few younger trees.

Griffin was forced to make a U-turn and follow the man again. He fumed silently instead of cursing repeatedly inside the helmet. No sense in letting Rico know how frustrated he was by their current situation. Then Griffin noticed how easy it was to follow Rico's tracks as they wound through the trees. Maybe Griffin had lucked out, after all.

All the zigzagging felt like a never-ending carnival ride. When he thought he wouldn't survive another minute of the great outdoors, the path straightened and Rico picked up speed as one small incline turned into a hill and then a mountain.

Griffin glanced down at the GPS. They had to be getting close, since they'd been traveling for well over an hour. The gas gauge hovered below three-quarters of a tank, stemming his other concern that they might not have enough fuel to make the return trip.

Even from several miles away he noticed something sparkling in the distance. The blinding brightness of the newly fallen snow was reflecting off a few windows. He stopped his machine and whistled into the mic for Rico, who stopped a hundred feet or so ahead of him.

Griffin unzipped his parka, located a pair of binoculars and raised them to his eyes, hoping to get confirmation they were headed to the right location. He was blinded by the initial glare and blinked a few times before spotting the house.

"Is that the place?" Rico asked a bit too loudly.

Griffin nodded before lowering the binoculars. "Looks like we found it."

Rico turned his machine around and approached him. "Are you sure we don't want to wait until dark to move in?"

"What?" Griffin wasn't waiting any longer to end the bitch's streak of luck. Plus, how would they ever find their way after dark?

"When the sun sets, the element of surprise will be on our side," Rico insisted.

Was the Mexican a moron or what?

"The element of surprise is already on our side. They think no one can find them."

"In another kilometer they'll hear us."

"Probably. But snowmobiles are common around here."

"I think we should wait."

Griffin didn't care for Rico's opinion. The bastard had no right to question his authority. Griffin was the one calling the shots. He shoved the binoculars into his pocket and quickly zipped his coat before replacing his glove.

"We're moving in now," he instructed. He wanted to

lead the way again, but his snowmobile died as soon as he hit the gas. He could have sworn Rico was smirking as he pulled away, and Griffin's temper flared again. One way or another, he was going to put him in his rightful place.

# *Chapter 15*

When Kira finally exited the bedroom, she was dressed in a navy turtleneck and jeans that had suddenly materialized on her bed. The tags were in place and she'd breathed a sigh of relief, knowing Dalton's wife had never worn the clothing.

The scent of coffee was a bit less overwhelming when she entered the kitchen and found Dalton retrieving waffles from the toaster. She paused long enough to admire the way he filled out a pair of jeans. He'd changed into a dark gray long-sleeved shirt, but his feet were bare. She noticed a battery lying on the ceramic tile floor and paused to retrieve it before approaching him.

"Thanks for the clothes." She stepped up behind him and laid the battery on the counter. "This was on the floor."

"Better than thc thumbtack I stepped on earlier." He glanced over her shoulder. "A casualty of my great condom search last night."

Kira laughed and he gave her a disapproving frown. "It could have been very serious."

She laughed louder and watched him drop two more waffles into the toaster.

"I'm going to remember how heartless you can be," he threatened.

"And I'm going to remember how thorough *you* can be," she replied, briefly eyeing the counter behind them.

Arms full of waffles and extra plates, Dalton gestured to the glasses on the table. "Unless you'd like a repeat performance, you should probably grab the orange juice out of the fridge."

She quickly stepped out of his reach and retrieved the pitcher of juice, all the while knowing he was watching every move she made. She filled the glasses, noticed that napkins were missing and retrieved some from the counter.

"Check the cupboard in front of you for syrup," Dalton instructed.

Kira found it and carried the real Vermont maple syrup and napkins to the table before seating herself. She took a sip of her juice. "Did you have orange juice on the plane?"

He shook his head. "Frozen concentrate, frozen waffles and some freezer-burned ham. I pitched it in the trash. The breakfast options were pretty limited."

"I'll survive," Kira said.

He placed the plate of waffles on the table and refilled his coffee mug. Kira divvied up the waffles and was pouring syrup on hers when he reached over with his fork and stole one.

"Hey, give me that," she said.

He placed the syrupy waffle on one of his and then covered it with another before raising the resulting sandwich to his lips and taking a hefty bite. "I'm starved," he mumbled around the mouthful of food.

"Yeah, me, too," Kira said, sliding her plate a little farther away from his. Wasn't there some unspoken rule about hosts waiting until guests ate their fill before taking all the food they wanted? Kira scowled across the table at Dalton while using her knife to saw through the two remaining waffles on her plate.

He'd polished his off by the time she'd cut her waffles into bite-size pieces. He smiled over at her. "If you're not hungry, I can finish those for you."

She stabbed two pieces, shoved them into her mouth and nearly gagged. Vermont maple syrup was really strong and the waffles had a too-long-in-the-freezer taste to them. She chewed, swallowed and washed everything down with the remainder of her orange juice.

Kira dropped her fork onto the plate and shoved it toward him.

"I'm full." Ignoring his greedy smile, she grabbed her glass and went to the sink. She was still hungry and definitely in need of some chocolate fortification. She squeezed a little dish soap into the sink and turned on the hot water, then started searching for a dishcloth.

Dalton appeared behind her holding both plates, which she retrieved and stacked on the counter.

"I'll clean up," she offered. He found a cloth and dropped it into the bubbly water before setting a couple dish towels nearby. Then he walked to the coffeemaker and filled his cup again.

"You know that I believe you, right?" Dalton asked.

Kira glanced over her shoulder. "Yes, I know." The expression on his face had her reaching for a towel to dry her hands. "But…?"

"But nothing." Seconds later, he was pulling her into his arms. "Don't doubt my allegiance, Kira. I'm doing everything in my power to clear your name."

"I know you are, Dalton." She stared up at him, wishing she could hold on to him for more than a minute.

"You don't sound very confident in my abilities."

She knew he was teasing her. "I'm completely confident in your abilities."

"Then tell me what's the matter."

She couldn't admit that being with him made her want things she could never have. Made her think about loving someone who thought she was worth loving in return, and building a life and a family with. She swallowed the tears clogging her throat. "I've caused you nothing but trouble. I'm sure you wish I'd never found you."

He eyed the counter behind her and laughed. "You'd be wrong."

"Really? You're going to embarrass me to death, talking like that."

"You weren't talking very much last night."

Kira clamped her hand over his mouth. "Please, stop."

He tugged it away. "I think what you meant to say is please *don't* stop."

She shouldn't allow him to kiss her again. Shouldn't kiss him back. The taste of coffee on his lips wasn't the deterrent she'd hoped for. And his gentle touch was the exact opposite of the way she clutched his shirt.

She forced her fingers to release him and took a step back. "I, um, really need to finish the dishes." *Walk away, walk away, walk away.*

Dalton mumbled something about checking the Weather Channel forecast, before disappearing from the room.

Almost an hour later, Kira stood in the doorway to Dalton's office, watching intently as he read on the laptop. Could it be more of Lauren's journal? Had he found more entries about the time she'd spent with Josh, or was it all too painful for him to relive? Before Kira could voice the question, he'd lifted the cell phone to his ear.

"Hey, Ethan, what have you got for me?"

She couldn't help the feeling of hope in her chest. Perhaps Dalton meant it when he said he wanted to help.

The chair squeaked as he stood and then lowered his voice. "What do you mean?"

Kira held her breath at his tone, taking a step back into the hallway.

"There must be a birth certificate, Ethan. Try looking under Josh's name."

Kira couldn't exhale the breath in her lungs and her body shook with the effort to remain silent. This wasn't about clearing her name.

There was a lengthy silence, then Dalton spewed a string of words she'd never heard used with such disdain. Something thudded to the floor and she almost peeked around the corner to make sure he was all right.

"Let me do some more checking on this end." He ended the call.

Kira clung to the wall for another moment before easing into the room.

"Who were you talking to?"

Dalton slowly turned to face her. "My computer guy at Buckshot's."

She nodded. "Sounded like a serious conversation."

He started to respond and then motioned to another chair. "Sit down for a second. We need to talk."

She hesitated, the tension ratcheting up another notch. She knew it wasn't good news.

"I think I'd rather stand."

Kira hadn't ever seen him looking so unsure during their brief time together. He was definitely choosing his words carefully.

"Tell me about the day your son was born."

"What?" She pressed a palm against her chest, almost certain her heart had quit beating.

"I want to hear all about the day you went into labor."

"You can stop right there." Kira held up her hand. "I've spent the last three years trying not to think about any of it. I'm not giving you a play-by-play." She'd never shared the whole story with anyone.

"I'm on your side here." Dalton's voice dipped to a soothing tone. "Take your time."

Time. It had been years, and yet grief could still bring her to her knees. But this was Dalton, and he'd already seen her fall apart. Comforted her when she'd initially told him about Brandon.

Dalton watched and waited while Kira picked invisible lint from her shirt. She was stalling, or maybe having trouble putting all the events in some kind of order. He wished he could do something to make this easier, but he needed to hear the whole story from her.

"The entire pregnancy was absolutely normal. I did everything right." She took a fortifying breath. "Maybe I worked a bit too much, but we needed the money. And then Josh sold a painting." Kira dropped into the chair across from Dalton. "We got some extra money and Josh insisted on an ultrasound. He wanted to know if we were having a boy or a girl."

"Did you want to know?"

"No. It didn't matter to me. But he was so excited when we learned it was a baby boy." There was another long pause, but her features remained the same, almost as if she was watching it happen to someone else.

"And then what happened?"

"I never went into labor on my own. I was induced when I was twelve days overdue."

He'd have to check with Tate, but so far it didn't seem unusual. "Did your doctor order any tests to make sure everything was okay?"

She shook her head. "Finn said some women never go into labor."

"Finn?"

"Yes, Finn Barnes, my doctor."

Dalton found a notepad on his desk and quickly scribbled down the name. "And he was an ob-gyn?" He glanced up when Kira didn't answer him.

"What hospital were you admitted to?" he pressed.

"I think he was studying family practice."

Every sense Dalton possessed went on high alert. The hairs on the back of his neck stood up. His arms broke out in goose bumps and his throat tightened. He reached for the half-empty cup of coffee and downed the remaining liquid before he felt composed enough to continue.

"So Finn was a friend of yours?"

"A friend of Josh's."

"Was he a med student?" Dalton tried and failed to keep a neutral tone of voice.

"I know what you're thinking, but Finn was at the top of his class. He answered all of my questions and assured me everything would be okay."

Dalton cleared his throat. "What hospital?"

She was immediately defensive. "Lots of women have babies at home. It's a calmer setting and everything I read said I might feel more relaxed in my own environment."

"Brandon was born at home?"

She finally looked as though her mind had caught up with her mouth. "I think so."

"But you aren't sure?"

"I went to Finn's clinic for the Pitocin. He said I could go home as soon as my labor started."

"Why couldn't you have the baby there?"

"Josh insisted that his son have a home birth. He couldn't stand that antiseptic smell that lives in every hospital."

"What about what was safest for his wife?" Dalton shifted in the chair. "Was there another doctor or even a nurse assisting?"

Kira seemed surprised at the question.

"There was no one else helping," Dalton surmised.

"I should have gone to the hospital. I know that now, but at the time…" She dropped her face into her hands.

"Kira, you did what you believed was right." He pulled her from the chair, wrapped his arms around her and held her tightly.

"Oh, God, this is my fault. If I'd stood up to Josh then, Brandon would be alive."

"We don't know that."

She drew away from Dalton. "But you think so, right?" Her voice was softer than he expected, almost emotionless. "Why else would you be asking all these questions?"

"Kira, I'm trying to understand."

"What does any of this matter now?" She swiped the tears from her cheeks. "I know how much it hurts to be betrayed, but I hope you know I never intended to reopen that wound for you." She took a step away. "I'm sorry."

"You need to stop apologizing for everything." His hands shifted to his hips. "Where's the woman who fought with me from the moment we met?"

"Not my usual behavior."

"Too bad. She could take care of herself, even if she sucked at planning." He leaned against the desk and crossed his arms over his chest. "I told her I wanted to

keep my brother's name out of the news, and do you remember what she said?"

"We can't always get what we want."

"Exactly." His gaze pinned her in place. "Do you even
know what you want, or have you been in survival mode
so long you can't remember what it's like to live?"

What gave him the right to examine her life, when he'd
been avoiding all human contact for months? At least she'd
continued to work and maintain relationships. She froze
as the realization hit her.

"You want to know what I'm avoiding."

He waited.

Her first instinct was to turn and collect herself. After
a moment's hesitation, the words jumped from her lips. "I
can't handle being around kids, especially preschoolers. I
look at every little boy and think he could have been mine.
One time I even took a chance and introduced myself to a
new neighbor, because she was single, like me."

Kira couldn't stand still any longer. She straightened
a picture frame, adjusted a lampshade. "I stopped by her
apartment one day and her refrigerator was covered with
baby pictures. She's an adoption attorney, and we will
never be friends because I can't handle the constant reminder of what I'm missing. I've gotten used to being
alone."

"That's not what I asked." The sternness returned to
his voice. Kira pivoted to glare at him, and those warm
brown eyes were nearly black. What did he have to be
angry about?

"I miss a lot of things, but I'll be fine." If she'd managed to survive the past few years, then wasn't it proof she
could live through anything?

"I don't want you to be fine. I want to know you have a

goal beyond clearing your name and returning to Midwest Mutual. I want to hear you say you will be happy again."

"I'll be happy again."

"You'll be happy at Midwest Mutual? You'll be happy living alone? Or you'll be happy seeing dozens of kids at the grocery store every week?"

"Damn you, Dalton." She never meant to yell and certainly never meant to continue her four-letter-word free-for-all. "You don't know what it's like to lose a child. Not just a child, but a baby that grew inside me for nine months. A helpless little person I should have been able to protect."

"I do understand what you're talking about. No one knew, but Lauren was pregnant when she died."

"I'm sorry." The words seemed too hollow for his announcement, but all Kira could think was how lucky Lauren was to have ended up with Dalton instead of Josh. Dalton was respectful and honest. Her thoughts skidded to a stop. "If Lauren and Josh were together in the weeks leading up to her death, could he possibly have fathered her baby?"

"I'll never know if it was my child or Josh's. But I won't close myself off to the possibility of having another child because I might lose again."

"Good for you." Her response was definitely lacking enthusiasm, even though she pasted an encouraging smile on her face. "I'm not going to set myself up for that heartache."

"You're planning to spend the rest of your life avoiding kids?" Skepticism laced his words. "Are you sure?"

"I'm not sure about anything. And we both know planning is not my strong suit."

"You'd be a great mom, Kira, regardless of whether you gave birth to the child or not. What about being a foster parent? Or adoption?"

She couldn't think about children of any kind without experiencing a major panic attack. She wasn't returning to her darkest place, whether or not Dalton understood her feelings.

"Maybe someday things will change, but right now I need to fight for my freedom and my job."

"Kira, you don't have to worry about money anymore. Josh's estate is worth several million dollars."

"I don't care!" she yelled. *So much for remaining calm and rational.* This whole conversation had quickly turned from uncomfortable to ugly.

Dalton watched her as if he'd cornered a rabid raccoon; torn between letting her wander off or shooting her and putting her out of her misery.

"After everything he put you through, I think you deserve some security."

"The one thing he took from me can't be replaced by money. Holding *my* child would have given me a measure of closure." Kira hugged her arms tightly around her middle and drew a deep breath, trying to calm her nerves. Why was it such a struggle to move forward?

Dalton took a step closer and then Kira heard a high-pitched beep that could only be a cell phone. He paused, yanked the phone from his pocket and studied the screen.

"I need to take this."

Of course he did.

She stormed to the hallway, determined to get as far away from him as possible. She probably didn't need to slam the door as she left, but it felt good to make a little noise.

# Chapter 16

Dalton shoved the cheap phone against his ear and released an impatient sigh. "Your timing sucks, as usual."

"And I'm saving your ass, as usual," Tate barked. "You and Kira need to get to a safe spot and hunker down."

Dalton reached for the rifle hidden behind the bookcase and then swept a shelf clean, revealing two boxes of ammunition. "Why? We heard the snowmobiles. Your guys can't be too far away."

"Those aren't my guys."

Dalton loaded the rifle and shoved extra shells into his pockets while mentally mapping the house's layout. Getting Kira to the second floor was the only answer. From there they'd be able to spot anyone approaching on foot.

"Talk to me," Tate insisted.

Dalton glanced out the window and spotted a figure stomping through the snow. Kira. Her name stuck in his throat. She was marching across the yard, wearing one of

his coats and an oversize pair of boots, completely oblivious to the danger.

"Kira is outside."

"I'm on my way, Dalton. Don't do anything crazy."

"Crazy? What part of the last seventy-two hours hasn't
been crazy?" And now a woman who three days ago he
hadn't known existed was the most important person in
his life. It shouldn't matter at all if he ceased to exist; he'd
barely been living before she stumbled into his world. But
Kira deserved more.

"I'm sorry, Tate, for everything." Saying the words
was much easier than Dalton expected. No bitterness.
No blame. Nothing left to do but flip the phone closed
and drop it in his shirt pocket. He would get Kira out of
harm's way. And then he'd destroy the reputation of his
only brother to clear her name.

Gunshots echoed through the house as he heard the
front door being kicked open. Kira must have disarmed the
alarm. The intruders were already inside, but if there was
any luck left in his world, Dalton would take them out before they discovered she was gone. *Stay smart, Kira. Run
for cover.* He eased to the doorway, rifle barrel extended
and finger on the trigger. At least two men. He listened,
moved carefully and noticed the shadow making its way
up the stairwell.

Divide and conquer. They were splitting up. His odds
improved. Dalton waited impatiently for the squeaky floorboard over his head to signal the man's location, before
creeping down the hallway toward the kitchen.

*One Mississippi. Two Mississippi.* He propped the rifle
against his shoulder as he focused his attention on the
other doorway. One good shot. It was all he needed. His
heart pounded as he silently prayed for Kira to remain far
from the house.

A gun barrel appeared in the opening, followed by bare fingers and then arms encased in a white parka. An alarm beeped on the far side of the kitchen, and only then did Dalton notice the scent of freshly baked bread. The bread machine finished its cycle. The intruder turned his assault weapon toward the noise and fired at least ten times as he entered the room.

Dalton fired once, the rifle's blast propelling the man and his weapon against the island countertop. He was dead before he hit the floor, the white parka streaked with crimson. Dalton dragged the body behind the island, buying an extra minute before the second gunman could see that his buddy was dead.

Digging through the guy's jacket, Dalton's fingers latched on to a cell phone, which he quickly discarded. No sense in possessing a device that was certain to announce their location to whomever it was linked to. He unzipped one of the coat's pockets and collected two sets of keys. One of the key chains advertised a ski shop, the other, a national rental car agency. Shoving both into his own pocket, Dalton peeked around the corner of the kitchen's island.

No sign of the second intruder. He retrieved the dead man's weapon from a few feet away and then remained hidden behind the island, sliding closer to the door and the alarm panel. It seemed as if another minute passed, but in all honesty it was probably only a few seconds before he heard footsteps at the top of the stairwell.

"Rico?" a voice called.

Dalton would have answered, if only he knew what Rico's voice sounded like. Instead, he opted to hit the alarm panel and set off a deafening wail of sirens as a distraction, before he sprinted through the door and across the snow-covered yard in search of Kira.

Following her tracks, he prayed he'd make it to the shelter of the trees without getting shot. The thought of Kira being unarmed, and facing the remaining man alone if anything happened to him, propelled Dalton forward.

The sirens behind him were silenced faster than he expected. Only someone with the code should have been capable of deactivating the alarm. The last few strides to the cover of the trees were made in a panic-fueled haze. What if she was gone? What if another man was posted outside, to prevent anyone from escaping? Dalton stopped and pivoted, the assault rifle at his shoulder, to check the area he'd covered, in case someone was close behind.

Nothing.

"Kira, where are you?"

The brisk wind shook the branches over his head and released chunks of snow. She emerged from behind a tree trunk about a dozen feet away, clutching a large stick in her hands.

"I didn't know what to do," she said, dropping the make-shift weapon and rushing to his side. Kira had Dalton's stocking cap pulled low over her ears, while his over-size gloves engulfed her hands. She'd also latched on to his coat, he noted distractedly as he searched her for any sign of injury.

"Are you hurt?" they asked each other simultaneously. He shifted the rifle to his side, using his free arm to pull her against his chest. Only a second or two to confirm she was okay and then reality interceded.

"We've got to move." He paused to reload the rifle before handing it to Kira. "The safety is right here." He indicated the switch.

She stared at his hands. "Is that blood?"

"Yes, but not mine," he answered. It sounded heartless to speak so callously of taking another's life. *The intruder's blood or Kira's blood, which would you rather have on your hands?* The thought iced Dalton's veins. He needed confirmation that she was living and breathing, and his mouth sought out hers. When her chilled lips parted beneath his, he allowed himself a brief taste before pulling away and then ushering her deeper into the forest.

"Where are we going?"

"Those snowmobiles we heard can't be too far away."

Kira stumbled through a drift of deep snow and he stretched out an arm to catch her. Doubt flooded his mind. Maybe he should be in front and leading the way instead of bringing up the rear. Another look over his shoulder didn't reveal anyone behind them. Would the other intruder immediately know Dalton had swiped the keys from the dead man's pocket? If they managed to locate the snowmobiles, would he be waiting to finish them?

"What happened to those security guys Tate was sending?"

"Don't know."

"So nobody is coming to help us?"

How could Dalton tell her Tate wouldn't reach them in time to make a difference?

"Have I ever let you down?" When Kira didn't respond, Dalton tugged on her arm and turned her to face him. "Look at me."

"This isn't right. You shouldn't have to sacrifice anything for me."

"Tell me what I should do. You've made it impossible for me to walk away." The words sounded completely wrong to his ears, and judging by Kira's shocked expression, hers, as well. It was also the moment his brain caught up with his heart. He loved her, but it wasn't the hearts-and-flowers kind of love he'd shared with Lauren. No, this woman dared him not to love her. She claimed she didn't deserve it.

He'd insisted he wanted her to be happy when this ordeal ended. But he'd never painted himself into the picture. Suddenly, his mind was working to ensure she remained in his life, not because it was the right thing to do, but because he loved her.

"Then by all means, let me do the honors." She made an about-face and started running at an angle away from him.

"Kira! Don't be a fool. He's coming this way." Dalton knew he could handle sassy Kira, the woman who refused to back down, but he hadn't expected her to choose this moment to stake her independence.

He heard the crack of the rifle a second before a bullet whizzed past his ear. A few more peppered the snow at his feet, sending him diving for cover.

"Dalton!" Kira screamed his name.

He rolled to his stomach and shifted the assault weapon into place, but didn't have time to fire before his opponent released a torrent of bullets into the trees above his head and then the ground surrounding him.

Dalton's ears ached from the noise while adrenaline pumped through his body. When the gunfire stopped, he had to be ready to move. Clumps of snow fell on his head while a cloud of white blocked any vision more than two feet away.

Kira was screaming, but now her words were directed at the man who'd grabbed her.

"Let me go!" She was making as much noise as possible, reminding him of their cemetery scuffle. As she had that night, she released a bloodcurdling scream, but was quickly silenced.

Dalton's racing heart seemed to collide with a wall. She couldn't be dead. He had to get to her, help her. The weapon shook in his hands and his fingers refused to follow his commands. What was wrong with him?

He shifted his elbows, trying to lever himself higher. Sweat dripped down his face and burned his left eye. He swiped his cheek against his shoulder, hoping to clear his vision, but to no avail. The gun fell from his hands and he stared down at the red snow. It looked like a snow cone from a summer carnival. But instead of annoying carnival music, all he heard was Lauren's voice, humming to him.

The tune wasn't familiar, wasn't soothing. Dalton fought to remain conscious. Kira's voice echoed in his brain, a scream, and then silence.

Griffin glanced over his shoulder to the path he'd made in the snow, wishing there was a way to cover his trail.

On the other hand, there were so many tracks leading around the house and through the tree-covered areas to the east and west, it would take several hours for someone to sort out who'd gone where. Canceling the response to the burglar alarm meant it could be days before Rico's body was found. And even longer for anyone to retrieve Dalton's body from the woods.

Who was he kidding? The frequent snowstorms in Colorado would bury anybody until a late-spring thaw. Change of plans. There was no need for him to fumble with the woman and a snowmobile when there were several other modes of transportation at his fingertips. He circled the house, keeping the woman balanced on his shoulder. He kicked the front door open with his booted foot and made his way to the kitchen.

The garage was packed with all sorts of toys. He adjusted the load on his shoulder, strode confidently to the key rack on the kitchen wall and, after a brief hesitation, chose the keys to the remaining four-wheel-drive vehicle.

On second thought, he swiped all the keys and shoved them into his pocket. No sense in making it easy for anyone to follow them. He smirked at Rico's body on the floor, the rivers of blood intersecting on the tile.

He shouldered his way into the garage and strode to the SUV. Dropping the woman onto the passenger seat, he clicked the seat belt across her chest to hold her in place.

He paused long enough to locate a spool of twine hanging over the workbench. After securing her hands in front of her, he quickly tossed the rest of the twine at her feet and placed his weapon on the rear floorboard, covering it with a travel-sized blanket.

He raised the garage door and opened the rear hatch of the SUV. A storage compartment held a bag of ice salt, a shovel, road flares, matches and a combination radio-flashlight. He shut the back and went around to climb into the driver's seat. Yanking the ski mask from his face, he tossed it onto the console between the seats and shoved the key in the ignition.

One more trip for old time's sake. He glanced to his right and studied the woman beside him, who'd made the game interesting for so long. It might have been easier to kill her and dump the body, but he needed to savor his superiority one more time.

Then he'd truly be free.

Tate Wilson knew he was the person to blame if either Dalton or Kira were harmed.

*The only way anyone knows where we are is if you told them.* Dalton's words echoed in Tate's head. He flipped on the headset and questioned the pilot, Grayson. "How much longer?"

"Twenty minutes, sir."

It couldn't happen like this. Tate dropped his head into his hands and started to pray. *Please, God, do not make them suffer for my infidelities. I swear I will change. Let Dalton and Kira be okay. They have to be okay.*

And what were the implications of not finding them alive? Tate called the security company and learned the intruder alarm had gone off ninety minutes ago, but someone phoned in with the correct code and canceled the alarm.

Dalton wouldn't have done so, which meant someone else knew the code. Who was he and how had he gotten it? When the security guys arrived at the snowmobile rental place, they'd found it closed for the day. There must be a link between the two.

Patience was not Tate's strong suit and he was about to don a parachute if it meant getting to Dalton and Kira faster. He'd said a lot of things he couldn't take back. He'd thrown a lot of guilt on Dalton's shoulders when he knew there was no one to blame for his sister's suicide.

No one except Lauren. And if he was being completely honest, Josh. Tate should have told Dalton. He'd found Lauren's laptop months ago and many of his visits to her grave site had started as a trip to tell Dalton the truth. His sister had been unfaithful.

Who'd have guessed Tate would be the one groveling for a second chance to prove his worth? If he could have bartered away his fortune for the sight of Dalton's ugly mug giving him grief, he'd have done it in a heartbeat.

"Stay in the chopper until I give you the all clear," A. J. Atkins ordered from the seat beside him.

Tate could have decked him. "You had your chance," he yelled in reply. If A.J. had gotten his ass in gear, then maybe he would have been the first one to the snowmobile rental store.

"I wasn't busy getting laid when my best friend needed me, was I?"

Tate got in one good punch before A.J. knocked him to

the floor and shoved the rifle barrel against his ribs. "Next time, I'll shoot first."

Tate knew A.J. wasn't bluffing. They'd spent weeks together in the jungles of Central America, tracking drug runners and rebel armies with no respect for life. A.J. expected the worst from everyone and never tolerated the minutest threat.

The copter circled the house and Grayson located a place to land. He and A.J. were out the door and scaling snowdrifts before Tate could adjust to finally being on the ground. It seemed as if two lifetimes passed before A.J. whistled and gestured him out of the chopper. Tate's footsteps faltered in the uneven snow, but he trudged forward while chanting the Hail Mary prayer in his head. He stopped a few feet from A.J.

"Male DOA in the kitchen."

Tate swallowed the bile in his throat. Dalton was dead because of him. This could not be happening. Not now and definitely not here, where one tragedy had already occurred.

He cleared his throat. "Is it Dalton?"

A.J. jerked the sunglasses from his eyes. "You think I'd be standing here waiting for instructions if it was?"

It took Tate several seconds to process the remark. "Any ID?"

"Negative." A.J. replaced the glasses. "No one else in the house."

Tate swallowed, shaded his eyes against the setting sun as it reflected off the newly fallen snow. *Where are they?* He snapped his fingers. "Dalton said he saw Kira outside. Search the perimeter. Maybe they found a place to hide."

A.J. nodded to his buddy and they both disappeared around the side of the house. Tate headed for the entry, feeling the need to piece together what had happened after he'd spoken with Dalton.

The front door was riddled with bullet holes. Gun drawn, Tate stepped inside, weaving his way to the kitchen. The dead man was facedown. He was unarmed, which gave Tate a reason to hope that maybe Dalton had disarmed him and both he and Kira had made it out alive.

It was the only acceptable outcome.

Tate checked his watch before stomping to the back door and throwing it open. Numerous boot prints followed a path directly to the tree line. Two sets of prints or three? He hated not knowing, not being in control.

Whether it was divine intervention or not, three men emerged from the woods a few minutes later. Two men walking and one being carried.

"He's alive," A.J. announced.

Tate sprinted across the clearing and offered his assistance getting Dalton to the house. His face was ashen and his jacket was saturated with blood.

"No sign of Kira?" Tate asked, taking over for A.J., who carried an extra assault weapon and a rifle.

"Signs of a struggle, but we couldn't find a body."

"We found another set of tracks sweeping across to the east," the pilot said.

"It must mean something if they took her, right?" Tate needed to believe there was a chance they'd get to Kira in time.

"We'll continue the search after we get Dalton inside."

A.J. shifted sideways, easing Dalton through the door and into the kitchen. Tate followed.

"Put him up on the counter," Tate instructed.

It took all three men to complete the task. "Hey, Junior," Tate said and gestured to the second man. "Run to the chopper and get my medical bag."

The pilot nodded and headed to the front door.

"His name is Grayson," A.J. said.

"Yeah, whatever." Tate didn't have time for niceties. He searched through drawers for scissors to cut through Dalton's shirt.

"Check the hall closet for a first aid kit," he barked, ripping open the insulated flannel and tearing through the T-shirt underneath. Tate used a kitchen towel to wipe away the melted snow and blood before inspecting Dalton's chest and left arm. A bullet appeared to have ricocheted off a rib and lodged in his biceps. "I need your Maglite over here."

A.J. propped his AK-47 against the counter and retrieved the light from one of his vest pockets, holding it over Dalton's head. "I'd say he dodged a bullet, wouldn't you?"

"He may have dodged a dozen, but he'll have one for a souvenir." Tate handed A.J. another towel. "Apply pressure to his chest."

"I know the drill." He was silent for a few seconds before jumping back into the conversation. "Have you been using any of your superskills here in the States?" A.J. asked.

Tate ignored the question and focused on examining Dalton for other injuries. A.J. never tiptoed around a topic. He'd ask a question about the weather in the same tone he'd use to deliver a death notification.

"Haven't you heard I'm a globe-trotting playboy now?"

"Keep telling yourself that, because you're the only one who believes it." A.J. snorted.

Tate hummed, keeping the mood light for another moment or two. He needed his mind to drift to the place where everything came naturally, and if he thought too much about who he was treating, his emotions would take over.

This was Dalton. His best friend since childhood and the one person he should have been able to forgive after Lauren's death. Why had he carried that anger for so long? Why hold the grudge until he felt hollow inside? So hollow and empty he'd dropped any pretense of caring.

For himself, for his family, for anyone. Another night, another party, another faceless woman to use and then forget.

Grayson returned with the bag of medical supplies and plopped it on the counter near Dalton's head. Tate dug to the bottom, removed his stethoscope and checked Dalton's breathing. Shallow.

"Find some blankets," he barked. Grayson hustled from the room.

A.J. shone his flashlight on Tate's face. "Lay off the kid or we're gonna have a problem."

"You mean another problem, right?" Tate countered with considerably less venom.

A.J. moved the light to Dalton's wounds. "This is a cakewalk compared to Costa Rica. No bombs or gunfire, and a semisterile environment. You should be able to sew him up with your eyes shut."

Tate swallowed his retort and cleared his throat. A.J. was trying to keep him focused on the procedure instead of the patient. After retrieving a package containing sterilized instruments, Tate used the tweezers to pull the bullet from Dalton's arm.

By this time, Grayson had located a blanket that looked more like a bedspread. He covered the lower half of Dalton's body before following A.J. from the room.

Tate listened intently to the telltale footsteps overhead as the two men cleared the second floor. He expected to hear at any moment that another body had been located. His mind filled with images of Lauren's motionless form at the morgue. Medical school and his stint in the Coast Guard had familiarized him with both peaceful and violent death. At the funeral home, Lauren had looked like herself. As if she was at a photo shoot and had to hold perfectly still.

He'd denied her death until her coffin was lowered into the ground.

Then it was over.

Staring down at Dalton, he got the same feeling. This was unreal and unacceptable. Someone would pay for the harm done to Dalton and Kira. Tate's finger itched to pull the trigger of his weapon and fire at the dead man on the floor, which signaled he needed to get his emotions under control. There was nothing to be gained by that behavior.

His gaze swept the kitchen once more, taking in the blood splattered on the opposite wall. This house was death personified. How many times had he visited, both invited and as a drop-in guest? How many meals had he shared around the dining room table, times filled with laughter, love and a good dose of sibling rivalry?

Dalton shifted slightly on the countertop, drawing Tate's attention. He slipped the safety on the weapon and rested his other hand on his friend's shoulder.

"Take it easy, bro."

Dalton's eyelids opened and immediately closed again. His body shuddered beneath Tate's fingers.

"I know you're cold." Tate reached for the bedspread and yanked it up to Dalton's chin. "But be a good patient and keep quiet for another couple minutes. Finding Kira depends on *your* cooperation. Understand?"

## Chapter 17

"Bossy bastard," Dalton grumbled.

Tate smiled. "I really thought I wanted you dead."

"Funny, I did, too."

A door slammed overhead, followed immediately by footsteps on the stairs.

"Where's Kira?"

"I don't know."

"How long has she been gone?"

"I don't know."

"So you're basically useless to me, right?" Dalton tossed the comforter off his chest and tried sitting up. Dizziness swamped him, along with a sharp pain that stabbed repeatedly at the left side of his body.

"Lie still," Tate ordered, pressing Dalton's shoulder down to the countertop.

"Your bedside manner sucks."

"Really? Make sure you fill out a comment card."

Dalton flexed the fingers of his right hand, paused and then reached to inspect the bandages on his left side. No doubt about it, he'd been shot. He could have lived the rest of his days without the experience.

His mind replayed the final sequence of events in the woods. All the words he'd left unsaid.

"She's definitely not here," Atkins announced as he entered the kitchen.

"Did you check every room?" Dalton intended for it to be a demand, but his voice was hoarse. He shivered, the chill of his wet clothing finally registering.

"The house has been cleared, twice," Tate said.

"So if they didn't take the snowmobiles, then where are they?" A.J. asked.

"Check the key rack," Dalton said.

"All the keys are gone," Tate stated.

Dalton swallowed his panic and glanced around the room, willing it to stop spinning. If they hadn't killed Kira here, then where was she taken? What had prompted the second attacker to let her live?

His stomach lurched as his mind flipped through the memories with Kira. Her small, soft fingers skating down his chest. Her bright green eyes questioning every one of his motives. The way she'd felt, pressed against him the last time they'd made love.

"Which vehicle is missing?"

A.J. stomped across the kitchen to the doorway to the garage. "The second and fourth stalls are empty."

Dalton had watched Tate drive away two days ago in the Jeep, which meant Lauren's SUV had been stolen by Kira's abductor.

"The Range Rover." Dalton looked up at Tate, feeling a burst of adrenaline firing through his veins. He'd get a location on the SUV and call in every resource to rescue Kira. "I want your phone."

"Take it easy. Give me the number and I'll make the call."

Dalton recited the number and Tate punched the keys. He turned on the speaker and a few moments later a service representative answered.

"How may I assist you?"

"I need to locate a stolen vehicle," Tate replied.

"May I have the vehicle identification number, please?"

"I don't have it. Can you use another method?"

"Name and date of birth, please?"

Tate rattled off the information while Dalton listened.

"Have you reported the vehicle stolen to local law enforcement?" the representative asked.

"Yes," Tate lied.

"Are you requesting the vehicle be disabled at this time?"

"Can you?"

"Yes, sir."

Tate looked to Dalton for permission. He shook his head. "We need the location."

"One moment, please." The connection was silent for all of thirty seconds before the woman returned to the line. "Your vehicle is currently parked somewhere in Benton County, Wyoming. The nearest intersection is Highway 6 and Blackstone Creek."

Tate and Dalton exchanged a surprised look.

"Thank you, darlin'. You've been a big help." Tate disconnected the call and stared at Dalton.

"They're going to the cemetery," Dalton announced. "Help me up."

"No," Tate replied, crossing his arms over his chest. "First the ground rules."

"Your concern is touching, but there's no way I'm staying here." Not while Kira was out there alone with the bastard who'd shot him.

Tate's phone blared an unholy noise. He fumbled to answer it, quickly turning the speaker off when Ethan's voice boomed through the kitchen.

Dalton shifted on the countertop, finally slipping his legs over the side and pulling himself to a sitting position. When he opened his eyes, A.J. was balancing him on his injured side, while his partner kept Dalton from falling forward.

"You look like hell, buddy," A.J. quipped.

"Thanks." He shifted in the wet denim jeans encasing his legs. "Find me a chair."

"What's the magic word?" A.J. had an ill-timed sense of humor.

"Please." Dalton gritted his teeth.

"The other magic word?" The man was a complete and total pain in the ass.

"Jet," Dalton said and sighed in resignation. "Get me a chair and you can fly the jet."

"Slide forward, Dalton," A.J. instructed. "We've got you."

The three-foot drop to the floor looked more like three hundred feet. It was easier to move when his eyes were closed. Dalton's feet briefly touched the tiles before he was seated in a chair. His heart raced from the effort it took.

"Are you okay?" A.J. asked.

Dalton nodded, keeping his eyes closed. His head didn't hurt, so the dizziness must be associated with how much blood he'd lost before they found him. Or maybe it was from the meds Tate gave him.

"Try opening your eyes."

Dalton squinted through one eye before popping the other one open and blinking repeatedly. Things were a bit hazy, but not spinning like when he'd been flat on the counter.

"I'm okay," he said. "But I'd like some dry clothes."

"Be right back." A.J. left the room and Dalton heard him climbing the stairs again.

He could also hear snippets of Tate's conversation. Ethan had found something important, judging by the way Tate was standing in the farthest corner of the room.

"You and A.J. have been friends a long time, huh?" Grayson asked.

Dalton merely nodded, his attention focused on the mumbled words floating from the other side of the kitchen.

A.J. returned with a pile of clothes, effectively breaking the sudden silence. "Dude, you really need to hire a stylist." He tossed a T-shirt in Dalton's lap. "Orange is so last season."

Dalton ignored the attempt at humor. He was able to remove his boots and jeans while seated, but had to lean against the counter to redress. He shoved one foot through the leg hole of the dry underwear, waited to regain his balance and then repeated the maneuver with the opposite foot.

He sensed Tate walking up behind him. "What did Ethan find out?"

"Could you give us a minute?" Tate glanced at A.J. and Grayson. The men quickly left the room.

Dalton reached for the clean pair of jeans on the counter. "I'm listening." He dropped onto the chair and worked at getting one foot through the pant leg.

"What's the special assignment you gave to Ethan?"

"He didn't tell you?"

"I want *you* to tell me."

"Get me a glass of water, would you?" Dalton shoved his other leg into the jeans and stood again, to yank the denim over his hips. Tate found a glass and filled it in the sink. Dalton gulped it down.

"This is all connected to Josh. As much as I hate to admit it, I didn't believe most of what Kira told me about him. In fact, if he wasn't already dead, I'd kill him." Then it hit Dalton. Nothing that had happened to Kira was pure coincidence or conjecture.

"This was always about Josh," he said. "He used her to guarantee a source of income. He figured out a way to embezzle the money and blame Kira."

"He didn't need the money," Tate said.

"Like he didn't need to be sneaking around with my wife?" Dalton spat out. He grabbed the socks and sat again, angrily yanking them on his feet.

"How long have you known?" his old friend asked.

"Not nearly as long as you, apparently," Dalton replied.

Tate sighed and paced to the other side of the kitchen. "I found her laptop on one of my trips up here."

"You knew how much I was hurting and you couldn't bring yourself to cut me some slack?" Dalton reached for one of his boots. "I feel like a dumbass. I never wanted to think that either one of them could betray me."

He silently laced the boot, then reached for the other. "Did you ever think maybe Lauren killed herself because she couldn't be with Josh?"

"No. Josh was an opportunist. He skated by because your mom refused to let him fail at anything. And Lauren was just another woman who couldn't tell him no. Dammit, Dalton, I always watched out for her and you promised—"

Dalton stood and kicked the chair away. "I kept my vows. She was everything to me and then she was gone." He snapped his fingers. "I lost my wife and my best friend on the same day. Your forgiveness and your friendship might have brought me back from a really dark place."

"You think I don't know that?" Tate shoved a few items

into his medical bag. "If I blamed you, then I wouldn't have to blame myself."

"So you've been *not* blaming yourself since she died? You've turned into a first-class man whore. Wouldn't Lauren be proud?" Dalton stared at Tate, daring him to deny the facts every tabloid in America had pictures to prove.

"Lauren would be proud I saved your life."

The sudden silence between them was deafening.

Dalton finally relented. None of this discussion was getting them closer to finding Kira.

"Who else would know about this place? Know the security code?" Tate asked.

"You, Lauren, me. And Josh," Dalton said.

"Should we assume it's only a coincidence every equation contains Josh's name?" Tate asked.

"Not anymore." Dalton pulled a coat from the rack near the door and gingerly shoved his arms through the sleeves. "Josh is the answer. Griffin was never a real person." Dalton smacked his hand against the counter in annoyance. "That's why Kira couldn't track him down."

"But he could have killed her out in the woods and ended all of this," Tate insisted.

"So why didn't he?" Dalton asked.

"Let's talk about this in the air. I have a chopper."

"It doesn't make sense," Dalton insisted, following Tate through the dining room. "He could have shot both of us. Why didn't he check to make sure I was dead?"

Tate turned and grabbed Dalton's arm, shoving him toward the door. "Run!" he yelled.

A.J. and Grayson were standing a few feet from the porch. But instead of running away from the house, as Tate instructed, A.J. ran toward them. Dalton was in no condition to sprint for his life, but A.J. bounded up the steps, threw an arm around his waist and hustled him into the yard. Tate was on the other side, hightailing it away from the house.

Dalton didn't know what they were running from or where they were running to, but the men surrounding him provided plenty of motivation. They had just passed a line of trees when a deafening blast propelled him forward. He was knocked to the ground, his face buried in the snow, while an enormous weight pressed against him.

The ground shook beneath him. He couldn't move, could barely breathe. And then there was a brief silence, as if the world had ended. In the next instant, fiery debris rained from the sky. Dalton couldn't see it, but could hear the sounds of various items landing on the snow with a definite sizzle.

Several moments passed before the weight pressing against him was suddenly gone and he was able to roll over to his side and brush the snow from his face. Tate and A.J. stood a few feet away, trying to hold a conversation using hand gestures. Dalton guessed all of them would be experiencing temporary hearing loss.

Slowly, he climbed to his knees and then to his feet. "What happened?" he asked.

Neither man turned to answer him. Black smoke billowed to the sky, churned by the wind.

He spotted the chopper approximately a hundred feet away and appearing undamaged. He whistled to get A.J. and Tate's attention before pointing to the aircraft. Tate gave a grim nod and Dalton picked his way through the debris field.

Grayson was already circling the chopper, making sure nothing would prevent them from taking off. Aside from a few dents and a crack in one of the side windows, it looked none the worse for wear.

Dalton opened a door and climbed into a second-row

passenger seat. Sitting eased the aching in his chest. The snow he swiped away from his face was tinted red, but there was so much adrenline pumping through his system that his entire head was throbbing. It felt as if a large chasm had been carved into his skull. It would only get worse when the chopper started.

He sat with his eyes closed for several minutes, saying a thankful prayer for surviving the bomb left by Josh. No wonder he hadn't worried if Dalton was dead in the woods. Josh had a backup plan in place to destroy everyone and everything that might send authorities on a manhunt for him.

Tate climbed through the door on the opposite side of the chopper. He handed Dalton a set of headphones. "Put these on." He did the same with another pair. Dalton followed the direction, which succeeded in cutting the noise in his brain to Mardi Gras volume.

"Can you hear me?" Tate questioned through the amplified mini speakers.

"Loud and clear," Dalton replied.

A.J. took his place in the pilot's seat, while Grayson donned the headgear for the job of copilot. They both flipped switches on the dash and the big bird started to rumble. Dalton could hear both men going through the preflight checklist and then A.J. gave a thumbs-up to signal they were good to go.

The helicopter lifted slowly into the sky, its backflow sending snow and black smoke spinning like a mini tornado beneath them. Nothing below them appeared salvageable. Only the shell of the house remained and it was quickly being consumed by the hungry flames.

"What's our ETA?" Tate questioned.

"Approximately seventy-five minutes," A.J. responded.

"My brother will be dead in ninety."

## Chapter 18

Kira awakened from unconsciousness to the scent of leather and the motion of a vehicle. Her cheek throbbed as the taste of blood registered on her tongue. She was still alive, but who'd taken her and why?

"I know you're awake." The words were uttered as strong fingers jerked her head toward the driver. His thumb pressed against her cheek and pain exploded behind her eyelids, popping her eyes open to focus on her captor. His voice wasn't familiar, but his profile brought memories to the surface. The slight dip at the end of his nose, the jaw-line and pointy chin… She knew that face, even without seeing his eyes.

"Let me go!" Her hands were worthless, tied together at the wrists. The seat had been moved forward and her legs were blocked in by the dashboard.

And Josh was alive.

The man who'd pledged his love to her forever and then

disappeared when they'd hit a rough patch. No doubt he wouldn't let her live through the night.

"You should have left it alone. You know that, right?" His hand thumped against the dash and her body jerked toward the passenger door. Her arms flew up to block her face, but he quickly knocked them to her lap and laughed. She'd thought he'd meant to strike her and had unintentionally allowed her fear to show. Now Josh would take even more pleasure in watching her suffer.

She hated him. Hated him. The anger built as her mind sorted through methods of escape. But would it do any good to escape, if Josh was alive?

Random thoughts became solid ideas. Kira was actually pondering ways to kill him. Maybe yanking the steering wheel when they crested the next hill, hopefully sending the vehicle down the embankment. Then justice would be done without anyone else being harmed.

When had she turned so heartless?

"I searched your apartment but didn't find anything incriminating, at least to me. Are you holding out?" Josh quizzed her.

She refused to answer him, continuing to chant *I hate you* in her head. She wanted him to think he had broken her. Wanted him believing she didn't have any fight left in her and that she'd resigned herself to losing to him once more.

Josh had shot his own brother and it was all her fault. Dalton would be okay if she hadn't gone to his cabin. She wasn't going down without a fight.

A few days ago, Kira had relished the thought of seeing Josh again and saying everything she'd kept bottled inside since the day he'd left. Now she believed he didn't deserve anything from her. She wouldn't give him the satisfaction of whimpering or begging for his favor.

But she couldn't get the prospect of never seeing Dalton again out of her mind. She'd behaved foolishly out in the woods, she knew that now. *You've made it impossible for me to walk away.* Dalton's comment meant she'd left him without a choice. And she had. He didn't have a choice because of the trouble she'd brought to his door. Even after he'd promised to keep her safe, and made love to her like nothing she'd ever experienced, it wasn't enough to bind them together.

Her heart ached over never having the chance to say how much he meant to her. She loved him and she should have told him while she had the chance. She, above all, knew how quickly love could recede and disappear. All the what-ifs crowded in around her. What if she'd never married Josh? What if she'd never had his child? What if she'd refused to be abandoned by him and made it a lot tougher on him to walk away? Would any of it have made a difference?

She might have been able to avoid the pain of Josh's rejection, but the truth was, he'd been having an affair with his brother's wife. On the other hand, Dalton might not have been privy to every dirty detail if it wasn't for her discovery of Lauren's diary.

Kira shivered beneath Dalton's jacket, pressed her face into the collar and inhaled his scent. The urge to feel his arms around her was overwhelming. If she had one more chance, she wouldn't let him think she was immune to the chemistry between them. She should have told him.

The sun was shifting low on the horizon as Kira was driven down the road to the Matthews family cemetery for the second time in less than a week. The newly fallen snow made everything look so different...

She let her eyes roam the vehicle's interior, wishing she could search the glove compartment or the console between the front seats. Leaning her head against the passenger-door window, she noticed something shiny lying in the armrest. She quickly looked away and held her breath. Was it a knife of some sort wedged in the small space?

Josh was flipping through the satellite radio stations and finally stopped on one of Lauren's songs. The bastard. His lips were moving, as if he'd memorized every word. He and Lauren had probably sung a couple duets for fun.

He was paying little attention to Kira, and she glanced to the armrest again. It was a nail file. Was it sharp enough to do any damage? No matter, at least it was *something* to use against Josh. Her eyes darted to the left. For the first time she noticed the emergency-communication button.

If the vehicle was in an accident, the deployment of the air bags would alert someone in a call center to send help. But if you had a flat tire or needed directions, you could also push the button and someone, somewhere, would answer. Kira itched to press the button and scream for help.

A few minutes later, after the final chords from Lauren's song faded, the bumpy lane they were traveling curved and she spotted the gates of the cemetery. Josh stopped the SUV and backed into a stand of trees about a hundred feet from the entrance.

Now what?

He sat quietly for a moment and then exited the SUV and stood by the hood, staring eerily at the cemetery. Kira quickly pushed the emergency-assistance button with her thumb.

"Range Rover client assistance. What is your emergency?" The voice was so calm, almost as if the woman was asking for her order at a McDonald's drive-through. Surprisingly, Josh wasn't paying any attention.

"I've been kidnapped by a man named Joshua Kincaid... I mean Matthews. He is armed and I need help."

"Ma'am, are you injured?" The woman's voice was

louder now and Kira was almost certain the sound could reach Josh's ears.

"No, I'm okay. But we are near a cemetery and…" She knew he wouldn't let her live. Knew she'd never see Dalton again.

"Ma'am, I need you to stay on the line with me, okay? For as long as it's safe, I need you to keep this line open. Do you understand?"

"Yes." Kira had to get out of the SUV and distract Josh so he wouldn't notice the emergency-alert button was flashing.

"I'm notifying the county sheriff and state highway patrol. They will be en route to your location very shortly."

"I have to go," Kira insisted.

"Tell me your name."

"Kira." She wasn't sure how much time had passed, probably less than a minute. The panic was subsiding and her anger was building. "Don't let this vehicle leave here. He's a killer and you can't let him hurt anyone else."

"Kira, I'm disabling the vehicle, but I need you to stall the kidnapper. Don't do anything to place yourself in danger. I promise I'm doing everything I can to help you."

Josh turned and stared at her, as if he knew he'd already won the game. Kira held her bound wrists up in front of her face. "He's coming for me. I have to go."

She swiped the nail file from the armrest before prying the door open and stumbling out of the SUV, right into Josh's arms. She quickly shoved the object up her coat sleeve before leaning against the door. It closed with a quiet thud, effectively preventing him from noticing anything out of the ordinary.

"What if she's gone by the time we get there?" Dalton tried turning in the seat to see Tate's expression.

"For the tenth time, hold still. Like I need you moving more than the helicopter," he complained.

"Your people skills are rusty."

"And your gratitude is underwhelming."

"You two are a riot," A.J. interjected with a grin.

"Shut up," they said in unison.

Dalton held perfectly still so Tate could finish up a few stitches to his head. Dalton couldn't stop thinking about Kira. Was she hurt? Was she scared?

There was a minute's silence before A.J. spoke again. "I'll do a flyover and make sure the SUV is there before I find a place to land."

"That kind of thinking earns big bonuses, right, Dalton?" Tate paused long enough to trim the thread to another stitch before gliding the needle through Dalton's scalp again.

"Definitely." He grimaced, fairly certain Tate was playing tic-tac-toe on his skull. But the pain and the price were inconsequential. Dalton had to find Kira. Had to tell her he couldn't imagine living another day without her. And give her the happily-ever-after she deserved.

"It should be just beyond the plateau." Grayson rummaged in the console and retrieved a pair of binoculars. He handed them over the seat to Dalton.

"If you can't see anything from here, I'll take a lap and try to get closer."

Dalton removed them from the case and raised them to his gritty eyes, hoping he'd be able to see anything at all. The sun's reflection on the snow was blinding and he was forced to stop and rub his eyes for relief. Then the chopper crested the final mountainside, where forest covered the land beneath them.

It took him several moments to gauge the copter's location and recognize the landmarks they passed. The county highway ran parallel to their route and Brookstone Creek flowed from north to south. The cemetery's location was exactly two point three miles from where the two intersected.

"Hand me those." Tate gestured to the binoculars.

Dalton passed them over and waited impatiently.

"There," Tate exclaimed. "Beyond those fir trees. It's your Range Rover."

Dalton grabbed A.J.'s shoulder. "Get me on the ground."

"Calm down, man," Tate said. "You can't run in there half-cocked and think this is going to end well."

Dalton ignored his statement. "Tell me you brought along some extra firepower."

A.J chuckled into his headset. "I'm always prepared. But with all your injuries and bandages, I'm thinking you should sit tight in the chopper."

"Not a chance." Dalton twisted again to look at Tate. "Are you done yet?"

"You're a horrible patient, but yes, I'm done."

The munitions locker in the chopper held a wide variety of handguns, rifles and assault weapons. Dalton chose a Sig Sauer 1911-22 and several clips of ammo. Tate took a handgun and a rifle. The decision was also made for Grayson to stay on board and radio the county sheriff to request assistance.

"Jeez, A.J., I'm almost impressed," Dalton said.

"Almost?"

"Yeah. Get us through this in one piece and I'll toss some real hero worship your way."

The snow surrounding the grave was pristine. The wind had blown a slight drift against the lower half of the headstone, but her husband's full name, Joshua Kincaid Matthews, was clearly visible. Kira was afraid to step any closer.

"You are the most determined woman I've ever known." Josh's voice startled her, even though she knew he was right behind her. "Aren't you going to ask me about the birth date?"

Her gaze jumped from his name to the dates etched on the stone. She'd never known the day Josh had supposedly died—August 29, according to this. But she'd celebrated two of his birthdays, on the fifteenth of July. So why did the headstone read March 21? She turned to face him.

"July 15 is Rembrandt's birthday." Josh shifted from one foot to the other. "I'm surprised you never made the connection."

She almost swallowed the retort. "Oh, because you painted two pictures, you're in the same league as Rembrandt?"

"Kira, Kira, such resentment." Josh mocked her in the same tone he'd used to imply she wasn't smart enough to tie her own shoes. There was absolutely nothing appealing about either his appearance or his personality. What in the world did she ever see in him?

"Should I thank you for all the lies?" She scanned the cemetery, hoping to see any evidence law enforcement was nearby.

"Of course not, but you should have known when to let it go." He shook his head. "When to admit defeat." He smiled in a predatory way, all his teeth showing as if he was promoting a new brand of toothpaste. His hands were tucked in the pockets of a white ski parka and the collar was turned up against the cold wind. She'd seen the outline of a handgun in his jacket pocket, but evidently he believed she posed no threat at the moment.

He'd changed his hairstyle, made it much shorter and added some highlights, probably meant to make him look a bit more distinguished.

It was pure vanity. He thought he'd won their battle of wits. "You son of a bitch."

He laughed. "I don't remember you being this feisty. It would have made things so much more interesting. Maybe I'd have stayed around a bit longer."

She laughed in response. "Well, thank God for small favors." She felt the rage building in her chilly toes and radiating up her legs. How dare he imply she'd done something to drive him away?

"You should have been smart enough to leave it alone." A cold mask slipped over his face and disgust radiated from every pore. He took another step toward her and she backed into the headstone.

"I should have ignored all the money you embezzled, *Griffin*? Or maybe I should have covered your tracks?" One of her hands came loose beneath the material he'd used to tie her wrists and she carefully retrieved the nail file from her sleeve.

"Life has a way of evening the score, wouldn't you agree?" He smirked in obvious pleasure, a move meant to infuriate her further.

"You tell me. What would a good wife do?"

"You were never supposed to be my wife," he bellowed. "But you got yourself knocked up." He shrugged. "What choice did I have?"

He couldn't have said anything to cut deeper than those words. She'd gotten herself pregnant and he *had* to marry her. Or what—the game would have ended?

"You should have been man enough to tell the truth instead of walking away."

"Eventually, I did." His smile of triumph was what sent her over the edge. Kira palmed the nail file and lunged forward, stabbing his thigh. He stumbled backward and she raced for the gate, not bothering to check to see if he followed.

She could hear his shout of outrage, knew he would trail her. But it wasn't until a gunshot whizzed past her and ricocheted off a headstone that she realized he'd kill her before she ever reached the exit.

She swerved to the left, dropped behind Great-grandpa Matthews's diamond-dusted headstone and worked her other hand free from the twine. The sun had finally set. The surrounding trees still held enough leaves to cast shadows. The walls around the family graves prevented the wind from doing more than swirling the snow around like a cotton candy machine. If she avoided the areas with heavier drifts, Josh wouldn't be able to follow her tracks. She needed to stay away from him long enough for help to arrive. Or maybe make her way to the larger cemetery, which would provide a few more hiding places.

"You bitch," he hollered. "You're not leaving here alive."

*Hopefully, neither are you.* She kept her mouth shut, scurrying to the other end of the monument and peeking around the corner. Josh was nowhere in sight, but she spotted a trail of blood leading in the opposite direction. Was it wrong to hope he'd bleed to death?

An unfamiliar noise sounded in the distance, and Kira prayed the woman from the Range Rover's emergency assistance had followed through on her promise to send help. Kira should have told her she was a wanted felon. Surely that would have gotten the FBI's attention.

Something rustled behind her and she quickly shifted to the other side of the headstone. Where was Josh? She narrowed her eyes and listened closely. Another sound came from the same direction, so she darted toward the mausoleum.

She needed another weapon. Her hands shook as she

brushed away the snow on the ground in front of her and felt for anything sharp or heavy. The best she came up with was a thick branch about two feet long. There were several small rocks she scooped up and dropped in her pocket. She'd seen a movie once where the hero had thrown something in the opposite direction to distract the villain, while he escaped.

The distant rumble of a helicopter came progressively closer and Josh's taunts resumed. "Why don't you surrender before my security team gets here?" His voice was less robust than earlier. She knew he was blowing smoke. "No one's coming to save you, Kira. Dalton's dead."

She swallowed the first wave of panic and ordered herself not to react. Josh was a liar.

Josh was a good liar. He would lie to extract himself from any situation.

The helicopter was definitely landing somewhere nearby. Snow flew from the tree branches and softly fell to the ground as the *whomp, whomp, whomp* of the copter's blades dominated the air. And then, just as quickly, it retreated toward the highway.

Was it Josh's band of semicompetent armed killers? She'd already survived two attempts on her life, and wasn't the third time the charm?

*Luck be a lady.* Kira swiped her runny nose across the sleeve of Dalton's coat and waited. All sorts of crazy ideas filled her head. If she killed Josh, would they charge her with murder, or would it be self-defense? Could she dig up his grave and roll his body in there without anyone knowing the difference?

"On the bright side, Kira, you gave me a beautiful son." His voice seemed closer. "Such a shame you didn't get to watch him grow."

She was ready to dig a hole with her bare hands and toss Josh's lifeless body into it.

*Josh is a liar. Liar.*

"He used to ask for you."

*What?* Josh truly was crazy if he assumed she'd rise to the bait. Brandon had been stillborn. Tears of anger filled her eyes and she counted how many ways she could kill this man for such extreme cruelty.

"He loves football."

She heard Josh's footsteps on the mausoleum stairs, so she tossed a handful of stones in the opposite direction, before retreating behind another headstone several feet away.

"Josh?" Tate Wilson's voice called. "We know you're in here. Let Kira go."

Silence.

"Kira, baby?" Dalton's voice was about the sweetest sound she'd ever heard.

"She's already dead," Josh yelled in triumph. "Kind of poetic, isn't it, her dying in our cemetery?" His voice was muffled, sounding more distant than before. "She wasn't worth saving, anyway, dear brother. Not a loyal bone in her body." His chilling laughter left her searching for another hiding place.

She had to be quiet, but tears of anger and resentment were washing down her face with renewed vigor. Dalton was alive and he must truly love her if he was risking his life, if he was facing down his own brother to protect her.

"Let her go, Josh. Or do you prefer Griffin?" Dalton questioned.

The cemetery was turning a somber gray as the last bit of light disappeared from the sky. Kira inhaled Dalton's scent from the collar of his coat again and began praying. If they survived this day, she wouldn't squander another chance at happiness. She'd tell him she loved him, and she'd do whatever it took to make things right between them.

"It took you long enough to figure out," Josh said. He chuckled. "Guess we know who got all the brains in the family, huh?"

"Josh, you didn't have to kill anyone."

"I wouldn't have if those two idiots I hired had done their jobs. Sometimes if you want something done right, you have to do it yourself."

"I understand." This time it was Tate's voice, continuing to pacify him. "The sheriff is on his way and you can explain the whole story to him."

Silence prevailed and Kira's thoughts became jumbled. She could barely remember to breathe in and out. There were at least two silhouettes moving within the walls of the cemetery, but she couldn't tell the good guys from the bad.

She wanted to call Dalton's name and reveal herself. Wanted to run directly for the gates and keep running until she was miles away. She tightened her grip on the stick, ready to whack the next person who caught up with her. But the cool metal of a gun barrel was suddenly pressed against her temple, and she froze, too shocked to react.

"Shhh," Josh whispered against her frigid ear. "One word and you'll be dead."

Her muscles contracted in fear as he plucked the stick from her shaking hands. It was over. He would kill her before making his escape, and she was helpless to stop him.

"Call to my brother."

She shook her head, and Josh trailed the barrel of the gun down her temple and along her jawline.

"Now, before I splatter your brains against this headstone."

"Dalton," she whispered.

Josh grabbed her in a headlock. "Louder."

"Dalton," she repeated, a noticeable quiver in her voice. Blood dripped from Josh's leg onto her borrowed boots.

"Kira? Are you all right?"

No, she wasn't all right. But it didn't matter, because she'd been granted a second chance to tell Dalton the truth before her life was over.

"I love you."

# Chapter 19

Josh's grip tightened around her neck, cutting off the rest of her words. And then he was dragging her to the trees surrounding Grandma Alice's tomb.

"Josh. Tell me what you want." Dalton was inching closer. Kira caught his outline skirting a row of pine trees and then dropping behind another headstone.

"Suddenly you care about my happiness? You're a decade too late, brother."

A decade? What did he mean? She hadn't even met Josh back then.

"You've been angry with me for ten years? Tell me why."

Kira choked as Josh's arm tightened around her throat even more and then he dropped behind a large oak tree and propped her in front of him to use as a shield.

"Okay, Dalton, I'll reminisce with you. But if I see you take one step closer, I'll shoot darling Kira."

"Josh, nobody has to get hurt."

"Somebody always gets hurt when you're around, bro."

Josh's frigid hand pressed against her cheek. His grip on the gun grew unsteady as his anger escalated. "You never once deemed me as your equal."

"Not true and you know it," Dalton replied.

"Really? Remind me who took over Buckshot's."

Silence ensued.

"What's the matter, Dalton, cat got your tongue?"

"I was always going to take Dad's place. You know that."

"I could have done the job, but you never gave me a chance." Josh's bitterness was boiling over.

"Why didn't you say something before?"

"You mean why didn't I come running to you for a raise in my allowance?" Josh's self-deprecating laughter scared Kira almost as much as the gun barrel pressed to her cheek. "I figured out a way to get a bigger paycheck, with Kira's help, of course."

"Kira was helping you?"

"Jeez, Dalton, I can't remember the last time you showed any interest in my life. But after I stole her Midwest Mutual computer pass codes, it was easy enough to siphon out the data I needed."

"Why would you—" Kira couldn't finish the question because Josh shoved the gun against her chin.

"If I treated you unfairly, I'm sorry. Tell me what I can do to make it right," Dalton called.

"Hmm." Josh pretended to ponder the idea. "You can't make this right. It's too late."

"It's not too late," he said. "We're all here. We can fix this together."

"Wrong," Josh yelled. "We aren't all here. You touched the one thing I loved."

After a lengthy pause, Dalton said, "Are you talking about Lauren?"

"You know I am."

"Okay, how did I take Lauren from you?"

"Playing dumb only makes you sound guiltier, brother." Josh rested his hand against Kira's shoulder and she tried not to think about how easily he could kill her. "Those songs were for me, not you. Those emails were about me, not you. You swooped in and took everything that should have been mine."

"Should have been yours?" Dalton cleared his throat. "I read Lauren's diary. You two were having an affair."

"I was the one she turned to when you were too busy running your coffee empire to show her any attention," Josh raged. "I was there and Lauren loved me."

"You're delusional," Tate interjected. "Did you overdose her when she wanted it to end?"

He'd been quiet the entire time. Kira had forgotten about his presence. But his voice came from the opposite direction of Dalton's, and she felt a slight rise in confidence, knowing they were both trying to save her.

"You don't understand the connection that we shared. Lauren should have been with me forever. I made her happy. But when she found out about Kira—"

Kira's quick intake of breath stopped him from sharing more. What if she'd remained quiet? Would Josh have revealed more of the story?

"It doesn't matter." He waited another heartbeat and then regained his arrogant demeanor. "Aren't you going to ask me about my lovely bride?"

"Kira already told me," Dalton said.

"It didn't take her long to jump into your bed, did it?" Josh chuckled in her ear.

"Stop it," she hissed, elbowing him.

His arm tightened across her windpipe and he repositioned the gun to the middle of her spine. "Did she tell you about our son?" Josh asked. "What was his name?"

Kira's lips moved, but no sound escaped. The bastard couldn't even remember their child's name?

"Brandon." Dalton's steady response gave her strength.

"Right," Josh said. "I always hated that name, so sissy sounding. I knew you wouldn't let him do anything," he said to Kira. "You made me baby-proof the apartment before he was even born." Josh scoffed. "You were going to be one of *those* mothers who wouldn't let their kid get dirty. Probably dress him in pastel shirts because you really wanted a girl instead."

"I wanted a healthy baby. *You* were the one who had to have a son, even though you refused to get a real job and help support us." She was getting even angrier thinking about all the extra hours she'd worked to keep them afloat, while he was spending a fortune entertaining Lauren.

"You trapped me into marriage. Doesn't mean I ever wanted a kid."

"Is that why he's not buried here, in your *family* cemetery?" Kira already knew how this was going to end. Josh wasn't going to surrender. But if she distracted him enough, then Dalton might be safe when the shots were fired. "Answer me."

For once, Josh had no quick response.

"I read Lauren's diary. She never loved you." Anger was bubbling in every cell of Kira's body. "You couldn't even get her to leave Dalton."

"Shut up," Josh ordered.

"Go ahead and shoot me!" Kira squirmed against his hold.

"Kira, Kira, I do prefer this spirited side of you," Josh whispered against her ear while releasing the safety on his gun.

"You won't last a week in prison." She threw her head against his chin, then jerked sideways, trying to avoid his shot. She screamed as the bullet tore through her flesh.

Two more gunshots echoed at close range.

Her body dropped to the ground and her skull thumped against the base of the tree.

Face buried in the snow, Kira felt her warm blood oozing through her clothing and pooling under her stomach. She wasn't dead yet. Pain meant life and life meant the possibility of seeing Dalton one last time.

Then she heard his voice calling to her.

"Kira! Dammit, Kira, you don't get to die on me."

Dalton clutched Kira to his chest and prayed for a miracle. His brother's lifeless body lay at the base of an ancient oak tree, and A.J. was removing his weapons while Tate checked for a pulse.

"He's dead," Tate confirmed.

A.J. searched Josh's pockets and removed several items.

"Why, Josh? Why did you have to do any of this?" Dalton moaned. What had turned his brother into a soulless bastard? Had Josh done all this to get even with him? Could Dalton have prevented any of it by allowing Josh to suffer the consequences of his actions growing up, instead of letting their mother shelter him? He'd destroyed Kira's life without any remorse. In fact, he'd sounded proud of what he'd done. Would Dalton ever know the truth about the day Lauren died?

He raised his head and stared at the sky. "Where is Grayson?"

Kira's blood soaked through his shirt, and Dalton lifted her against his chest and ran for the cemetery gates. She couldn't die. He wouldn't allow it. Wouldn't survive losing someone else he loved.

The copter climbed over the mountain and settled into the clearing where Grayson had dropped them a few minutes ago. Tate appeared next to Dalton and they raced for the helicopter as if the hounds of hell were fast on their heels.

Snow blinded them as the copter touched down. Grayson threw open his door and jumped to the ground. He drew back the sliding door and helped lift Kira inside, carefully laying her on blankets he'd spread on the floor of the aircraft. Before long, they were in the air and headed to the closest hospital, in Casper. Tate knelt over her body, doing his best to stop the flow of blood.

Dalton felt useless. He kissed her forehead and took one of her hands, warming it against his lips. "It can't end like this."

"I'm doing everything I can," Tate said. "Grayson, I need an outside line to 411."

"You got it," he replied. "I've got an ETA of twenty minutes to the hospital."

Dalton donned headphones again and listened in as Tate requested the hospital's phone number and connected with an emergency room doctor. Tate started rattling off a bunch of numbers and relating what tests he needed to have run as soon as they landed. Dalton quickly lost interest and removed his headset.

"Don't you dare leave me like this, Kira. You owe me a house and a car. You even took my coat." He bent to kiss her cheek. "I'm going to wipe the slate clean. Open those beautiful green eyes and tell me again that you love me. Remind me how much you hate coffee."

How was she ever going to forgive him? She'd been right about Josh's erratic behavior and deep-seated cruelty.

But it didn't make any sense. What did Josh have to gain by deceiving Kira? Dalton's last phone conversation with Ethan replayed in his head. They hadn't found either a birth certificate or a death certificate for Kira's son. Could Josh have committed such an unspeakable sin? Could he have deceived Kira about their baby and then taken the child somewhere else, to raise him alone? And if so, where was the child now?

Grayson's whistle pierced the cacophony of noises filling the copter's cabin. He gestured to the headphones, then he held up three fingers, signaling a change of frequencies, once Dalton had put them on.

A.J.'s voice crackled across the connection. "I found a bunch of fake IDs and credit cards in his wallet."

"Tell the sheriff," Dalton said, before he could continue.

"Dalton, listen to me," A.J. insisted. "He has several pictures of a small boy."

Oh, sweet God in heaven. What had Josh done?

A whirlwind of activity met them at the emergency room entrance and Dalton was eventually separated from Kira. Even Tate, with his massive amount of charm, was refused entrance to the treatment area, and settled for keeping Dalton company while he was examined.

Tate's charm worked, however, in acquiring some clean clothing. Dalton paced in the small exam room, sparing an occasional glance at Tate and the clock ticking away the minutes on the wall. He was one tetanus shot away from freedom and it couldn't happen soon enough.

"You shouldn't jump to any conclusions," Tate warned, as he flipped through a free copy of *AARP Magazine*.

"Yeah, I'm sure there are oodles of explanations why A.J. found all those pictures of a little boy in Josh's billfold."

Tate glanced at him over the top of the magazine. "I'm

actually more shocked you managed to use the word *oo-dles* in a sentence."

"Bite me."

Nurse Betsy McNeil breezed into the room and all conversation between them ceased. "Mr. Matthews, I am so sorry for the delay. We had a little trouble tracking down all the injections your family doctor said were due."

Dalton counted six syringes lined up on the metal tray she set on the counter. *Family doctor?* He glared at Tate and offered the woman his shoulder.

"We'll do two in each arm and two in the bottom." She smiled as she wiped the alcohol square against his biceps and reached for the first injection. "We normally don't give all these shots at once, but Dr. Wilson was very insistent."

Dr. Wilson was also going to get his ass kicked, sooner rather than later.

Tate dropped the magazine and eased to his feet. "I'll wait outside." He grinned from ear to ear. "All those needles give me the heebie-jeebies." He faked a shudder and hauled ass before Dalton dropped his pants for shots three and four.

Nurse Betsy was a chatterbox. The shots took three lifetimes to administer and by then Dalton knew all about her marital status, single. Her education, Peakside Nursing School. And her overwhelming desire to visit New York.

She also loved Buckshot's Coffee. Go figure.

Tate was nowhere in sight when Dalton exited the exam room. Law enforcement officials from at least three agencies were waiting to speak with him, however, along with the attorney he'd called as soon as Kira was taken into surgery. Dalton couldn't risk saying anything that might get them in more trouble.

The sheriff of Casper County got in the first round of

questioning. Ninety minutes later it was the FBI's turn to grill him inside out.

Then Dalton tracked down Nurse Betsy for some pain-killers and asked for an update on Kira's condition.

"I shouldn't be telling you this," she confided. "But Mrs. Kincaid has been moved to recovery and downgraded from critical condition."

"Do you know her room number?"

"Not yet. But it will be somewhere on the sixth floor."

"Sixth floor?"

"Yes, our high-security level. There's a police officer stationed outside her room." The nurse's eyebrows rose dramatically. "She's wanted for murder, you know."

Dalton started to protest, but Nurse Betsy cut him off. "Excuse me, hon. I've got a patient waiting in exam three." She hurried away, leaving Dalton alone in the hallway.

The elevator doors opened and Tate emerged.

"Where have you been?" Dalton demanded.

"Hello to you, too, Mr. Personality. How's your bottom?"

"Not funny." He shoved Tate into an adjoining corridor and lowered his voice. "Did you know Kira can't have any visitors?"

"She's fine," he replied.

"And how would you know?"

Tate wisely took a step away from him before responding. "I've checked on her and spoken with both her doctors and nursing staff. We're all on the same page."

"No, we aren't," Dalton said. "I want to see her."

"You can't do her any good here."

"Really? Because I don't have an MD after my name?" He took a menacing step forward and Tate punched him in the shoulder.

"Ouch." Dalton rubbed his arm in annoyance.

Tate smirked. "Is your butt sore, too?"

"I'm not leaving."

"Planning to pitch a tent in the lobby?"

"If I have to, then yes."

"You need to meet with the board and assure them you are in charge. Plan another funeral and hire Kira some attorneys with clout." He shrugged. "You can't do that from here."

"There isn't going to be another funeral."

"Does your mother know that?"

He'd completely forgotten how Josh's actions would affect the rest of his family. The paparazzi would descend again, like when Lauren died. The very last thing Dalton wanted was for his mother to suffer through another round of invasive questions. She'd be inconsolable and looking to him for support.

"Grayson is waiting on the roof," Tate said. "Make him your right hand and get everything squared away in Denver. You need to handle damage control."

"I can't leave Kira like this." Dalton was sickened by the thought of her waking up and finding him gone. She needed him.

"They won't let you see her until the charges are dropped. You can help Kira the most by being in Denver." Tate shrugged. "Let me help, Dalton. I can keep you apprised of her condition. Try making amends for my behavior."

Dalton had never witnessed humility in his old friend before, so it took him a moment to accept his offer.

"All right," he finally agreed. "Tell her—"

"Tell her yourself. I'll call you when she's ready to talk. Until then, go put out the fires."

# Chapter 20

Dalton stormed over to the liquor cabinet in his office. He reached for the closest bottle, dumped some in a glass and swallowed it before repeating the motions. Kira wouldn't see him. Or they wouldn't let him see her. He didn't know what law enforcement agency was keeping them apart today.

The family had been in the headlines every day with new developments. This could not be happening. *But it was.* His mind rewound through the past week in fits and starts. Jumbled bits of conversation with law enforcement agencies, attorneys for Kira and himself, and the team of private investigators he'd hired to dig into every element of Josh's double life.

After everything his brother had done, Dalton wasn't certain he'd be capable of forgiving him. And honestly, if he didn't have a front-row seat to the show, he never would've believed Josh was capable of such deception and hate.

Kira had collected enough documentation to show a

possible link to Josh. Then Ethan stepped in and provided the authorities with a road map of sorts, which led straight to Josh and his alter ego, Geoff Griffin.

A sharp knock sounded at the door and Dalton looked across the room as A.J. entered and slammed the door closed behind him.

Dalton raised his glass in mock salute. "Well, if it isn't the famous underwear model posing as a mere mortal."

"I need your computer."

"What's wrong with *your* computer?"

A.J. stormed to Dalton's desk and dropped into the chair. A few seconds later he was tapping away at the keyboard.

"Julie," he said distractedly.

Dalton smiled. Yesterday it had been Heather and the day before, Monica. A.J. had the whole building abuzz. Searching his name retrieved enough eye candy to crash computers all over the office. Ethan was having trouble keeping up.

"Is your fan club meeting in the copy room?"

"Don't know." He continued punching away at the keys.

"I heard they were taking over conference room C because it has a projector in high-definition."

"Don't care." He smirked at Dalton. "Are you jealous or something?"

"I didn't think you cared." Dalton set his glass on the counter and dropped into the closest chair.

"And I assumed you'd appreciate my distraction techniques."

It took a moment for the statement to sink in before Dalton responded. "You posed in your underwear for my benefit?"

More keyboard tapping. "No, you're benefiting because I posed in my underwear."

"How exactly?"

"Are you kidding? No one even notices you're here. No one is gossiping about you or Josh or even Kira." He checked the supply of printer paper before continuing. "All they care about is little old me."

"And you're eating this up, right?"

"It feeds my ego." The printer started spitting out page after page of information and A.J. reclined in Dalton's chair. "But more important, it allows me access to the entire building without argument from anyone."

True. Plus, employee morale was higher than ever.

"And what have you learned from all this access?"

"First of all, hiring the private investigators was a waste of money. I could do the job blindfolded." He crossed his arms over his chest and shifted his feet onto Dalton's desk.

"How so?"

A.J. teemed with smugness. "Everything is on the internet. You just have to know where to look."

Dalton copied A.J.'s posture as the liquor loosened his muscles and his mind. "And you know where to look?"

A.J. nodded and tilted his chin toward the printer. "I've got everything you need right there. Josh and Kira's marriage license, copies of bank statements from the time they were together, Brandon's birth certificate."

"You found the birth certificate?" Dalton stormed to the printer and started riffling through the pages.

"Josh was pretty smart. I thought about all the possible ways to hide a child. The easiest was changing the baby's name. So instead of searching for a baby named Brandon, I started searching for any baby with the last name of Matthews born in the same year."

Dalton scanned the document in his hand. It was from the state of North Carolina and as soon as he located Josh's name he glanced at A.J.

"Aren't there plenty of men named Joshua Matthews out there? Did you find anything with Kira's name listed for the mother?"

"If he used Kira's name, it would be easier to track, because it's unusual."

"Who names their baby Rembrandt? This seems a little far-fetched, don't you think?"

A.J. grabbed a few sheets of paper from the stack and flipped them onto the desk. He plucked a highlighter from Dalton's penholder and systematically circled items on at least six separate pages. "Take a look at the date on their marriage license."

Dalton nodded.

"Now look at the date Josh opened this bank account and what he listed as his birth date."

So far, they all had one thing in common. The fifteenth of the month was listed on every document.

"I'm sure I don't need to show you Josh's birth certificate, right?" A.J. paused.

"March 21, 1986," Dalton automatically replied. And then he grasped the inconsistency. "So he lied about his birthday. Probably the smallest lie he told."

A.J. snorted. "Well, yeah. But what's so special about July 15?"

Dalton finally glanced up at him. "I don't know, but I bet you're going to tell me."

"I ran an internet search for the date and found a slew of famous people. I think your brother was trying to channel Rembrandt."

"Rembrandt?"

"Famous Dutch painter from the 1600s," A.J. prodded.

"Don't be a smart-ass. I'm familiar with the name."

Silence filled the room as Dalton scanned the rest of the documents A.J. had collected. There was a joint checking account with a paltry amount of money direct deposited every two weeks. Kira hadn't been lying about surviving on next to nothing.

The next statement was from a different bank and showed only Josh's name. He'd maintained a substantial balance during the same time period. Two major withdrawals had been made a few months after their marriage and then again around the time Brandon would have been born.

"Any idea where these withdrawals were spent?"

"A large part of both were transferred into this account." A.J. circled another name.

Finn Barnes, the doctor who'd supposedly delivered Kira's baby. Son of a bitch. And since Finn had disappeared around the time Josh faked his death, more than likely the man had outlived his usefulness in Josh's eyes.

Dalton grabbed the sheets of paper and slapped A.J.'s back. "Still want to fly the jet?"

"Of course."

"It's past time for me to meet my nephew."

Kira peeked out the blinds of her sixth-floor room and stared through the bars covering the window. This was utter madness. The paparazzi occupied the parking lot adjacent to the hospital, and orange plastic fencing had been installed to keep them away from the entrance. At least a dozen large news trucks with giant satellite dishes filled the cramped area and it looked more like a bunch of tailgaters at a college football game than the media event of the year.

Plus, Dalton hadn't called. It was probably all too painful. Josh was dead and now the press was rehashing Lauren's suicide, using everything but a flow chart to connect all the pieces. Scratch that. CNN had a color-coded chart filled with pictures of all the main players and dates going back to the moment Lauren had become an overnight sensation. Kira couldn't blame Dalton a bit for keeping his distance.

He was probably wondering if she planned to go after Josh's stake in Buckshot's. If she was smart, which there was overwhelming proof to the contrary, she'd leave him alone.

She turned at the knock on her door, undoubtedly another nurse checking another set of vital signs and making progress notes in her chart. Kira had spent six days being a model patient and answering questions of numerous nosy doctors and interns.

Instead of a nurse, Tate Wilson stepped through the doorway and greeted her with his trademark lady-killer smile. His face probably hurt from constantly schmoozing with the nursing staff, who treated him like some sort of god.

"Good afternoon, Sunshine." He used the same greeting every day and yet it still caught her by surprise, how easily it flowed off his tongue and how much she enjoyed the endearment.

"Dr. Wilson." Finding out he was a real doctor had been a minor shock compared to everything else she'd endured. But it also meant he was either trying extra hard not to upset her or secretly feeding her Valium in her IV bag.

She felt pretty levelheaded, so it was probably the drugs.

"Are you ready to blow this Popsicle stand?" He flipped the wooden chair around and dropped onto the seat, crossing his arms over the back to stare at her.

"And go where, to a real jail?"

"I'm deeply offended you'd think such a thing."

"I'll bet." She wheeled the IV stand to the bed and sat down, wincing slightly as the stitches in her side tugged uncomfortably.

"A majority of the charges against you have been dropped."

"Majority?" She adjusted the red silk bathrobe he'd given her and tilted her head to the side. "But not all?"

"A little gratitude would be nice."

"I want to go home." It might have sounded firmer if her voice hadn't ended on a whisper. She was miles from home and a million miles from normal. And after everything she'd put him through, Dalton probably hated her.

"Dalton doesn't hate you," Tate said.

Had she said that part out loud? Evidently, yes. "Really? Is he too busy saving the family's good name to even pick up the phone?"

"You aren't allowed phone calls or visitors." Tate delivered the line with a frown.

"You're losing your touch, Dr. Wilson, if you can't find a way around hospital policy and smuggle me a cell phone."

He ignored her comment. "You're being discharged tonight."

"And?" She wasn't foolish enough to believe she'd gain any measure of freedom, whether in darkness or daylight.

He rose from the chair and turned his back long enough to retrieve something from the hallway. He handed Kira an oversize shopping bag loaded with clothes. "Pick out something cheery to wear and I'll be back at seven."

She hadn't expected him to leave so quickly. There were many more questions she wanted to ask. Instead, she dumped the contents of the bag onto the bed and plucked the brightest colors from the pile. A red shirt with three-quarter sleeves caught her attention, but then she spotted an orange V-neck sweater.

It was October. She could wear orange if she wanted to, no matter if it was Dalton's favorite color. She checked the size, yanked the tags free and quickly discarded her hospital clothing. She flipped through a few more items and located a pair of black casual pants of stretchy material. Spandex was a girl's best friend.

After pulling on socks and a pair of wool-lined boots, in size eight, she folded the leftover clothes and returned them to the bag. A while later, one of the nurses stopped by to remove her IV and pulled a handful of items from her pocket.

"I always feel better when I wear a little makeup." She laid a few tiny bottles on the bedspread. "I brought these from home, but if anyone asks, you didn't get them from me, okay?"

Kira nodded. It was the first time all week that anyone had spoken to her as more than a patient. She'd been allowed to walk up and down the hallway twice a day, but always under the watchful eye of the two armed guards who patrolled the floor.

After the nurse left, Kira spent some time in front of the bathroom mirror, carefully applying the makeup and adding a bit of color to her lips. It was the most normal thing she'd done in days. And then she waited as the final two hours seemed to drag by. Even the delivery of her supper tray offered little distraction.

Her door opened again a few minutes after seven. She stood, bag in hand, waiting for the next part of her journey.

"Showtime." Tate held the door wide-open and plucked the bag from her hand.

"Don't I have to be handcuffed or something?" she asked, resisting his attempt to usher her into the hallway.

"Do you want to be handcuffed?" Tate said.

"No."

"Then let's go." He grabbed her right hand and led her down the hallway to the elevators.

Ten minutes later they left the hospital from the rooftop helicopter pad, under the cover of darkness. Tate evidently had paid big money for a private flight to take them to the Casper airport, where an unmarked private jet was waiting.

Tate conversed with the helicopter pilot about current weather conditions while Kira watched the changing terrain below and remained quiet. She had nothing left to say. She probably should have asked where they were going, but she wasn't convinced jail wasn't in her future.

She wanted to go home. Wanted to sleep in her own bed and wear her own clothes. Wanted to spend some time mourning everything she'd lost.

Her throat tightened and tears filled her eyes each time she reflected on Dalton.

It hurt to think of the years she'd locked herself away from everyone who brought her happiness. Josh had robbed her of interacting with the rest of the world. But in her new life, after jail, she was going to be a different person.

She would give her opinion. She'd allow herself to feel emotion again and not stay locked in a cycle of unhappiness. In a nutshell, she was going to live.

Had it really been less than a week since they'd argued in his study? Since Dalton had forced her to think about her future, and she hadn't been able to give him the answers he wanted? He'd said he wanted her to be happy, but hadn't said that her future would include him.

Had she read too much into his behavior at the cemetery? She'd announced that she loved him and hadn't seen or heard from him since.

The ride to the airport took less than ten minutes and then they were on solid ground. Tate helped her from the helicopter and hustled her toward a familiar hangar door. Once inside, the bright lights were almost blinding and she clung to his arm for direction. Was he taking her home to Kansas City?

Instead, she saw the Buckshot's jet and jerked to a stop. "You never said it was Dalton's plane."

"You never asked." The contours of his handsome face reflected his tiredness before he winked at her.

Tate had stayed with her at the hospital, and now she couldn't show a hint of gratitude for his sacrifice? She followed him across the hangar. It was silly to be afraid of a plane. Okay, maybe not silly, because planes could crash. But being leery of anything associated with Dalton would be exhaustive.

The man standing next to the stairs looked vaguely familiar. He was almost Tate's height, but with hair as light as Tate's was dark. His smile insisted they were old friends, but it was his turquoise-blue eyes that flashed through her memory.

"Are you trying to picture me with my clothes off?" he asked Kira.

Tate punched him in the arm and his smile was replaced with a scowl. "Clean it up, A.J."

"What? I'm very recognizable."

"Not always a good thing," Tate replied. "Kira, this is our copilot, A. J. Atkins."

She extended her hand, but Tate hustled her up the stairs before she could complete the gesture.

"I can speak for myself," she insisted.

"I know you can."

Kira almost imagined Tate was jealous of the attractive man at the bottom of the stairs, which was a ridiculous assumption. Women fawned over Tate as if he was the last tasty morsel on a sinking ship. And he'd used that to his advantage more than once at the hospital.

He followed her to a gathering of seats and watched intently as she buckled herself in.

"Is something wrong?" Kira asked. He was hovering again.

"Nope." He winked at her. "I'll let you know when it's okay to move around." He hurried to the front of the plane. A.J. secured the door before following him.

Why was the man so familiar? Had they met before?

The plane taxied down the runway and was airborne within minutes. She'd forgotten to ask Tate where they were headed. She didn't care, as long as she never set foot in Wyoming again. She rubbed her eyes, yanked a magazine from a nearby seat pocket and absently thumbed through the pages.

Halfway through the magazine she came across an ad for Buckshot's Coffee. She quickly flipped past it, swallowing the knot in her throat. Why did she have to notice their advertising now, when she'd happily avoided it for years?

As the plane leveled off, she sighed, turned one more page and recognized a familiar pair of turquoise eyes. That was him, the copilot. He was A. J. Atkins, the spokesmodel for Bare Briefs underwear.

Kira laughed for the first time since the ordeal had begun. No wonder he'd made a joke about picturing him with his clothes off.

"I really thought you'd choose the red," Dalton said from somewhere behind her.

The magazine slipped from Kira's hands. She turned sideways in the seat, the tightness where she'd been shot pulling enough to keep her from jumping up. She watched him emerge from the rear of the plane. Her eyes locked on his face and she immersed herself in the dark brown depths of his eyes, his clean-shaven face and much shorter hair.

"It's a power color, you know," he added.

"I've acquired an unhealthy attachment to orange." She absolutely didn't mean to say that, at least not as the first words out of her mouth.

"Really?" He stood several feet away from her with his hands shoved in the front pockets of his jeans. He looked worried, almost as if he had a vested interest in each of her answers. "They wouldn't let me see you. Or talk to you. First one law enforcement agency, then another. Tate convinced me it was better to stay put and sort through the mess. I had to make certain all the charges were dropped."

Kira wanted to jump from her seat and straight into his arms. It would have been so easy. But she couldn't expect that Dalton was there for anything more than closure to an extremely unpleasant set of circumstances. None of this was his fault, and yet he'd borne the brunt of the pain.

"Dalton, I'm so sorry." Could she make him understand she'd never meant for him to get hurt? For his family to weather another storm of unwanted public scrutiny.

He rubbed his chin. "I thought we were past all of this."

"But you don't deserve—"

"What about you? What do you deserve?"

He was doing it again. He was forcing her to think about what she truly wanted. It wasn't fair to tell him she wanted him.

"I'll be fine." She forced perkiness into her voice.

He was keeping his distance now. His eyes grew darker as his shoulders tensed.

"You mean you'll be fine alone, right?" His voice rose for emphasis. "Because you're never going to give anyone a chance to make you happy?"

"No one else should have to pay for my mistakes." Her voice sounded convincing, even to her own ears. "You've lost enough."

"What about what I want?"

She laughed. Dalton certainly must wish for a time when he didn't know she existed. When his life was quiet, simple and free of constant drama.

"You don't want me," she said. "We may have needed each other for a night, but nothing more."

"Does that happen to you a lot? You get lonely and find someone's bed to warm?"

"No!" She denied the question and immediately recognized her mistake. He knew their intimacy had touched her deeply. Knew she wasn't experienced enough to believe what they'd shared was run-of-the-mill sex.

"So which is it? You're either lying to me or lying to yourself."

She released her seat belt and slowly stood, balancing heavily on the seats next to her. "There's no reason for you to care about what happens to me."

She would have been fine if he'd nodded in agreement and then walked away. A smart man would have bade her farewell and run for an exit.

"I can think of one." He slowly eliminated the space between them until they were mere inches apart. "I remember what you said at the cemetery."

Kira's heart beat erratically and she couldn't force her eyes to do more than stare at the center of his chest. They stood that way for a dozen lifetimes. Her voice felt rusty, clogged with emotions when she finally said, "I didn't want any regrets."

His hands gently framed her face and tilted it up to meet his gaze. "I'm brave enough for both of us." His lips barely brushed against hers. "And I love you."

Then he was kissing her with enough tenderness that her body ached with wanting him. His lips roamed from her temples to her eyelids and cheeks, before returning to her mouth. He dropped onto the seat she'd vacated and pulled her onto his lap.

"I love you." He kissed her soundly, wiping the tears from her face with his thumbs.

"I love you, too," she whispered against his lips.

"You don't know how much I wanted to be with you at the hospital."

"You did?" Her hands latched on to his wrists and squeezed. "Why didn't you call?"

"I called. Believe me, I phoned morning, noon and night." He shook his head. "Tate didn't want me to raise your hopes about getting everything cleared up. He thought it was best if you focused on getting better."

"Dalton, I would have been better just hearing your voice."

"And if I heard *your* voice, I wouldn't have been able to stay away. I'm sorry this was so hard on you, babe, but I know now it truly was for the best." The tone of his voice changed again and she couldn't quite judge what it meant.

"I have to go to jail, don't I?" She knew there would be repercussions for everything that had transpired in the past month. But allowing Dalton to shoulder any of the blame was out of the question. She would take whatever sentence the courts gave her, as long as he wasn't held accountable for helping her.

"There will be a court hearing," he conceded.

She'd go to court and tell the truth, the whole truth and nothing but the truth. Everyone would know how Josh had played her for a fool. Oh, Lord, what if the press got wind of his affair with Lauren?

"What if I plead guilty to all the charges?" she insisted. "We could keep some things private."

Dalton pulled her closer, pressing her face against his shoulder. "Trust me, nothing has been private. I only wish

I could change that for my mother. She's been through the wringer."

"I'm sor—"

"No more apologizing, Kira," Dalton said. "I mean it."

"Um, okay." A habit from her old life she needed to break. Would break.

The silence between them lasted a minute or so, long enough for him to shift her in his lap. Her cheek pressed to his chest, the steady beat of his heart resounding in her ear. She inhaled his scent, focused on the strength of his arms wrapped around her. Memorizing the moment would have to be enough to get her through what was sure to be a long separation.

Then it dawned on her, the reason Dalton was being so quiet. It must be very bad news and he was trying to figure out a way to break it to her. She cleared her throat. "Just tell me."

"I want to marry you," he said. His heartbeat suddenly raced beneath her ear.

Kira didn't move. Wasn't even sure she'd heard him correctly, but his statement deserved some sort of answer. "I'm not very good at being married."

"No, you were married to the wrong person."

"But it's not necessary," Kira said. She'd read how traumatic events could bind two people together, but she also suspected he was trying to make up for all of Josh's deceptions.

"Necessary?"

"Sure, we can love each other and not be married."

"What would that look like?"

"I'm guessing it would involve a few visits a year at a women's prison in Kansas City."

Dalton laughed and she immediately twisted out of his embrace. The action tugged uncomfortably at the stiches in her side and she winced while sliding into the seat across from him.

"Kira, you aren't going to jail, or prison, or even to Kansas City," Dalton said.

Her anger was quickly replaced with fear. What other options were left? "But you said I'd have to go to court."

Dalton shoved a hand through his hair and glanced to the ceiling. "This would be a whole lot easier if you'd agreed to marry me."

"I've already rushed into one marriage."

Dalton dropped to both knees between the seats and removed a small box from his front pocket. "Kira, I love you and I want to spend the rest of my life with you and our family. Will you please marry me?" He flipped the box open and extended it to her.

She nearly fell out of her seat as she leaned forward to stare at the massive diamond-and-emerald ring nestled there. Dalton reached for her hand and slid the ring onto her finger. She sat and stared at the sparkles of light reflecting from the stones.

"Dalton, it's beautiful," she whispered. "Emerald is Brandon's birthstone." Tears clogged her throat again.

"I think you mentioned it."

Dalton was giving her permission to remember her son every day. When she looked down at the ring, she could see her future and her past.

"A piece of paper isn't going to make much difference."

"I'm making a commitment. You deserve to finally have a family."

Kira tried connecting all the pieces in her head and something still wasn't adding up. If they got married, wouldn't they be a couple? Why did he keep stressing the fact they would be a family? "Dalton, what aren't you telling me?"

"Do you love me? You said you did, but maybe you've changed your mind."

He was stalling and they both knew it. But she couldn't for the life of her figure out why. "I do love you, but can we be engaged for a while? I've already had one quickie wedding and I don't want to rush into this."

"Yes." He reached for her hands. "If you want to be engaged, then we'll be engaged. But if you want to get married tomorrow, I can make it happen."

Kira may have been too harsh in judging him. There were many moments in the past month where she'd felt like a passenger on the train of life instead of the conductor. Hadn't she promised herself things would be different if she survived Josh's final attempt to kill her?

"I love you, Dalton. I'm not taking another day for granted."

"We're going to make every day count," he said, as he slid into the seat next to her and hugged her tightly. "Give me a chance."

"I think the whole happiness thing is a partnership, though. Right?" She giggled as he gently kissed the column of her neck.

"Definitely." He planted another string of kisses along her jawline before jumping to his feet. "We can do better than this." He took her hand and led her toward the rear of the plane.

A smile tugged at her lips. "Refresh my memory."

He pulled her into the bedroom and quickly shut the door. "Gladly."

# Chapter 21

An hour later, they were both naked underneath the covers when Tate made an announcement via the intercom. "Checking to see if we're on schedule."

"Yes, everything's a go," Dalton responded. The intercom went silent and Kira rolled to her side.

"On schedule for what?"

"We'll be making an important stop later, nothing to worry about right now," he assured her.

"A secret stop? Like maybe someplace warm with a sandy beach?"

He laughed. "I really have turned you to the dark side if you're pondering tropical vacations instead of letting me keep you warm."

Kira slid closer to Dalton, gliding one hand down his rib cage to rest upon his hip. "How warm?"

He repositioned her hand a bit farther south. "Hot, maybe even steamy."

\* \* \*

Kira awoke to an empty bed, with Dalton's scent lingering on her skin. She slowly stretched beneath the covers. Were they in the air?

No, it was too quiet.

She yanked the sheet from the bed, wrapped it around her body and padded to the window. Sliding the blind up a bit, she peeked outside. No snow.

Wherever Dalton had taken her, it was bright and sunny and probably close to noon. The plane was parked near an airstrip, but Kira couldn't see anything else through the small window.

She closed the blind and stepped into the bathroom. There on the counter was a duplicate of the cloth tote bag she'd gotten the night they'd met. She laughed. It was filled to the brim with all kinds of goodies, including chocolate mini doughnuts, a travel mug and a fancy assortment of tea bags. An overwhelming sense of relief washed over her as she spied her reflection in the mirror.

It was real.

This was real.

Dalton loved her and they were going to be together forever.

In two weeks' time, everything wrong in her world had righted itself. She paused, stared down at the beautiful ring he'd chosen.

Almost everything.

She flipped on the tap and splashed water against her cheeks, hoping to distract herself from the errant notions. She knew it was okay, probably normal, to ponder all the what-ifs, but it didn't make the questions any easier to think about.

Focus on the positive. She had Dalton, and they'd both earned a second chance at happiness.

* * *

"Stop doubting yourself." Tate walked through the plane's living room and closed the hallway door, offering them a small measure of privacy.

"Maybe I shouldn't spring this on her until—"

"Until what? She's already lost three years of his life."

"I know, I know." Dalton paced to the couch, tried sitting and immediately popped up.

"And you're sure it's him?" Tate asked.

"I pulled some strings, got a DNA test pushed through." He reached for his briefcase and removed a dog-eared folder. "Here are a few pictures Grayson took."

Tate flipped through them. There were several photos of a small yellow bungalow with leaves piled high in the front yard. Next came a twenty-something girl, taller than average, her long blond hair pulled into a ponytail.

The remaining pictures were those of a little boy, maybe three. He was wearing jeans and a purple Panthers sweatshirt, and he was having a blast playing in the leaves.

"He's not a baby anymore." Dalton flipped through a few more items in the folder and pulled out another page. "The girl is Lacey Connor. She's a senior at North Carolina State, and from all indications, she's been his nanny from the start."

"Was she involved with Josh?"

"Grayson interviewed some of their neighbors here in Raleigh, and it doesn't sound like it."

Tate reached for a bottle of Scotch and poured a good measure into a glass.

Dalton jerked the glass from his hand. "I thought you gave up drinking."

"If I had, a *good* friend wouldn't have a fully stocked liquor cabinet," Tate said.

Dalton downed the liquid. "Then let me pour you another drink while you explain exactly how Josh found us."

Tate quietly capped the bottle and exited the room without another word.

"Yeah, thought so," Dalton mumbled, semi-tempted by the empty glass. He tossed up a silent prayer and headed to find Kira.

The bed was empty and the bathroom door was closed. Dalton sorted through the bag of Kira's new clothes and quickly chose the least wrinkled ensemble for her to wear.

He wanted her feeling as confident as possible when he told her about her son.

Together they'd escaped two attempts on her life and together they'd learned about Josh's deception. It only made sense that together they would put all the pieces in place and make a family of their own.

"Dalton?"

"Yeah, babe, it's me." He watched her exit the bathroom draped in a towel.

"I wanted to help you choose an outfit for today."

She eyed him skeptically before sauntering toward the bed. "Isn't your goal to keep me undressed as long as possible?"

He grinned. "Normally, yes, but today we need to stick to a schedule."

She let the towel slip farther south. "Are you sure?"

"Stop tempting me or you'll miss your surprise."

"It's a good surprise, right?"

"Very good." He inched toward the door. "If I were you, I'd choose the red."

She smiled and dropped the towel. "Thanks, Santa."

"Don't thank me," he said and frowned. "I'm adding your name to the naughty list."

* * *

Thirty minutes later, Kira primped one last time in front of the mirror and then slipped from the bedroom in search of Dalton.

He was on the phone when she walked into the living area, and she patiently leaned against the wall. Hearing his voice brought calmness into her world and gave her a sense of belonging.

He winked at her, motioning her over to sit next to him. When she got within arm's reach, he pulled her onto his lap.

"Yeah, Grayson, thanks." He ended the call and set the phone on a nearby table. "You are so damn cute." He pressed his lips to hers.

Kira returned his greedy kiss, wrapping her arms around his neck as his hands slipped beneath her blouse. She laughed. "You had your chance, remember?"

"Yeah, I remember." He kissed the tip of her nose and sighed, adjusting her top. "This isn't how I wanted to do this."

Kira immediately tensed and tried to stand. "More bad news? Were some charges against me reinstated?"

"Babe, it's nothing bad." He pulled her closer.

"Are you sure? Please tell me the truth."

"Just remember, we couldn't do this until right this minute. You had to be here. And I thought if you knew before, there'd be more complications or the court would want a waiting period."

Whatever the truth was, Dalton was acting less confident than she'd ever seen him.

"Dalton…tell me. I don't understand, so just tell me."

"Josh lied to you."

"That's not new news," Kira retorted. She really didn't

want to ruin the day with more talk of what Josh had done to both of them.

"Kira, Brandon is alive."

She must be dreaming. She'd watched his lips move and heard the words, but they didn't make sense. It was the only explanation. Maybe she'd never left the hospital, and they'd given her a strong sedative and her mind went haywire. She was rewriting the ending because she couldn't face the reality of losing everything again. Or she was dead, and being in heaven meant nothing but happy endings.

"How is that possible?" Her voice sounded remarkably calm and reasonable.

"Kira, look at me."

She glanced over to Dalton and choked at the emotions painting his features. He was dead serious and obviously having trouble breaking the news to her.

"Are you certain?" she asked.

"Absolutely certain." His hands framed her face and he pressed a kiss against her lips. It was a kiss promising they were a team. He wasn't leaving her side and he'd already taken care of everything. If she trusted him.

"I don't want to understand anything. I don't need to know any of the details," she insisted. "I want to see my son."

The rational part of her brain was taking over. When she saw the child Dalton found, she'd know if it was true. A mother could tell, right?

Dalton stood and pulled her to her feet. He intertwined their fingers and squeezed her hand, raised it to his lips and kissed her knuckles.

"I knew you were an aggressive risk taker." He winked.

Dalton parked across the street from the house at 112 Hanover Drive and lowered the windows on the rented

SUV. The afternoon breeze shook a few more leaves from the maple tree shading half the perfectly manicured yard where Brandon lived.

Dalton tapped the steering wheel nervously before turning to face Kira.

"Where is he?" she asked.

"He lives in the yellow house." Dalton pointed across the street.

The front door opened and Grayson stepped onto the porch, quickly followed by a little boy with a mini football clutched in his hands.

"That's Grayson, a new member of Buckshot's security team." Dalton unlatched his seat belt and did the same to hers.

The child squealed excitedly as a young woman, presumably the nanny Dalton had told Kira about, followed on his heels. He raced to the other side of the yard and tossed the ball into the air.

"Catch it, catch it," he hollered.

The woman waited for it to bounce off the ground, retrieved it and tossed it to him. He caught it and ran past her to the other side of the yard.

"He's adorable," Kira commented.

"He's three and a half, just got potty trained and loves the *Jungle Book* movie."

Kira nodded and cleared her throat nervously. Dalton could see the tears welling in her eyes and reached for a box of tissues. He placed it on the console between them and waited until she'd removed one.

Grayson slipped into the yard and stole the football, tossing it to the girl at the other end.

"Okay, Remy, are you ready to catch it again?" she asked.

Kira silently reached for Dalton's hand. "His name isn't Brandon?"

"No."

"But you said you were sure." Her eyes darted to his, searching.

"I am sure. DNA test came back positive. Lacey said that Josh would usually take a business trip once a month. Be gone for four or five days in a row. It appeared normal to her, and what she did question, she wrote off, because he'd supposedly lost his wife when Brandon was born. Let's go meet him so you can decide for yourself."

Kira leaned over and pressed her lips to his. "I love you." Dalton kissed her soundly, wiping the tears from one cheek with his thumb.

"I love you, too. Remember, we're a family. All the way. All of us." He waited for her to make the next move. She flipped the visor down and opened the mirror. After dabbing away the moisture beneath her eyes, she tossed the tissue aside and squared her shoulders.

"Okay, then. Let's go play ball with our son."

# *Epilogue*

Kira shifted on the front porch swing as she watched Dalton and Brandon playing catch. Dalton had started out a few weeks ago with real baseball equipment and then quickly switched to a sponge ball and plastic bat. Poor Brandon had gotten her nonathletic genes, but bless his heart, he wasn't giving up on copying everything Dalton did.

They'd spent a week together in Raleigh, North Carolina, at the house where Brandon had lived since he was born. His nanny, Lacey, did a wonderful job of keeping Brandon's routine in place while Kira and Dalton learned everything they could about his life. She'd answered an online ad for a widower needing full-time care for a newborn and had been with Brandon ever since.

Dalton immediately started proceedings to get Kira's son returned to her, and to change his name. Rembrandt Griffin would have been a horrible reminder to them all of the years they'd missed together. She'd been willing to keep the nickname Remy—as his nanny called him—but her son said he liked Brandon better.

Kira sniffled, but fought the urge to cry. She'd shed way too many tears already, but when she thought she'd gotten beyond the grief of losing her baby, something else would happen to stir the pot.

After weighing the pros and cons, she and Dalton had decided that moving to his family's ranch in Texas was the best solution for all of them. The media continued to be a thorn in their sides, vying to fabricate stories on a daily basis. The ranch offered them privacy and security. And after meeting her new mother-in-law for the first time, Kira understood the family dynamics a bit better. Dalton's mother, Stella, was a soft-spoken woman who'd suffered repeated loss. She needed someone to give her purpose. The sadness etched on her face seemed to ease a bit when she met Brandon.

After a few days of watching him from a distance, Stella had asked him to help her bake cookies one afternoon. The next morning, Brandon was helping with pancakes. Everyday since, the two of them were up at dawn and filling the house with laughter.

The ranch became a fresh place to start, where they could make their own memories, together. Last night, Lacey had given Kira a baby book for Brandon. She'd used the stories and pictures from her online scrapbook page to make a paperbound book that included stories about his first tooth, word and steps. The amount of love in that book helped Kira realize that although Brandon hadn't been with her, he had been well cared for and loved.

A whistle pierced the air and she snapped out of her musings to see Brandon connect the bat to the ball and send it sailing over Dalton's head. He dropped the bat and darted across the yard toward third base, stopped halfway there and changed direction for first. She stumbled off the porch, clapping and hollering his name. "Go, Brandon!"

He ran over first and made a loop for second base. Truthfully, the bases were almost as big as he was, and his little arms were pumping with the effort to run. He stomped on the base and glanced over his shoulder to see where Dalton was before squealing in delight and racing to third.

Kira almost peed her pants laughing. She hurried to home plate and waved him past third. "Come on, Brandon, you can make it. Run."

Dalton had the ball, but instead of racing across the infield directly to home plate, he followed Brandon's path with a ferocious growl. Kira planted her feet near home plate and extended her arms to catch Brandon when he crossed. He hurried to her while Dalton continued the chase. She lifted her son into her arms and swung him the other direction.

"You did it!"

"I got home, Mommy."

Kira twirled him a couple times in a circle to celebrate and then Dalton was grabbing her and twirling them both in the air. Everyone laughed, and Dalton said, "Yeah, Mommy, we made it home."

"Yes, indeed, we did," Kira agreed.

\* \* \* \* \*

Available June 2, 2015

## #1851 Colton Cowboy Protector

*The Coltons of Oklahoma* • by Beth Cornelison

Widow Tracy McCain wants to bond with her deceased cousin's son, despite the concerns of the child's attractive father. But when she becomes an assassin's target, the only man who can save them is the one cowboy who might break her heart.

## #1852 Cowboy of Interest

*Cowboys of Holiday Ranch* • by Carla Cassidy

Nick Coleman's best friend is murdered, and the grieving rancher knows he's the number one suspect. Public relations maven Adrienne Bailey is positive that Nick murdered her sister. When sleuthing suggests Nick isn't the culprit, it puts them both in the real killer's crosshairs.

## #1853 Course of Action: Crossfire

by Lindsay McKenna and Merline Lovelace

Set in exotic locales, these two stories feature military heroes who must overcome devastating odds if they are to survive long enough to pursue the extraordinary women they've fallen for. Thrills, passion and danger—romantic suspense at its best!

## #1854 King's Ransom

*Man on a Mission* • by Amelia Autin

As king, Andre Alexei IV of Zakhar has everything he wants... except the one who got away. Actress Juliana Richardson is lured to his castle by a prominent role. When sinister plots for the throne unfold, will he be able to save her?

---

HRSCNM0515

# REQUEST YOUR FREE BOOKS!
## 2 FREE NOVELS PLUS 2 FREE GIFTS!

**⬧ HARLEQUIN®**

# ROMANTIC suspense

**Sparked by danger, fueled by passion**

**YES!** Please send me 2 FREE Harlequin® Romantic Suspense novels and my 2 FREE gifts (gifts are worth about $10). After receiving them, if I don't wish to receive any more books, I can return the shipping statement marked "cancel." If I don't cancel, I will receive 4 brand-new novels every month and be billed just $4.74 per book in the U.S. or $5.49 per book in Canada. That's a savings of at least 12% off the cover price! It's quite a bargain! Shipping and handling is just 50¢ per book in the U.S. and 75¢ per book in Canada.* I understand that accepting the 2 free books and gifts places me under no obligation to buy anything. I can always return a shipment and cancel at any time. Even if I never buy another book, the two free books and gifts are mine to keep forever.

240/340 HDN GH3P

Name _____ (PLEASE PRINT)

Address _____ Apt. #

City _____ State/Prov. _____ Zip/Postal Code

Signature (if under 18, a parent or guardian must sign)

### Mail to the **Reader Service:**
**IN U.S.A.:** P.O. Box 1867, Buffalo, NY 14240-1867
**IN CANADA:** P.O. Box 609, Fort Erie, Ontario L2A 5X3

**Want to try two free books from another line?**
**Call 1-800-873-8635 or visit www.ReaderService.com.**

* Terms and prices subject to change without notice. Prices do not include applicable taxes. Sales tax applicable in N.Y. Canadian residents will be charged applicable taxes. Offer not valid in Quebec. This offer is limited to one order per household. Not valid for current subscribers to Harlequin Romantic Suspense books. All orders subject to credit approval. Credit or debit balances in a customer's account(s) may be offset by any other outstanding balance owed by or to the customer. Please allow 4 to 6 weeks for delivery. Offer available while quantities last.

**Your Privacy**—The Reader Service is committed to protecting your privacy. Our Privacy Policy is available online at www.ReaderService.com or upon request from the Reader Service.

We make a portion of our mailing list available to reputable third parties that offer products we believe may interest you. If you prefer that we not exchange your name with third parties, or if you wish to clarify or modify your communication preferences, please visit us at www.ReaderService.com/consumerchoice or write to us at Reader Service Preference Service, P.O. Box 9062, Buffalo, NY 14240-9062. Include your complete name and address.

*Jack Colton wants Tracy McCain as far away from his son as possible. But when she becomes an assassin's target, the stakes have never been higher…*

Read on for a sneak peek of
*COLTON COWBOY PROTECTOR*
the first book in the
*COLTONS OF OKLAHOMA* series.

"Excuse me."

Jack pushed to his feet, his knee cracking thanks to an old rodeo injury, and faced the woman at eye level. Well, almost eye level. Though tall for a woman, she was still a good five or six inches shorter than his six foot one. He recognized her as the woman he'd seen earlier lurking in the foyer, practically casing the main house.

"Are you Jack Colton?" she asked.

"I am."

"May I have a word with you?" she asked, her voice noticeably thin and unsteady. She cleared her throat and added, "Privately?"

In his head, Jack groaned. *What now?*

"And you are…?"

He suspected she was a reporter, based on the messenger bag hanging from her shoulder. He had nothing to say to any reporter, privately or otherwise.

"Tracy McCain." She added a shy smile, her porcelain cheeks flushing, and a stir of attraction tickled Jack deep inside. Hell, more than a stir. He gave her leisurely scrutiny, sizing her up. She may be tall and thin, but she still had womanly curves to go with her delicate, china-doll face.

"Am I supposed to know you?"

Her smile dropped. "Laura never mentioned me?"

His ex-wife's name instantly raised his hackles and his defenses. His eyes narrowed. "Not that I recall. How do you know Laura?"

"I'm her cousin. Her maternal aunt's daughter. From Colorado Springs."

Jack gritted his back teeth. Laura had only been dead a few months and already relations she'd never mentioned were crawling out of the woodwork like roaches after the light was turned off. The allure of the Colton wealth had attracted more than one gold-digging pest over the years. "You should know Laura signed an agreement when we divorced that ended any further financial claim on Colton money."

Tracy lifted her chin. "I'm aware."

"So you're barking up the wrong tree if you're looking for cash."

Tracy blinked her pale blue eyes, and her expression shifted, hardened. "I'm not after money," she said, with frost in her tone.

Jack scratched his chin and tipped his head, giving her a skeptical glare. "Then what?"

"I wanted to talk about Seth."

Jack tensed, his gut filling with acid. He squeezed the currycomb with a death grip and grated, "No."

"I... What do you mean, no? You haven't even heard what I want to—"

"I don't need to hear. My son is off-limits. Nonnegotiable."

*Don't miss*
*COLTON COWBOY PROTECTOR*
*by Beth Cornelison,*
*available June 2015 wherever*
*Harlequin® Romantic Suspense*
*books and ebooks are sold.*

www.Harlequin.com

HRSEXP0515

# HARLEQUIN®

## A *Romance* FOR EVERY MOOD™

# JUST CAN'T GET ENOUGH?

Join our social communities
and talk to us online.

You will have access to the latest
news on upcoming titles and special
promotions, but most importantly,
you can talk to other fans about your
favorite Harlequin reads.

Harlequin.com/Community

 Facebook.com/HarlequinBooks

 Twitter.com/HarlequinBooks

 Pinterest.com/HarlequinBooks

**HARLEQUIN®**

A *Romance* FOR EVERY MOOD™

Stay up-to-date on all your
romance-reading news with the
*Harlequin Shopping Guide,*
featuring bestselling authors, exciting new
miniseries, books to watch and more!

The newest issue will be delivered right to you
with our compliments! There are 4 each year.

Signing up is easy.

## EMAIL

ShoppingGuide@Harlequin.ca

## WRITE TO US

HARLEQUIN BOOKS
Attention: Customer Service Department
P.O. Box 9057, Buffalo, NY 14269-9057

## OR PHONE

1-800-873-8635 in the United States
1-888-343-9777 in Canada

Please allow 4-6 weeks for delivery of the first issue by mail.

# THE WORLD IS BETTER WITH

## *Romance*

Harlequin has everything from contemporary, passionate and heartwarming to suspenseful and inspirational stories.

Whatever your mood,
we have a romance just for you!

Connect with us to find your next great read,
special offers and more.

**f** /HarlequinBooks

**t** @HarlequinBooks

www.HarlequinBlog.com

www.Harlequin.com/Newsletters

**H HARLEQUIN**®

A *Romance* FOR EVERY MOOD™

www.Harlequin.com